EVERYTHING LOOKS IMPRESSIVE

EVERYTHING LOOKS IMPRESSIVE

A NOVEL

HUGH KENNEDY

New York London Toronto Sydney Auckland

PUBLISHED BY NAN A. TALESE
an imprint of Doubleday, a division of
Bantam Doubleday Dell Publishing Group, Inc.
666 Fifth Avenue, New York, New York 10103

DOUBLEDAY and the portrayal of an anchor
with a dolphin are trademarks of
Doubleday, a division of Bantam Doubleday Dell
Publishing Group, Inc.

Book design by Viola Adams

Grateful acknowledgment is made for permission to reprint excerpts from the following:

"Notes towards a Supreme Fiction" and "The Idea of Order at Key West," from *Collected Poems* by Wallace Stevens. Copyright 1954 by Wallace Stevens. Reprinted by permission of Alfred A. Knopf, Inc.

Correction by Thomas Bernhard, translated by Sophie Wilkins. Reprinted by permission of Alfred A. Knopf, Inc.

"Making Flippy Floppy" (David Byrne, Tina Weymouth, Chris Frantz, Jerry Harrison). Copyright © 1986 by Index Music, Bleu Disque Music Co. Inc. All rights administered by WB Music Corp. All Rights Reserved. Used by Permission.

Male Fantasies, Vol. II by Klaus Theweleit, translated by Erica Carter and Chris Turner. Copyright © 1989 by the Regents of the University of Minnesota. Reprinted by permission of the University of Minnesota Press.

To the Lighthouse by Virginia Woolf, copyright 1927 by Harcourt Brace Jovanovich, Inc. and renewed 1954 by Leonard Woolf, reprinted by permission of the publisher.

"Fall Term Calendar of Events," © the Yale Record, Inc., and Michael Gerber.

Library of Congress Cataloging-in-Publication Data

Kennedy, Hugh.
    Everything looks impressive / Hugh Kennedy. — 1st ed.
       p.   cm.
    I. Title.
  PS3561.E4264E94   1993
  813'.54—dc20   92-17809
                                        CIP

For my parents,

Katherine MacLellan Kennedy and

Hugh Donald Kennedy

Author's Note

The bulk of this novel was written under the mentorship of Sheila Schwartz, whose exceptional insight and support made its completion a reality. For their fine editorial comments on earlier drafts, I also want to thank Tom Augst, Michael Chabon, Neal Chandler, Michael Cooke, John Gerlach, Barry Hannah, Tamar Lehrich, Doug Nygren, Richard Reinhardt, Paula Resch, Richard Selzer, the late Carol Rinzler, and Rita Watson.

Special thanks to my agent, Fred Hill, to Jesse Cohen at Doubleday, and to my wonderful editor, Nan Talese.

Ev'rything is divided
Nothing is complete
Ev'rything looks impressive
Do not be deceived

    —David Byrne,
     Tina Weymouth,
     Chris Frantz,
     Jerry Harrison,
     1983

1

I met Jill Lanigan on the last day she ever pimped for Yale. That's how she put it.

This was also the last day of "Camp Yale," the lazy settling-in week at the end of August which ushers in the fall term in New Haven. I'd forgotten to set my alarm the night before, and as a result I woke up five minutes late for a squash match at the gym. I opened my eyes, rubbed the sweat off my forehead and formed two conclusions: I was late and it was ninety degrees out already. It occurred to me as I lay there staring at my clock radio that I'd just been dreaming about squash, about winning, too, the way I would wake up on exam days in prep school thinking that vacation had already started. In fact, vacation was just about to end.

I was supposed to be playing squash with a sophomore named Lyon who had graduated a year earlier from my prep school in McMurtry, the dim Maine resort town near Penobscot where I'd grown up. Since Lyon was a popularity monster when I knew him at school, and I was a new freshman and knew no one but my roommates, and knew them hardly at all, I didn't want to take the chance of standing him up. Everyone I'd met in my first week had Lyon's intimidating aura of self-confidence and privilege, and in calling him out of the blue to set up the match I was making it clear that I had no intention of being left out. As a day student at a school where almost everyone boarded and was from New York, Boston or Connecticut, I'd already spent three years hanging between indifferent peer acceptance and casual peer ostracism, and now that I'd kicked ass and gotten into the Ivy League, I wasn't about to do it half baked. Neither was I blind to the irony of attending a hugely expensive college on full scholarship when my parents wouldn't have been able to afford any of the second-tier schools in Maine that could only offer to foot a quarter or a half of their bill. Knowing, too, how it felt to walk three miles with your mother in the cold to get food stamps while your father is out looking for work, or how to look down at the lawn and want to disappear when five unexpected guests arrive at the going-away party your parents throw for you, and your father has to borrow the money from a neighbor to buy more booze. These reflections brought me to the point of being ten minutes late, and I saw that I would have to explode out of my bedroom, down four flights of stairs and halfway across the campus if I wanted even outside odds on getting to the gym before I became a no-show.

I remember shoving the heavy walnut doors of Lawrance Hall right back on their hinges, as if the corresponding doors to Success and Achievement might already be closing against me. Coming out into the sticky slam of sunlight, though, I glanced from one arched gateway to another around the Old Campus quadrangle and saw that I was already lost. My roommates had taken me on one trip to the gym, but I'd been too preoccupied looking bored to watch where we were going. After a minute of trying to choose which path to take, I wandered up to a piece of glossy blue paper that had been taped to an elm tree a few feet from the edge of the green. I held out a distant hope that this sign might contain directions to the gym. In fact, it said, FRESHMAN ORIENTATION 9:00–2:00 TODAY: *LAST* CHANCE TO SIGN UP FOR CLUBS AND ORGANIZATIONS. I took another step toward the green and fell in love.

My eyes had stopped on a tall, slender woman with porcelain skin who was brushing a ring-studded hand up through her short blond and red hair. She was stunning. She sat apart from the double row of canvassers at a small card table, not twenty feet from where I stood, and just by sitting there she made everyone else on the green look repressed. In fact, she looked as if she might represent a coalition whose goal was to undermine all the other organizations. I watched her uncross her long legs and stand, then kneel with perfect posture and add a thumbtack to a poster on the front of her table. Our eyes met for a moment and I felt my chest tighten. She had clear Irish features which made her stare seem knowing and distant at the same time. My ex-girlfriend Katharine from McMurtry was Irish too, but Katharine and this woman could have come from different planets.

While I looked on, two large men who had wandered off from the crew team's recruiting display arrived at the woman's table, and she began to talk with them. I found myself dropping my racquet and taking a seat on the upper wooden crossbeam of the Old Campus fence.

She had an oval face and a thin nose that gathered into a bulb at its tip and nudged upward. Her eyes were bright green against a skin even paler than mine, which as the product of four hundred years of purebred Scottish melanin deficiency I hardly thought possible. Her hair was blond at the roots and rusty orange-red on the tips, slicked straight back and then shaved close on the sides, almost like a cap. She looked about five-nine, my height, but couldn't have weighed more than a hundred pounds. She reminded me of one of those boyish, unstable-looking haute couture models who can put rags in their hair and smear their faces with oatmeal paste and still get you turning back and turning back to the page where their picture is.

One of the crew rowers who had stopped at the display squatted down and pointed to the poster on the front edge of the card table. The poster said, YALE WOMEN'S CENTER DEMANDS DIVESTMENT FROM SOUTH AFRICA. He pretended to read a small sheet of paper taped to it, but out of the woman's line of sight I saw that he was actually writing on it with a pen he brought out of his pocket. After he repocketed the pen he looked up.

"Where do I sign?"

"Here." Her smooth, low voice was almost lost in the crowd. "Right here in front of you."

The larger guy stepped forward in his bright yellow T-shirt and blue and white striped shorts and read over his friend's shoulder. "Hey, you're *demanding* that Yale divest from South Africa? Don't you think it would be nicer to request it?"

"Where's it say that?" The other guy tipped back on his haunches and read the sign again. " 'Demand'—huh."

"Yes, 'demand,' " she said pleasantly. "We've found a surprising correlation between continued Western investment and people being clubbed to death trying to get the right to vote. I don't think 'demand' is too harsh."

"Wow," the standing guy said. "Do you think you should sign it if it says 'demand'?"

"Hey, dude." The squatting one looked up at his friend. "I'm not sure. What do you think?"

Before his friend could answer the woman slipped the petition away and held it at the edge of the table. "Tell you what; why don't you come back after you've hashed out all the fine points? Ask for Jill Lanigan." She held up a small pin with her name on it.

She added something that I didn't catch. Whatever it was, it wiped the smiles off the faces of both men. For a long second no one moved. My first impulse was to jump in, but since this woman was a stranger I stopped short. By the time I was ready to ease down off the fence and walk over, both guys had smirked at each other and turned to go. She watched them as they wandered off. Then she pulled a half-finished Granny Smith apple from a paper bag on the grass behind her and bit into it.

I wasn't sure what I'd just seen, but my heart was pounding and I felt a rush of guilt as if my own mother had nearly been roughed up on a street corner and I hadn't been able to act. I'd never felt protective toward anyone outside of my family except Katharine, and certainly not toward someone who looked so capable of taking care of herself.

When Jill had finished her apple, she slid her folding chair back over the uneven ground and stood. She was wearing a black tube skirt and a white pocketless scoop-neck T-shirt with several necklaces underneath. She shook her head once, as if to dislodge the incident from memory, then stepped back from the table and slowly stretched two long arms up over her head. She looked out into the crowd, gave an amused, I guessed, vegetarian smile to a yellow circus tent belching hamburger fumes and exhausted parents far down the green, and then scanned the perimeter of the fence carefully. Her eyes stopped on me, and I turned around, blushing, and stared at a trash can until the blush passed. When I turned back Jill was already halfway toward the can and me, balling up a white napkin and the remains of the apple in her hands. She walked through the alternately lush and trampled grass as if descending from a 747 on one of those portable outdoor stairways, with the effortless, irresistible confidence some people still have at airports. I knew, I had predicted to myself, somehow, that she would choose my trash can. The fact that it was closer than any of the others seemed irrelevant. I was very curious to see what she was about or, as my new roommate Peter would put it, see what her deal was, and in a rush I extended my hand.

"Here, I'll toss that."

"Thanks, I've got it." Jill leaned over the fence and underhanded the napkin and apple into the trash can. She didn't smile but let her eyes rest on me for a moment and acknowledged my courtesy. Then she smoothed her hands over her hips to dry them. "If you really want to help, you might come over and sign our divestment petition. After your game."

"Great." I looked down at my racquet in the grass. Chasing a small green ball around a hot room covered with boundary tape suddenly seemed ridiculous. When Jill turned and walked away I slid off the fence. If I hadn't been a no-show when I woke up, I was definitely one now. At least I didn't have to worry about the doors to Success and Achievement for the rest of the day.

I walked down to the other end of the green and approached Jill's display like a nervous teenager working from the news magazines to the pornography in a bookstore; one glance at what was in front of me, one quick glance over at that card table. She was definitely older than I. My brother Marty had married a woman almost a decade older than he, and she'd worked the macho coldness crap out of him in about three months. Along my route I paused at a neofascist group called the Party of the Right, a square-dancing club called Bulldog Sets, and a comedy magazine that was distributing cards with their version of the fall schedule on it. I took one of these cards from a short, black-haired guy who looked like he was going to charge me for it and read it through:

Your *FALL TERM* at Yale

15	Jul	M	Crippling tuition payment.
10	Aug	S	Building anxiety, Freshmen. Tepid sense of enthusiasm, everyone else.
30	Aug	F	Freshman Registration; crying.
3	Sept	T	Upper-class Registration. Euphoria, which dissipates as you see all the people you hate.
4	Sept	W	Fall term classes begin. "Camp Yale" ends.
15	Nov	F	Thank God, fall term recess begins.
16	Nov	S	The Game. Loads of drunken alums.
29	Nov	F	Another tuition payment is levied by Yale. Parents now on their knees.
12	Dec	Th	Incredible shrinking Reading Period begins.
18	Dec	W	Final examinations begin. Are you in a state of grace?
23	Dec	M	It's over. Go home and lick your wounds.

"Terrific," I said to the guy. "Can't wait to get started."

I pocketed the card and walked up to Jill's table. The foreplay was over.

"Hi, here I am."

Jill glanced up at me from her book. She looked a bit surprised to see me. I glanced from her bare, white collarbone to the delicate bones that led in a V from there up to her neck, and picked up the tart, lemony scent of a men's cologne. Since Jill's display stood off by itself, though, the fragrance was almost certainly coming from her. I could hardly believe how nervous I was.

"Thanks for stopping by. We were selling bran muffins a while ago, but we're all out. You're in luck, actually, they were awful." She spoke in a coy, almost candied voice which struck me as so ironic that it might not have been ironic at all. Maybe she aimed for ambiguity; that way, no one could pin you down.

"I bet you're from New York," I began.

"How'd you guess?" she said. The answer came back as if I'd moved a pawn and now she was moving a pawn.

"All the people from New York I've met are like Europeans somehow, and you seemed that way."

Jill slid her index finger between the pages of her book and folded her arms over it. "You may be the break I've been waiting for. You're a freshman, right?"

I smiled. "That's right. Is it so glaring?"

"It's charming, actually. Let me be the first member of the senior class to express my sentimental envy."

"Thanks. . . ." The open way Jill stared at me made me uncomfortable, so I cleared my throat and read over the divestment petition. As I added my name, the three hundred and twelfth, I wondered how many of the other three hundred and eleven people had asked Jill out for a drink. Then I squatted down to look at the page taped to the poster. On the top line it read, YALE WOMEN'S CENTER SURVEY, and underneath this title and the word SAMPLE, which had been written in in black marker, there were fifteen questions. Several of the sample's blanks, I noticed, had already been filled in. Under the question, "What do you think women really want?" someone had written, "Ten inches and a commitment." Under the last question, "Do you have any advice for the Women's Center?" someone had written, "Disband."

"Have you seen this thing?" I said.

"Yes." Jill laid her book aside entirely now and perched her

head on an upturned palm. "Thank God for the First Amend-
ment, right?"

"But this is horrible."

"You should have tasted our bran muffins."

"No, I mean it," I said. "I'm completely for women's rights."

Jill gave me a searching look. I guess she assumed I was being
ironic, though irony was always unintentional where I came from.
"My experience has been that there are no male feminists, only
recovering sexists." She glanced at her watch and began to clear
the completed surveys and the petition off the table.

I stepped back. "Whoa, don't leave on my account."

"It's not you," she said. "I just reminded myself of lunch. I
haven't had a thing to eat today."

"What about your apple?"

Jill glanced over at the trash can and then back at me. "That's
right, the apple. You don't expect me to live on eighty calories a
day, do you?"

"Of course not. Can I have a survey though? May I?"

"A survey, yes. I'm blinded by malnutrition here." She took
one from an envelope beside her on the ground and slid it over
the table. I reached for a pencil stub while she swept the rest of
the pencils and her name tag into the envelope.

"Can you wait a second while I fill it out?"

"As I said, we're closing for lunch."

"I know, you told me." I scribbled the date down, fighting a
smile. "I'll just be a minute."

Jill stopped packing up and met my eyes. "Seriously, I've
really got to meet someone, okay? If you want to man the table for
lunch, then I can wait."

My mouth hung open. She had placed a heavy emphasis on the
verb "man." "Uh, actually—"

"That's all right then." She slid the pencil from my hand. "It
would be much more productive for us if you took the survey
back to your room and thought it through. You can pass it in at

the Women's Center when you're done. You can even join if you want. We're sex-blind. Weren't you completely for women's rights a couple of seconds ago?"

"Is the Women's Center far?" I took another reluctant step back from the table. "I'm having problems even finding the gym."

"You got this far," Jill said. "I can tell you'll go much farther."

I watched as she packed a black leather book bag with her supplies and found that I didn't want to let her out of my sight. If she stayed for another minute, or a few more minutes, maybe we could move out of the repartee into something more significant. I had gone past curiosity and was already dabbling my toes in the deceptively calm waters of fascination. She was so chic and so real at the same time. The combination was intoxicating.

"Are you coming back after lunch?"

"No." She zipped the bag shut. "My political pimping is at an end, thank God. I've got a senior essay to write."

"Pimping?"

She gave me a parting smile. "I don't enjoy screeching to the unconverted any more."

"You ought to use that smile more often," I said.

"I think you might need to get out of the sun." She slung her book bag over her shoulder and strode off. "Bye . . ."

I watched as the distance between us increased, then I picked up my squash racquet and my survey. "Hang on! Could you give me directions to the gym? I'm sort of late too."

She looked back at me, the parting smile still playing over her lips. "The gym is easy, come on."

I ran down the green and caught up with her as we entered the throwing path of two sunglassed women who were hurling a lacrosse ball into the webs of each other's sticks. Once safely past them, Jill slowed her walking pace considerably and picked at the front of her shirt.

"This is not a day for rushing, don't you agree?"

"It's not. What could we have been thinking?" I relaxed at the friendly tone in her voice now that we'd stepped away from the tables. Canvassing obviously wasn't her favorite thing to do. She was probably pimping as a favor to someone.

"Sorry about being snappish," she went on. "William F. Buckley and his sidekick back there were not what I needed."

"That's all right," I said. "Did you really mean it when you said you were envious of me?"

"I meant freshmen as a whole, but yes." She moved her book bag to her opposite shoulder, and I strolled the tiniest bit closer to her. "This is one of the only places left in the country where you can come and be an insufferable, self-involved artiste for four years without provoking general ridicule."

I laughed, and she raised her eyebrows. "You think it's funny now, but wait a few years."

"No," I said. "I just love the way you talk."

"In that case you won't forget my directions. Here." She put a hand on my shoulder as we went through the Elm Street gate. "All the way down straight, keep right when it becomes Broadway, and Tower Parkway intersects it a block later. The gym is the last cathedral-shaped building before the ghetto starts."

"Thanks a lot," I said. "And for the survey. I will fill it out."

"Good." She stepped back out of the flow of people, across the gate from me, but lingered momentarily on a flagstone. Maybe she wanted to see if I could follow her directions. I raised my racquet.

"You don't play, do you?"

She squinted. "Sorry?"

"Squash."

"Can't say I have."

"Well," I said, and backed into some sort of moat wall, "maybe we'll bump into each other."

She raised her eyebrows again and nodded. "Inevitably."

I spun my racket in my hand and started jogging off toward the gym. I got less than halfway there when it occurred to me that I hadn't even introduced myself, and while deriding myself for

such a stupid, freshman mistake I turned right too soon and
ended up at the gates of the local cemetery. Somehow I didn't
mind. I was thinking of Jill's slim, guiding hand on my shoulder.
There was no way that hand could have been ironic.

2

When I next woke, light was still slanting into my bedroom. I glanced down at my clock radio and read "7:47." I scrambled into a sitting position, panicking without a particular reason,
and watched a folded piece of paper that had been tucked between my toes float down to the floor.

> Alex, meet us at Mory's for cups at 8:30 if you're free.
> Coat and tie. Brook's dad is treating, then we get to clean
> out his attic tomorrow in Darien. But we also get old furni-
> ture for the common room. See you later?—Peter. P.S. If
> you don't plan to wake up, can we rent your room and store
> you in Brook's attic?

I read the note again and tried to remember what and where
Mory's was. If it was in an invitation from Brook Morehouse it
had to be exclusive. This was, after all, the guy who called our
common room with its polished hardwood floors and windowed
brick turret "a dump," and referred to his one-year-old Wagoneer
as "a heap." I sat up with my sweaty back against the cool white
plaster wall and listened to my stomach rumble. Then I remembered the encounter with the platinum- and red-haired senior
and shuddered.

I leaned forward on my knees and pulled the Women's Center
survey off my desk. Underneath the survey was a small framed
picture of my ex-girlfriend Katharine, a memento of a hiking trip
in the Appalachians we'd taken with my parents, my brother

Marty and his wife on a freakishly warm May weekend. Marty, the star photographer for Associated Press, had snapped the shot five minutes before we crossed the path of a seven-hundred-pound black bear and he'd nearly wet his pants. This picture kept landing on my desk because I couldn't find a suitable place for it in the room. I really didn't remember packing it at all, and wondered if my mother hadn't slipped it into my suitcase thinking I'd forgotten it. Neither of my parents knew that I was on the skids with Katharine until we were three hours gone on our journey down to Yale in the station wagon. I caught hell for it then, of course, through the entire state of New Hampshire.

In the picture I was sprawled on my back on a large slab of granite while Katharine climbed over me in low hiking boots, looking off toward an imaginary peak. I brought the picture up to my eyes and frowned. Straight-A Katharine: my archrival in spelling bees all through grammar school; my meticulous yearbook coeditor; my fellow server on all the Student Council committees at Hollier Prep; and then, surprising both of us, my coconspirator in our first exhilarated attempts at sex during a Student Council ski trip to Stowe. Yet ten weeks after the photograph was taken we weren't even speaking to each other. I wondered if the person grabbing Katharine's sunburned calf was really me, or if I was looking at the Zen me, or whatever the hell she called the human essence, the pure, love-informed self that nudged aside the daily self and acted without error or doubt. The whole scene was unreal—or as unreal as real now was. There had been the photo, and a summer spent together with Katharine, night after night, with no copy deadlines or meetings to run to, only the tiny social scene of a dull Maine tourist town; there had been me saying that I was bored one August afternoon, as Yale loomed closer, and when pressed, that everything had become boring. I felt something snap between us before the whole sentence was out of my mouth. Then there had been Katharine's sudden, complete silence and those passing stares as if she'd never known me; seeing her in a pew in our local church protected by a brother on either side rather than next to me; watching her mother come to the O'Brien door to say that no, Kate wasn't home, though I could hear the stereo playing in her bedroom. Until that moment, sitting on my sweaty, Ivy League bed with a Women's Center survey in one hand and a picture of two quietly transported lovers in the other, I had preferred to understand Katharine's acceptance of the fact that she had become boring. Reflecting on Jill's knowing stare, though, it came to me that my ex-girlfriend was by no means boring or defeated, but in her silence she had craftily denied me the satisfaction of being told that I was an asshole. By not acting at all Katharine had gotten the upper hand. Now that I really thought about it, she used to do the same thing in the final rounds of spelling bees in the sixth grade, staring hard at the floor while I struggled with "cemetery" or "malign."

After a few minutes I laid the picture back on the desk and looked out my ivy-clogged window. A couple was walking down one of the flagstone paths together, tiny from four stories up, their voices so distant they reached me only in fragments. I felt a sudden ache in my chest, as if I'd slept through the wildest party of the year or, worse, had never been invited. The best thing to do was get dressed and join the roommates before despair set in. If I could find them.

3

At Mory's a waiter showed me through to a dining room near the center of the club, and I saw my roommates Brook and Peter talking together at a small table. Brook, the taller, black-haired one, was in a lightweight double-breasted blue blazer and red go-to-hell pants, while Peter, who had sun-bleached blond hair and a permanent sailor's tan, wore an old gray check-plaid suit and a pink tab-collar shirt. Brook was in highly polished black Gucci loafers without socks while Peter wore a pair of Tretorn sneakers with his toes sticking out from tears on either side. He must have known how to get around the finer points of the dress code.

Peter and I had arrived in New Haven first, actually, and moved into our suite several hours before Brook showed, so we had a chance to walk around downtown and then get acquainted at the Old Campus fence. Peter was a fourth-generation legacy whose family hailed from Boston. He spent the summers in East Hampton, Long Island, with his father, who edited a small newspaper, and lived the rest of the year in New York with his mother, who ran an interior design firm. Peter didn't get along well with his mother, who was "too tightly wound" for his tastes, so he had attended Yale summer school since his sophomore year at Exeter. As a result he could fill me in on every Yale factoid from the number of draftsmen required to build Sterling Library (eighty-five) to the best off-campus dive, a time-frozen lounge on College Street called the Anchor. When I accidentally called the Anchor by the name of an identical time-frozen lounge around the corner from it, Peter slid down the fence and pretended to give me the cold shoulder. But he broke into a smile about two seconds later; he loved the place so much that he didn't mind sharing his expertise.

At the height of the moving-in on that first afternoon Peter and I had spotted a six-foot-three-inch guy with short black hair, a tan, perfect body, a Roman nose and a chin you could have landed jets on, wearing Ray Bans and an Andover shirt. He was striding across the green looking superior and openmouthed, as if heading for the nearest playing field.

"My God," I'd said to Peter, "can you imagine having him for a roommate?"

Now, at Mory's, Brook and Peter stood and Brook extended his hand to me. "It's about time. Did you get lost again?"

"No, I just woke up." I sat down and Peter reached over to grip my arm in greeting. He and Brook were talking about their respective crew practices from earlier in the day, and since they didn't provide any immediate openings for me to comment, I surreptitiously looked around. Mory's is a two-story clapboard house from about 1850, and has brown painted floors which creaked like an old porch as waiters and members strolled around on them. The walls are covered with crew photographs, oars, plaques and signed cartoons from the turn of the century. We seemed to be the only party of people there under fifty years of age, so we were getting some interested glances. In fact, we were probably the first illicit freshmen of the fall.

Brook leaned back in his chair and looked over at me. He had that kind of aggressive friendliness that my brother, who is a soccer star, gets when he talks about sports.

"Alex, what are you going out for?"

"Squash," I said.

"When are tryouts?"

"Actually," I said quickly, "I blew off the first round. You play?"

"Yeah," Brook said, "and I'd kick your ass too."

"I don't know," I said, falsely confident, "I think I'd run you around a bit."

"I'll take you on," Peter said. "Brook's just been playing in his basement since he was four. It's essential that everyone know that."

"Fuck you." Brook balled up a napkin and tossed it at Peter. "You should've seen this guy trying to deal in an eight-oared shell in Branford today. He nearly tipped the thing over three times."

I looked at Peter. "Weren't you trying out for the swim team?"

"Well . . ." Peter leaned way back in his seat. "I thought I'd try this, until I drown someone. I'm going out for the *Daily News* at some point, and the Political Union too, so I'm sure I won't have time to keep it up."

"Better get your game together," Brook said to me. "I want to see all of us walking into Lawrance wearing team jackets."

"Yeah, right," I said. "If everybody didn't cancel on me I might get some practice." I didn't mention Lyon, of course, but Brook had lost interest anyway.

The waiter returned and confirmed that Brook's father had left his membership number at our disposal and that we could use it to our satisfaction for the evening.

"Cups are served for the next hour, gentlemen. What would you like to begin with?"

Peter and I looked at Brook. "Let's start," he said in a deep, of-legal-age voice, "with a red cup and the menu for dinner."

"Good choice," Peter said. "Dad always started with a red cup."

We dove hungrily into a bowl of oyster crackers while Brook explained Mory's cup drinking to me. It was like hearing about the best off-campus dives again.

"Here's how you do it. You sing a song for the person who's sucking on the loving cup full of booze, and that person has to keep drinking until the song is finished. Then you pass the cup along. The person who drinks the last bit out of the cup has to spin it dry on his lips, rotate the rim on his head, and slam it down onto a white napkin. If there's a ring of booze on the napkin after all of us have slammed on the bottom, then that person buys the next cup."

"How much are cups?" I said. The idea of working backwash into my hair wasn't very appealing.

"Seventeen, aren't they?" Brook turned to Peter.

He shrugged. "I heard golds are twenty now."

"They must be huge," I said.

"Enormous," Brook said. "That's where the terror element of the game comes in. You've really got to drink past your limit."

Presently the waiter reappeared with a gallon-sized silver cup. It had neoclassical, earlike handles and had been inscribed in 1902.

"You can hand that to the man in the paisley tie," Brook said.

The cup was brought under my nose. It smelled like the cherry ale from Belgium that my uncle broke out when I visited him in Boston. I gripped both handles and looked inside at the frothy pink head and the red liquid underneath it, then sloshed the block of ice around. After a second I moved to put the cup down for a better grip. Was I really expected to drink out of this thing and spin it on my head?

"No!" Brook protested. "Don't let it touch the table. That's not allowed."

"That's right," Peter said. "They'd have to melt it down in the kitchen and get us another one."

Brook glared at him. "Come on, stay in the spirit, okay?"

"Hey then, let's go!" Peter clapped. "What Yale songs does anybody know? How about 'Take Take Take from the Old Third World'?"

"I know all the songs," Brook assured us. "Just follow my lead. They're all in C anyway. You start on that cup, Alex, and we'll get you moving. Let's do 'Down the Field.' "

I stuck my head into the cup. The enthusiasm felt forced.

Drinking from a Mory's cup was like plunging your face into an armored helmet full of spiked Orangina. Enough of my head fit inside the cool silver dome that I felt it was just me and the sloshing tide of liquor put together for a private showdown. The cups were mixed to give you the impression of tying on a neat little buzz, so that when you got up from the table and found that you couldn't walk, you felt sure that it was the world which had pitched sideways while you remained upright. There was also a placebo syndrome involved since the cup recipes were a secret and no one had any idea how much booze each one contained. By the time we emptied two red cups and a green forty minutes into Cup Hour I found myself liking Peter and Brook extraordinarily, more than I would have thought possible when I met them. This was so even when they persisted in cutting each other down in little offhanded comments as we got more and more smashed. Especially Brook, who somehow knew an old girlfriend of Peter's from Exeter named Jane, who'd apparently spilled every intimate bean about their relationship to their common friend Joan, who'd bumped into Brook's sister Olivia in Hong Kong—I lost track of the lines of connection somewhere. I also found, after a fourth cup had passed from me, that I was lurching in my attempt to reach the men's room.

"Hey, Alex!" Brook yelled behind me. "Where are you going?"

I turned back and was amazed at how little progress I'd made through the club. The air around me was cloudy with steam from plates of hot seafood. "I'm slouching toward Jerusalem, whaddaya want?"

"It's Peter's turn!" he called back. "He hasn't gone in this round. Now we've got to sit here and wait for you. You should've skipped your turn, man."

"Christ, you'll live," I said. As I walked off, I heard Peter say that this was probably my first time drunk, and that Brook should take it easy on me.

"That's not true!" I called.

Brook looked up at me, his face red. "Just use the can and get back here, would you?"

"Sorry." I tiptoed away and waited for Peter to laugh at me, but he didn't. I guessed that we were doing the Behave Like Gentlemen routine. Maybe I would suggest some Mahler songs for Brook's next turn. I pushed into the men's room and wished to hell that I'd eaten some dinner.

In the mirror nook just past the door I noted my cup-shaped hair. There was a loony grin on my red face. Well, Katharine, I thought, if you could only see me now. Hi, Alex, I smiled, you have cup head. Hey, butthead, you've got cup head! I leered and saw my greenish-stained teeth and my red tongue stuck out between them. Then I put on a tragic frown. Thank you, your red tongue has been brought to our attention. There are no men's rooms, by the way, only Recovering Sexists' Rooms. Bleah. Excuse me for being male, Queen Women's Center.

I stepped around the metal partition and walked toward the

urinals. I saw that everyone in the men's room was hammered, because they swayed to and from the toilets as if they'd received several mallet blows to the head. One fortyish guy stepped up to the urinal on my left and started describing to his friend how stupid the blond he had the eye on at his table was. Then a much older man in a wrinkled blue seersucker suit stepped up on my right, farted and began to tell everyone about the honor he'd once had being in a line of British colonels pissing off the back of some King Somebody's balcony in Kenya at the end of "the War." I looked down at my shoes; all I'd ever done was take an occasional pee in the Atlantic.

While I was standing there Peter stepped up on the far side of the youngish guy and unzipped.

"Hey." I caught his eye.

Peter nodded, waited about ten seconds, sighed and flushed. I stared over at him. Everyone else was about three quarters of the way through a long, three-drink piss. The youngish guy even had his eyes closed in pleasure.

"You know, Alex," Peter said, leaning forward slightly, as if we were at the end of a serious discussion, "I still don't think you should have let the guy fuck you. You just met him, after all. That's just the way I feel." He stepped away and walked back to the sinks along the opposite wall.

"What?" I tried to turn my head back. When I did I came face to face with the older guy in seersucker. He was looking down on me with such unmitigated contempt that I couldn't get out another word. All three men finished quickly and stepped away. I stared at the American Standard symbol on top of the urinal, fuming, and waited for them to wash their hands and go. The men muttered at the towel machine, then left together.

I found Peter standing at the mirror near the door, wetting down the few blond hairs which were sticking up at the crown of his head. I watched his tanned reflection rather than him. Was this the same guy who'd slipped me a note during the President's Freshman Address that said, "Are you just shopping this class?"

"Was that supposed to be funny?" I said.

"No," Peter said breezily, "not really."

"Well then, what the fuck?"

He shrugged. "Nothing, all right? I just really wanted my turn. Don't pay attention to those old farts."

"Who cares about the old farts?" I leaned back against the pale green stone wall. "Did I break another rule here? Is this worse than letting the cup touch the goddamn table?"

Now Peter seemed apologetic. "No, no. It's just courtesy. It's my fault. Don't lose any sleep over it."

I followed him to the door and put my hand on his arm. "Peter, I'm sorry. I was drunk. I *am* drunk."

His smile was almost bashful. "Alex, don't worry about it. Come on back to the table."

His tennis shoes squeaked over the floor outside and receded as the door swung shut. I walked back to the sinks with a crushing sensation in my chest and wrestled with an impulse to leave the club which dispersed when I got back out to the dining room.

Back at our table I noticed that many of the couples seated around us had moved on to dessert and become interested in our table's progress with its cups. Some of the older men joined in with our songs, then gifts began to arrive on the waiter's tray, all of them booze in some manifestation, all of them to be imbibed before we left the club. In response, and against my stated judgment on the matter, Brook and Peter put on more steam. They each got a fresh cup and started singing "Down the Field," then going under for the alternate verses, which I and the alums supplied. The alums smiled at us as if they knew exactly who we were and what we were doing, and we smiled back and more drinks came. Smiling back at alums can be a dumb move.

Nine-thirty came and went and Mory's began to empty out. Brook gave strong handshakes to the men and kissed the hands of all the ladies who stopped by the table. One couple, John and

Susan Madeira, even lived down the street from Brook in Darien. Brook sent the Madeiras a bottle of champagne on his tab, but they sent it back to us since they were on their way out. We also had a run of complimentary gin and tonics and bourbon and sodas—most of them long, whatever the hell that meant—and then another green cup and a velvet cup, which tasted like mop water spiked with Stoli and almost sent me running back to the men's room again.

When the main dining room was empty except for bus boys and waiters, Peter popped our champagne and stood to make an announcement. I applauded before he started so I'd have it out of the way.

"Excuse me, excuse me for a minute! Could I get something in, please? Could I just propose a toast?"

"Go for it." Brook held up a glass.

"All right." Peter wiped his lips. "This is a toast for Price, my roommate last year, who finally showed some sense and turned down Princeton."

"Hear, hear!" Brook tipped the champagne bottle up to his lips and drank while keeping a full glass in his hands.

I stood up. "One more bathroom run. If you're done, Peter."

Peter turned halfway to me. "Almost. My only other announcement is that we head over to Naples right away. The Zeke initiation is tonight, and they should be passing free beer around."

Brook banged on the table. "Naples it is! Don't get lost again, Alex, or I'll stick you with the check."

"Impossible." I smiled at him and staggered off. "This is Daddy's treat."

In the men's room I gave back my cups. At first I only ducked into a stall to avoid the old man in seersucker who had the revelatory piss in Kenya, since he was back at the urinals again. I faintly entertained the thought of walking up and saying, "Good evening!" in a big friendly voice. The minute I laid eyes on the open mouth of the toilet bowl, though, it was all heaves and flushes.

After about five minutes I got my breath, wiped my face off and rose to my feet. My legs were shaky, but to my relief the men's room was empty. My face had gone gray in the mirror, and I splashed water on it before going back outside.

The waiter was bending over our table mopping it off, but Peter and Brook were gone. He spoke up before I could ask.

"Your friends have asked me to tell you that they will meet you at Naples restaurant. Are you feeling all right, sir?"

"I'm fine, thanks," I said. "I'll catch up with them. The bill's been taken care of?"

"Yes," the waiter said. "The doctor's son forgot to add in gratuity, but we will just include the standard."

"I know the Morehouses," I said confidently, though I was swaying. "Make it twenty-five percent, please. You were wonderful."

The waiter bowed smartly. "Thank you indeed, sir. Have a nice evening."

"Thank you, you too." I stood at sloppy attention in my blue blazer until the waiter turned, but as he walked away I hesitated and called him back. I pretended to be looking under and around the table.

"Yes, you've misplaced something, sir?"

I shook my head. "Maybe not. I was just sure that I ordered an extra bottle of champagne before I went to the men's room. Mr. Morehouse asked me to bring one along. Hm, I don't remember if I talked to you or not . . ."

The waiter looked a little surprised. "If you did, sir, it must be on its way. I'll be happy to check in the kitchen, though, and review the bill."

"Thank you." I met his eyes and pulled out my seat at the table. "It was the gold-labeled bottle, I think."

"The '78 Veuve Clicquot, I remember, sir." The waiter spoke

over his shoulder as he rushed away. "Terribly sorry about the delay."

"It's no problem." I watched the waiter plunge through the swinging doors at the far end of the room, then I picked up a small folded card on the table which told me the prices of champagne by the glass and bottle. Screw you too, Brook, I was thinking; screw both of you.

4

I went straight from Mory's to my room and, refreshed by the cooler air, I finished Jill's survey before returning to bed. At a quarter to three Peter decided to jump on my bed. I was glad to see him only because I didn't remember making it to my room before I passed out. In fact I was amazed to wake up and find myself there, even if I was still wearing a shirt, paisley tie and trousers. I could already smell the alcohol evaporating from my pores. To defeat a headache, Peter forced a half-gallon orange juice carton full of cold water on me and told me to pound it. While I drank he described the woman he'd met at Naples Pizza in vivid detail. Eventually he got around to telling me that an indirect invitation had been passed along which gave him the opportunity to return to this woman's room if he so desired. He looked eager to do this but too nervous.

"That's great," I said, between drinks. "She sounds great."

"Yeah, but oh, man." Peter ran his hands up through his bright blond hair. "Oh, man."

I couldn't tell how much of his anxiety was genuine and how much was Peter playing down his cockiness, but eventually we drafted a game plan—shower, change, walk to appropriate dorm, say hello—and he left me. Still, he didn't apologize for ditching me at Mory's.

I felt too woozy with bedspins to go back to sleep, so I slid out of bed and tried to stand. I saw my blazer lying in a crumpled heap at the foot of the bed and picked it up. The bottle of champagne rolled out from underneath the blazer, and I hid it away in one of the blanket drawers built into the frame of my bed. The only thing I could think of doing was to drop off the Women's Center survey, so after looking around for the address of their office I took a walk out to Elm Street to make a delivery.

A soft, warm breeze was blowing through the city and picking up pieces of gutter trash which had gathered at the rear wheels of parked cars. Deserted and lit by streetlights, the neo-Gothic corner of Elm and High looked like some run-down section of a Disney theme park after closing. I found the Women's Center's mail slot and slid the survey through, my name scrawled over the optional name line in large block letters. I had worked in reverse order on it, answering the first question last: "Women want what they deserve, and usually have a better sense of this than men." I liked the tone of that, which didn't sound at all like a recovering sexist. I hoped that Jill would be the first one to arrive at the Women's Center office the next morning, since I had also included a phone extension and dorm address at the top of the sheet in case she wanted to call me and talk about it.

Several hours later Brook and I shopped our first class together, something in the 200-level called "Postmodernism and Cultural Codes" that looked intriguing to me and like a solid Credit/Fail elective to him; thus we sat in the back row in case early escape became necessary. I took sips from a hangover cola that had to last for the next forty minutes and kept an eye peeled for Jill. Lots of smugly satisfied upperclassmen poured into the room, and more of the tall, boyish women I'd seen everywhere since I arrived, but Jill wasn't among them.

"You look like shit," Brook said, apropos of nothing.

I looked over. "What?"

"I said you're a corpse. You sure you'll be up to salvaging furniture at my place later?"

"Don't worry. I'm just hung over."

"Hung over," he said. "You didn't even go to the keg-suck."

"Well," I said, "don't you let me miss the next one."

When I sat back I spotted Peter standing just beyond the entry doors of the auditorium, holding hands with a short blond woman. His hair was sticking up in more places than at the crown of his head now; it was obvious that he'd just rolled out of bed. I was pleasantly surprised, however, to see that the woman wasn't some knockout beautiful phony, as his description might have led me to believe. What struck me about her was that she didn't stop talking to Peter for one second, even as they maneuvered down, over and up through the packed auditorium on the strength of Brook's beckoning wave. She seemed to be giving Peter highly complicated directions, which he was receiving with amused sobriety. Was it possible that they'd only known each other a few hours?

Brook elbowed me. "I knew he'd come. What do you think?"

"She's funny-looking," I said. "I mean she looks funny."

"Huh. Peter looks pretty couched too."

"He's got postcoital hair."

Brook grunted and went back to the syllabus. "I can see I'll be doing all the heavy lifting."

As Brook said this Peter grabbed his new girlfriend's arm and picked me out of the crowd with a melodramatically pointing index finger. She exclaimed, "Oh!"—whether disappointed or pleased I wasn't sure—and the two of them walked up the carpeted slope to where we sat. The woman took a deep breath and broke into a warm, almost mischievous smile, much the same smile that my Aunt Cassie produced during Christmas visits before she grabbed a couple of ounces of my cheek and tenderized it between her thumb and forefinger. I felt lightheaded and smiled back.

"Hey," Peter greeted us. "This is Flavia Nathan, guys. Flavia, meet Brook Morehouse and Alex MacDonald." Brook leaned forward in his seat, I stood, and we all shook hands.

"Hiii," Flavia said politely, "nice to meet you." She spoke with a deep, scratchy-throated Long Island accent that put me at ease. She had a long, straight nose, a round chin and huge brown eyes with thin brows. A coral gloss glistened on her full lips, and in the back of her curly blond hair sat a large pink bow. She wore an outsized T-shirt knotted at her right hip, and a pleated black miniskirt that showed off her sturdy if unmuscular brown legs.

"Peter thought this was the class," she continued, "but I made him find you to be sure. I have *to*tal stress on the first day, can I tell you?"

They squeezed in on my right. Peter winked at me.

"What's up?"

"You're almost late," I said. I leaned forward and glanced at Flavia. "You two look like you just walked off an airplane."

"What's that supposed to mean?" Peter gave the crowd a once-over and combed his bright blond eyebrows with his middle fingers. "Looks like this is the gut of choice."

I looked for Brook's reaction. "The air conditioning's a big draw."

"It's not a gut," Peter said. "I was *joking*. The prof is my adviser's wife; they're both great. She'll probably do some flashy, shopping-period lecture to get people to sign up, then she'll unload the real stuff."

I sat back in my seat. "So this whole week is like a curriculum payola thing?"

"Seriously. Flavia, didn't you say the Westerbrooks used to live close to you in New York?"

Flavia leaned forward and tucked some hair behind her left ear, revealing a Lucite fortune cookie earring.

"Who, Julia and Bob Westerbrook? They're awesome. They were in my building for ten years. Mom used to have them over for dinner."

"So they're pretty hip?" I said.

"Oh yeah." Flavia pursed her lips and nodded, as if the Westerbrooks were the salt of the earth. "Bob is this old-money Philadelphia guy who dropped out of law school in '68 and got his Ph.D. in metaphysics or something. Julia told me about meeting him at Berkeley when he was teaching a be-in seminar. Apparently once a week this class would meet under some tree and talk about Being and everyone would eat hashish cakes and exist. He walked in the first day and said, 'Hi, I'm your instructor Bob Westerbrook, and I've seen God.' "

Peter yawned over a laugh. "The psychedelic philosophy lab."

Flavia brought her manicured fingernails to her lips, and from there to the thickly veined back of Peter's hand. "That's exactly what it was. And then the final project was to construct some object and bring it in. It wasn't supposed to be a term paper or whatever, just produce a *thing*. So Julia, who was taking this class and had the hots for Bob, brought in an angel food cake she made, okay? That *night*, Bob drives over to Julia's apartment with the cake, gives her an A on her 'final project' and proposes to her. Of course they used the angel food cake at the wedding the next week. It was totally stale, but Bob said it was rich in Being. Oh, my God—queerer."

"Probably rich in hash," I said.

"Up the butt," Flavia agreed. "Julia used to put hash in her meat loaf in those days. They had some kind of pagan ceremony held in a state park where everybody tripped on mushrooms for three days, so they're not even legally married. . . . But the best thing was, apparently they went back to this picnic area for the reception where everything was laid out? And right on top of the picnic table there's a huge porcupine, and he's already eaten half the cake. Anyway, Julia's great. Not all the way on sometimes, but great. Bob's kind of, ehh, wacky-crazy-Waspy-strange. I think their daughter Aphrodite just swam around Manhattan."

"Flavia," I said, "you made all of this up."

"No, not a word," she said. "Can't you just see the porcupine, though? It's about two hours later and he's munchin' on a fern in the woods, and he looks up and says, 'Oh, my God, I'm *so* stoned.' "

When Julia Westerbrook walked up to the podium I couldn't help staring. She paused halfway across the stage and looked out at us as if she'd wandered into her bathroom to retrieve a brush and found five hundred undergraduates there instead. With a guitar, and without her glasses, she might have been mistaken for Joni Mitchell. The crowd grew quiet as she called for the lights and her first pair of slides in a smooth, deep voice.

"Slides, please." The polished way she said it made me smile with pleasure.

The lecture was entitled "Cold War Ideology in Modern Animation." We began with "The Rocky and Bullwinkle Show." I couldn't follow the lecture after this opening because Flavia launched into a contagious fit of laughter, interspersed with the line "Nothin' up my sleeve—*pres*to!" which she repeated several times in a moose voice to keep the flames fanned. Brook pinched his Roman nose shut with two fingers and turned red trying to hold it back. He wrote on the back of his syllabus, "We have found the gut of the CENTURY." I couldn't believe that anyone would take notes, but as one of Westerbrook's teaching assistants shut the doors and dim lights came up over the seats, quite a few people did get out their pens and binders. And ten minutes in, when the professor said, "This discourse is first codified in the activated political consciousness symbolized by the ticking bomb," a hush settled over the auditorium. At this point Peter nudged me, smiled with a finger over his lips and said, *"Shh"* like a homeroom monitor. I didn't know what to think. The lecture was half theoretical gobbledygook and half verbal play. And whenever my doubts began to override my admiration, Professor Westerbrook made a casual remark about the politics of the U.S. entertainment industry or the history of the relationship between societal mores and animation, and I was interested again.

With three minutes left in the hour, the professor put down her lecture notes, walked around to the front of the podium and took off her glasses.

"First of all," she said into the dim light, "let me apologize. What you have just seen is a rather arcane example of postmodern practice. The basic message behind it all is that modernism has now been absorbed, and the mandate becomes, change the object of focus itself, read everything as the cultural text it undeniably is. As we will see this semester, the line between what is critical and what is creative has virtually disappeared. Every stratum of culture can be, or *must* be, read as a body of codes and myths that obtain in all aspects of life. If we as part of an already privileged group become blind to these codes, we are in danger of becoming as a nation what Said calls the mediocracy. We'll look at some strategies to stave off the mediocracy this fall. Thanks."

A huge black and white image now flashed on the screen, a kitschy department store wig mannequin photographed in stark profile, with a caption down the left-hand side that said: YOUR GAZE HITS THE SIDE OF MY FACE. The applause was loud as the lights came up again.

Flavia took us down to meet Julia Westerbrook afterward. She gave Flavia a surprised hug, stood back to look at her and said that she should be thinking about retirement if Flavia Nathan was old enough to be in college. Then she fielded a question I had about the lecture, swinging her glasses back and forth in her hand. All I could think of was that the woman before me had once stayed up all night baking an angel food cake to ace a class.

As we stood there a voice spoke out behind me—"Julia!"— and Jill Lanigan walked up to our crowd in a tight black cotton dress with a deep scoop front. The dress hugged the slim curve of her hips and made a striking contrast against her white chest. Her intent, elegant presence assured me that Westerbrook had to be for real. I cleared my throat to get Jill's attention but she marched right past me and extended her hand.

"Hi!"

"Hi!" Julia Westerbrook said. She took Jill's hand in both of hers. "I loved your little note. How was your summer?"

"It was wonderful," Jill said. Her voice was hoarse, as if she'd been screaming a lot recently. "This all sounds like fun."

Peter and Flavia stepped back, and Brook got tapped on the shoulder by one of his Andover friends, but I didn't budge.

"It's an introductory survey for the most part," Professor Westerbrook said, "but the reading is wonderful. And we've got a couple of Yvonne Rainer films too." Her voice was starting to drawl a little.

"Fantastic." Jill folded her slender arms with satisfaction.

"Yeah," I added, "that sounds great."

Jill glanced over at me without really looking, but paused. Perhaps she realized that she had interrupted a conversation that was in progress before she arrived.

"Hi," she said unsurely.

"The lost freshman," I said, "remember?"

"Right, right." Jill snapped her fingers. "You're off to a good start if you found this class."

Professor Westerbrook smiled. "I feel that I'm about to be asked a favor."

"I was going to invite you for a coffee, actually," Jill said. "And I'd love to talk about my essay proposal before things get crazy."

"Sure, I've got half an hour." Professor Westerbrook stepped back to her podium and grabbed her shoulder bag.

"First let me see if I've got my copy . . ." Jill started searching through her black leather bag for something. As her search became pointed, and then almost frantic, a playful, guilty smile spread over her lips.

"Aha!" she cried. "Here it is."

"Good, we're set. Unless . . ." Professor Westerbrook paused now and stared at me, offering to draw me in, perhaps. For a moment I thought that she was going to introduce us.

"Did you have another question about anything?"

I opened my mouth but no sound came out. The auditorium was nearly empty behind me.

"I was just wondering," I sputtered, and felt a blush rising from my throat to my cheeks. "Are you going to be doing a discussion section of your own?"

"No, sorry." She smiled at me. It was an entirely different smile from the one Jill had been favored with. "I wish I had the time but I can't. I thought I mentioned that when I started. Sorry to keep you waiting." She turned to Jill, and I was outside again.

"Do you want to try that new place on Chapel?" Jill said. She smoothed one pale eyebrow with a pinkie finger. "I think they roast their own beans."

"Sure, I was running so late this morning that I haven't even had a cup. Did you see . . ."

Jill and the professor moved off and up the stairs. To make my mortification complete, some people who had arrived for the next class were looking down at me as if it were the most ridiculous thing imaginable that I was standing there by myself. I looked up at the double doors of the auditorium, and I left too.

Late that afternoon I found myself pulling into the wealthy Manhattan bedroom community of Darien, Connecticut, with Peter and Brook. Peter sat next to Brook in the front of his Wagoneer and the two compared notes on another crew practice. They made an amusing study from the back seat: Brook ramrod straight at the wheel, his hands at ten o'clock and two o'clock; Peter, with his postcoital hair, sprawled over the passenger side drinking Perrier. I rolled down both my windows and tried to ignore my headache as we roared past sporting goods shops and upscale malls whose low roofs shimmered in the hot sun. Brook became engrossed in his conversation and we leveled out at eighty-five or so. Occasionally Peter would look back, catch me staring at our driver and lift his eyebrows in mock terror.

After progressing through better and better neighborhoods we arrived on Brook's wide street and pulled up his driveway. The Morehouses lived in a two-and-a-half-story Georgian-style house with a stone portico. As we approached the end of the drive an old golden retriever squeezed through a line of bushes and hurtled itself across the lawn toward us. Brook gave it an innocuous scratch behind the ear when he got out of the Wagoneer. With no further encouragement, the dog lost interest in us and headed for the bushes again. Brook hadn't opened his mouth in the last five minutes.

"Brook," I said, "that's a beautiful retriever."

He body-checked his door shut. "They're standard issue around here." He kept his eyes on the front of the house as we walked toward it.

"What's it called?" Peter asked. "Brandy?"

"Yeah, right." Brook hesitated, then broke into a light jog. "Let me just check the front door. If it's locked I'll go around and let you in!"

"Forget your keys?" I called.

"No." Brook's voice floated across the huge, manicured lawn. The street was absolutely silent except for one sprinkler behind us and some far-off thunder from a pair of blue-black, anvilheaded storm clouds building in the western sky.

The front door was unlocked. Brook held it for us and slammed it shut after Peter. We stood in a cool, dark front hall. To my right was a large living room that held a chandelier, a pair of antique sofas, several framed botanical prints and a floor-to-ceiling secretary. It was the first living room I'd ever seen without a television set.

Brook looked around as if getting oriented. "Great. You can go right up, I think. The attic stairs are across the hall from the second-floor landing. I'm going to see who's around." He walked down the long front hall and disappeared through a swinging door at its end into another part of the house.

Peter and I stood for a moment without speaking.

" 'You can go up, I *think'?*" I said.

Peter led the way up the stairs. "Who knows? Maybe the ghost of some anal-retentive grandmother lives in the attic."

The walls in the stairwell were hung with framed Currier & Ives prints of Hartford and pastel sketches of a young, fierce-looking Brook, an older sister and the dog we'd just seen on the lawn. As we climbed, Peter ran a finger over the top of every surface.

"I can just hear Mom if she was called in to renovate this place. 'Oh, Mrs. Morehouse, what *your* rooms need is some choreography!' "

"It is kind of tight-assed," I said, "isn't it?"

At the top of the flight we heard Brook's voice, first below us, then behind us again. A woman called after him in a tone nearly as deep as his.

"Have a good trip, Koob!"

"Koob!" Peter turned to me and beamed. "Koobie. No wonder he wanted to cut his parents off at the pass. Yeah, that *does* have potential."

"You can try it out on him first," I said. "I don't want to look pushy."

Brook caught up with us at the attic door on the second floor. He moved Peter aside and half pulled, half lifted this door open.

"Sorry about the delay, guys. Après-golf games of cards. Everybody's a little sauced. . . . Actually, everybody got a little too sauced to get to the club. My dad the doctor trashing his body." He switched on the attic light and took the stairs by threes on his muscular legs.

"This shouldn't take too long. I just cleaned out this place two weeks ago."

The attic was sixty by ninety feet, smelled of pine, and was packed with Waspy junk. I saw cracked paddle tennis racquets, cracked woodsy toys, boxes marked FURS in black marker, sailing plaques, a stack of Yale and Dartmouth yearbooks and a pillow with a stained needlepointed cover that said, "Bridge is the Opiate of the Affluent." Brook wasn't pleased at the order of things, particularly since we'd promised to clear out all the items beyond keeping. He kicked a couple of boxes angrily.

"Jesus Christ! Has the maid been tripping up here or what? I had this neat before I left!"

"Brook, chill out," Peter said. "This is much neater than my dad's whole house." He wandered about, leaning over boxes and trunks, and paused at a chintz-covered couch. Here he dug around and brought up a two-by-four-foot sign on thick poster-board. There were three red, white and blue elephants linked tail to snout on it, over a slogan in large letters that read, BE A TRUE AMERICAN—VOTE REPUBLICAN. Peter hoisted this sign up in his hands, moaned and started toward me in a Frankenstein lurch. I backed up, pretended to fall and dragged myself backward.

"God, please, not that!"

"Yeah, we keep the mutilated girls up here too," Brook muttered. "Why don't you both stop whacking off and move some of this stuff down to the Wagoneer? I'm sweating my balls off already."

"Right-o." Peter leaned the sign against a box of furs and walked back over to the couch. He pulled off the chintz covering. Underneath, it was an off-white linen color. He punched its back.

"How about this?"

"Great." Brook nodded. "We used to have that at the shore place. What do you think, Alex?"

I pretended to arrive at an aesthetic judgment about the couch, though in fact it was nicer than the one currently in my living room at home. "That's good. As long as the bottom's not out."

"Looks pretty solid." Peter bent before the couch and grabbed an end. He had a thinner, less sinewy build than Brook's, but he looked pretty strong too. "Brook, you wanna give me a hand?"

"Alex, you go down first and direct traffic," Brook said. He bent down to the other end of the couch and got on eye level with Peter. They groaned the piece up together and started toward the stairs.

"The son of a bitch is heavy," Peter said.

"Feels like half the fucking beach is still in the bottom," Brook grunted.

"Maybe it's the maid," I said. I started taking backward steps down the wooden stairs and calling out directions for Brook to go a little left or right. He and Peter made it six steps down before we all heard a rude scraping noise in the stairwell. Brook pulled sharply, and an oar from the '56 Head of the Charles race that was hanging on the wall fell onto the cushions. A cloud of dust rose up over Brook's head. He cursed and pulled on the couch again. Now it was stuck fast.

"Off like a herd of turtles," I said.

Peter's head peeked down from the top of the stairs. "Alex— check your script!"

"Goddamn this thing," Brook huffed. He moved up to the fifth stair of the flight and gave a tremendous pull. There followed a sound of exploding wood and an ominous whisper of plaster like mice running inside the walls. Peter let go of his end. The couch stayed exactly where it was, pointing down at a thirty-degree angle.

"All right!" he called. "Who wants to go out with me and start pulling on the other side of the house?"

"It got up here," Brook said with annoyance, "so it's going to come *down*."

We were silent for a moment, trying to think of a new plan. While we stood there, a door creaked on its hinges far below and a deep male voice shouted: "Two spades, Gwen? For Judas' sake!" Then heavy steps started up the first flight of stairs. I turned to see a huge, glowing, middle-aged man in green corduroy shorts and a white polo striding toward me. He had a dark tan, a hawkish nose like Brook's and almost as much of the same black hair, slicked and combed back. He held a sweating highball glass in his left hand and was exhaling moist breaths that smelled of scotch. Brook craned his head around.

"Oh, fuck."

"Hi, boys." Dr. Morehouse met me on the third stair from the bottom and swallowed my hand in his. Peter gave a friendly wave from the top.

"Koob told us you were here, but we were playing for high stakes. Ten cents a point. What's all the ruckus, son?"

"Nothing, Dad, we're totally okay." Brook stared down at him. "You can go back to your game."

Dr. Morehouse started up the attic stairs. "You can have the couch, but leave the oar. What's your name, son?"

Peter looked quite impressed with Dr. Morehouse, and leaned down at a precarious angle over the couch to shake hands with him.

"Peter Cliffman. It's a pleasure to meet you, Doctor."

"Pleasure to meet you," Dr. Morehouse said gravely. He crowded the stairway so much that Brook had to back down two steps. "And you're playing some squash this year?"

"No, that's Alex, behind you," Peter said. "I'm rowing with Brook at the moment."

"Wonderful," he said. "I was a first in my heavyweight boat for two years."

"It still shows."

"Dad, if you don't mind," Brook interrupted, his arms tightly folded. "And we weren't planning on taking the oar. We're fine."

Dr. Morehouse examined both trapping walls. "Doesn't look fine, Koob. You're going to take half the plaster with you, you're so stubborn." He moved a little closer to the action and gripped the edge of the couch with one hand.

"I see your problem here. Just twist the thing, boys, you've gotta twist it! I delivered babies for ten years, I ought to know."

"Jesus Christ." Brook shoved harder. "We've got to get it back up to the top and start over."

"Hey now"—Dr. Morehouse swished the ice cubes in his glass as he pointed—"easy on that language."

Brook stared. "What language? Nobody here believes in him."

Peter was already creating a diversion by twisting the couch as Dr. Morehouse said he should, and it began to slide forward a little. Brook looked up at him as if he were trapped in a crevice, and Peter's twisting the couch was forcing him into a ravine. A man's voice called up from downstairs.

"Carter! It's been your bid for five minutes!"

"On my way!" he called down. "Ah well, I guess you've got it now. Through no good of yours, Koob." He slapped his son's soaking back. "Drop me a line as soon as you get out on the water."

Brook stood under the arm of the couch and looked down to see his father's hand clapping on my shoulder.

"We already are on the water, Dad. Thanks a lot."

Now the same voice called up the stairs again. I turned and saw a tall, bearded man with tortoise-shell glasses and a bright red face. "Carter, no need to rush now! Betty's running down to the plaza to pick up some tonic water. Is that your kid's car in the driveway?"

"Are we out already?" Dr. Morehouse said incredulously. "Barry, don't break up the proceedings, I'll just send Brook."

Brook shook his head. "Can't do it, Dad, we just got started here. I haven't got time."

"Don't fret," Dr. Morehouse called down to his friend. "I'll be right with you." When the bearded man disappeared he took a few steps toward Brook. He nearly lost his balance on the last step.

"Koob," he began, "it'll take you fifteen minutes. Would you rather your mother went?"

"Dad . . ." Brook pleaded in a low, tight voice. "Send the goddamn maid, would you?"

"All right, Koob, you know this is Darlene's day off. And you'll have to move your car regardless."

"Dad—"

"I said all right, enough of this piffle!" I watched in amazement as Dr. Morehouse's thick arm lifted in an arc. He slammed his highball glass down onto a stair, but miraculously it didn't shatter. Peter stopped twisting and Brook blushed.

"You've got two able-bodied men here while you're gone." He threw a twenty from his wallet onto the stair in front of him and pointed up at Brook. "I want six bottles of tonic water from the Corkscrew. Get them from the cooler. And you get them back here in fifteen minutes or you can forget the furniture. I mean it." He picked up his glass, turned and stomped back down the stairs toward me, breathing hard through his nose. I caught a quick glimpse of his face and looked down at my feet. As he passed me he bellowed again.

"Did you hear me, Brook?"

Brook scowled at his retreating figure. "Yeah."

Peter raised an eyebrow at me. When Dr. Morehouse disappeared back into the first-floor hallway, Brook looked like the load he was about to carry down the stairs had been halved. On the other hand, half his strength seemed to be gone too.

"Alex!" Now Brook's voice boomed. "You want to take over? I've got to run this little errand for Dr. Jekyll. I'll be back as soon as I can."

"Sure, no prob." I ran up the stairs and took Brook's end. He grabbed the oar from the cushions without glancing up at either of us and started down the flight.

"Brook," I called, "you okay?"

"Save it," he said. He let the oar clatter to the bottom of the attic stairs, kicked it from underfoot and took the next flight in twos.

5

Over the next few days I caught glimpses of Jill slipping out of buildings or walking briskly up Elm Street, hand in hand with her friends. I saw her everywhere, it seemed, and the only thing clear to me was that I was hooked. Something about Jill made me drop out of conversation in a group of people and stare off, wondering how she spent her days and nights, or what her landscape and sensations might be at a particular moment.

The first opportunity to call her presented itself at the end of the week, at the first official private off-campus party of the year. Peter, Brook and I were going to crash it and hook up with Flavia and some of her Dalton School friends from New York and have some official fun. Flavia had only heard about the party, but even that was something, being freshmen as we were. *Everybody* was supposed to be at it, Flavia said. I already knew that when people say "everybody" they usually mean five or six people they envy or lust after, but I couldn't deny that even a rumored party beat another night of sitting in our common room killing a case of beer or playing Quarters at Naples, so off we went.

Brook briefed us on the party and its hostess Jiffy Smith in minute detail. He emphasized that if we found anyone selling coke to let him know, and that we could join him for a line if he scored. Brook had dressed in his whitest polo and greenest corduroy shorts, then slapped enough hair fixative on that he looked like he was wearing a wax wig.

I said, as we wove through the evening bustle on Broadway, "Do you actually *know* Jiffy, Brook?"

He shrugged and checked his hair again. "Haven't met her, no."

Peter looked at Brook in disbelief. "Well then, how the hell are we going to get in?"

"Our in," Brook said in his deep voice, "is that I have this friend from Andover, Mike Berwynd, who's been doing Jiffy. So we come in like we're just stopping by to take Mike over to Rudy's Bar and have a couple of pitchers. If he wants to hang out, we stay at the party and take him out later; if he's into going to Rudy's we'll buy him some drinks and he'll invite us back. Simple."

"Yeah," Peter said, "like we're really going to get past the bouncer at Rudy's. I was just carded today."

"I've got a picture from my twenty-first birthday party," I said.

Brook considered all of this. "Maybe Mike and I will just slip into Rudy's for a drink and you two can wait outside. I haven't been carded since I was fifteen."

I closed my eyes to the nighttime whirl and imagined the top of Brook's dresser lined with several years of prom photos, each one with an identical Brook and an increasingly taller date. When I opened my eyes again we had come up to Lynwood Place, the site of the rumored party.

Lynwood is a short, tranquil-looking street nicely set off from Elm, and roofed in with thick trees which spread their late summer branches right down to the tops of parked cars. It is laid out with about two dozen Victorian houses, some two- and some three-story. That fall, Lynwood was considered to be the Paris district of Yale off-campus life. I guessed this was because the apartments were spacious and expensive, or because a lot of the people renting there had been to Paris, or walked around trying to make you believe that they had been, or some combination of these things.

Before we got to Jiffy's we saw the varsity football team quarterback swaying back and forth at the door of his screened-in porch near the corner of Lynwood. He had an enormous head that was almost all cheeks and forehead and a circle of tight red curls that grew thin and sparse near the top of his skull. His arms and face were burned to a tan, but his big legs were white in their rugby shorts. He was about as Paris as I was. The house behind him was in the grips of a party so loud I swore I could feel the bass vibrations from the stereo on the street.

Brook walked up the steps of the house and they knocked each other around in greeting for a moment. Another huge guy with a pneumatic-drill chin cleft and blond hair emerged and put a cup of keg beer in Brook's hand. Peter and I walked up when Brook waved us forward.

"This can't be the right party," I said in a low voice.

"No chance," Peter agreed.

"Guys," Brook said, "meet Dave Freitag. My sister used to date his brother Pat. This is Peter and Alex." We shook hands.

"You're not throwing this party with Jiffy Smith, are you?" Peter said.

Freitag hissed out a belch. "Uh-uh, that's down at 18. We've been getting shitheads looking for her place all night. We just booted a couple of faggots who were drinking all our vodka. I was like, 'What am I, a rest stop?'"

"Oh, really," Brook said, nodding. "So what happened?"

Freitag gripped his porch railing and looked off down the street. "We just asked them if they were invited. Then Talbot here walks up and takes the drinks right out of their hands!"

"Talbot!" Brook shouted to the guy with the chin cleft. "You son of a bitch!"

"What are you standing outside for?" he called back. "It's pussy heaven in here!"

"We'd like to hang out, but we've got to meet some people," Peter said. He took a step back. "Including my girlfriend."

"Stop by later," Freitag said, though he looked only at Brook. "We'll be here."

"Take care," Brook said. We started down the street but paused at Freitag's call.

"Hey, remember—it's not a party till someone breaks something!"

The sound of a British synthesizer band grew as we ascended the long staircase between the first and second floors of 18 Lynwood. When my eyes adjusted to the dark I could see taped on the wall corkscrewed strips of glossy paper cut from a map of the moon. Over the door at the top of the stairs there was a red Christo poster of a wrapped Pont Neuf stuck with darts.

We walked in and soon were confronted by Jiffy. She had a perfect bob of chestnut hair, a deep tan and the kind of presence that demanded attention due to a rich dad. She also had a closed, tired face that could have been nineteen and could have been thirty-five. Jiffy's annoyance upon seeing us was obvious. Apparently her boyfriend Mike had invited fifty people at his crew practice that afternoon and gave them the address, and now he wasn't there. Brook improvised and dug up some very old but common ghosts from his and Jiffy's pasts, and eventually she allowed us into the party. After this she ignored us.

The second floor of the house was gloriously air-conditioned and, with its french doors open, long enough to bowl in. I smelled fresh wood, as if a new floor had just been laid in or some other renovations done. There were track lights turned low around the living room and several fluorescent black bulbs substituted into a junkish assortment of table lamps in the rest of the space. Dance music, very trendy and bass-heavy, was pounding out from a pair of passive radiator speakers that looked like pants presses. Once past the contingent of preppies, I saw that most of the people at the party were dressed in black. At Hollier Prep this meant that you were colorful and ran around with other people in black, looking cold. This crowd made mincemeat of any trendies from my experience, though—they were the most angst-ridden revelers I'd ever laid eyes on.

Peter went to find us some booze in the kitchen, and Brook slipped over to pay respects to Jiffy's friends, who were standing very close together in one large clump. I hesitated, grimacing at myself for falling into old habits, but drifted toward the least threatening people I saw. A short guy with a red bowl-cut was talking to a pretty Japanese woman in a long white silk shirt and British walking shorts that practically reached her ankles. They were standing behind a partial wall that cut out most of the music. I drifted past them a couple of times, pretending to get a lay of the place. The guy was talking about filming at Cape Kennedy with a cable TV station he had started at a high school in Florida. He looked pure 1600 SAT to me, but I forced myself to step closer. If filmmakers were the least threatening people at Yale parties, I had better get used to it.

"The crowds you get out there for a launch are always *incredible*," the redheaded guy said. "People take a week off from work to go down and camp out so they can get a good spot. And the whole launch doesn't even last ninety seconds."

The woman was taking little bites from the edge of a soda cracker and looking around too much to be paying attention, so I stepped in, unannounced but desperate to gain social mooring.

"I guess for a lot of people," I said, "seeing a space launch is a good modern equivalent of a religious experience. Without drugs, I mean."

"Yeah!" The guy looked up, blinking, and smiled brightly at me. "Wow, exactly, that's great! I'm George—who are you?"

"Alex MacDonald."

"I know you," the woman cut in, "you live with that Brook guy, don't you? I'm Miyoko. I live right downstairs from you in Lawrance."

"Of course," I said. "I should have remembered."

"Then I live *upstairs* from you in B51," George said.

"How weird," I said. "Brook and I thought that this party would be all upperclassmen."

"Hey, everybody." At the mention of his name, Brook walked up with a bottle of beer.

"Hey, Brook." I stepped back and widened our circle. "We were just talking about George filming space launches in Florida."

Brook lifted his head, rotated it thirty degrees toward George and dropped it again. "Which part of Florida are you from?"

"I just lived there for a year. I was going to a technical school," George said. "I've always lived in Providence."

"What's your name?" Brook took a swig of beer and wiped his mouth with the back of his hand—one swipe on each side.

"George Grabowski."

"I used to know a girl named Jess Diffendeffer from Newport. I remember she had a brother George."

George brushed his red hair away from his eyes and shrugged. "Nope."

Brook was less attentive now that George couldn't be mapped onto his network. He looked the same way at me on the first day when I told him I grew up in Maine.

"What are you interested in?" Brook said.

George looked at me. "I think I know your roommate, Peter Cliffman? We're in Directed Studies together."

"That's him. So, are you a science person?"

"Actually, I like Comparative Literature very much."

"Fantastic."

"In which languages?" Brook said, as if he was about to trip George up in a lie.

"French and Russian," George said, "or maybe Italian. I've actually picked up some Italian living in Providence."

Brook drained his beer, and on the downstroke with his bottle exhaled into: "Comp Lit's really an unusual major for someone from your socioeconomic background."

George froze. Miyoko pulled the cracker from her mouth and went to get a napkin.

"Yeah," George said. "I'll remember that."

"Good to meet you." Brook looked at his empty beer bottle and headed back toward Jiffy's group.

"Excuse Brook," I said as soon as he was out of earshot. "You've probably guessed that he's planning on business school."

George raised his eyebrows. "So he saves time and lets people see what an asshole he is?"

"No, not exactly. He's just like that."

"I just hope you're not in a double with him. How does a beer sound?"

"Anything," I said. "Anything would be good."

We started excusing our way over toward the distant kitchen. The wall to my left where people were dancing was covered with razored pieces of Warhol's *Marilyn*. Farther on someone had pulled all the tape out of a cassette and made a tall, messy cat's-cradle bridge between the edge of a Chinese screen and a hat tree. I saw a dimly lit back porch and thick trees at the far end of the kitchen, and to the right of the screen door a small group of mud-streaked Ultimate Frisbee jocks were hot-kniving hash on an electric stove. One guy in a Joy Division T-shirt was scraping down the cooler knives like a short-order cook and taking the hot, glowing ones off the elements, then dabbing a little chunk of hash onto the tip of one knife and sandwiching another one over it. Our friend Miyoko stepped in to take up the thick, concentrated trail of smoke this produced. She was a fast operator. George looked at her as if she were in for a nasty burn.

"Check that out," I said. "That's called hot-kniving. I didn't know they did it down here."

"Ha." He nodded.

"It's a fantastically fast way to get stoned."

George looked at his watch uncomfortably. "I guess that's better than a fantastically slow way."

"Sorry." I smiled. "We can stick to beer if you want."

"No, no, go right ahead. It just gives me a headache, that's all. Uh . . ." George suddenly looked half at me and half behind me. "Alex, I don't know if I should tell you, but someone's sneaking up on you."

"Really? Do you know who?"

"Excuse me," a voice said, close to my left ear, "would you mind cheffing for me?"

I turned around. Jill. She raised one eyebrow and smiled mischievously. Her voice was so coy that it came back full circle to sounding genuine again. Tonight she wore dark mascara with eyeliner and a pair of knee-length Lycra biking shorts with aquamarine roses on them. Flavia was right—everyone *was* here.

"Hi," I said. I hoped that my blush wasn't showing in the low light. "Cheffing?"

She nodded, a little drunk, and I caught a whiff of her cologne. Antaeus. My brother Marty used to brag about how it made him unstoppable. It was such a strange choice for a woman. I felt uneasy drinking in the scent from her skin and even more uneasy realizing I was aroused by it. I'm sure she knew it, too. Jill had that kind of manner that takes admiration for granted, and yet without the hair, the slim curve of her hips, and the slightest suggestion of breasts she could have passed for a tall twelve-year-old boy.

"Cheffing, yes," she said. "Don't you know what women *really* want?"

I reddened deeper. "Cheffing—do you mean hold the knives for you? Sure."

"Thanks." Jill surveyed the room and ran her tongue slowly over her upper lip. "My date is otherwise occupied."

"Oh." My heart dropped, and I could produce nothing more than a slight nod.

She guided me to the stove burners. The seven red-glowing people there were either holding their breath or exhaling smoke —it looked like a post-apocalypse campfire. My eyes lighted on Peter with Flavia, her hair in an enormous black velvet bow, which must have been her on-the-town bow. She was going like a teletype into Peter's ear, and Peter was grinning lazily. He must have forgotten the beer he had promised to bring out to me. Flavia dipped in front of the chic woman beside me and kissed my cheek. She was half canned.

"Hi, sweetie. Thank you for being a great roommate to Peter."

I pecked her back. "That's okay, he's low-maintenance."

Jill's eyes followed Flavia as she rejoined Peter.

"Everybody ready?" She dropped a small pinch of hash into my palm and closed the hand. I was so nervous that I could barely finger it up between my index finger and thumb and reach for the knives. I took two deep breaths and momentarily staved off the shaking.

"Let's do it," I said.

As she cleared her lungs of air Jill steadied herself with a hand planted against my chest. Her thumb grazed my left nipple and I felt a shiver that ran down to my waist. When I looked at Jill's chest I saw nothing but flesh underneath the thin T-shirt. My eyes dropped from the curves of her breasts to find that I'd already pressed the hash between the two hot knives, and that the magic smoke was billowing up.

She bent over quickly to inhale. "Thanks for warning me."

Ringed with smoke and red light, Jill flicked her head back and stood motionless, almost meditating, but looking as if she'd been outsmarted too. I looked directly into her green eyes and watched a thin squiggle of a vein in her left temple appear and recede under her skin. The look on my face—stupefied, animalistic wonder, no doubt—made her crack up in laughter momentarily. Then she swallowed and got her bearings back. Ten, fifteen, twenty seconds. She smiled as she exhaled. Almost no smoke came through her lips.

"Your turn." She popped another smidgen of hash into my hand. "I'm already too stoned to help you, unfortunately."

"No problem," I said. "You must have huge lungs." I looked around the stove. Peter and Flavia were now jamming and pulsing in the kitchen to a fast reggae number called "Police Officer." Everyone else looked heightened. The darkness of the party proper looked like the next town. I was getting baked just from the heat and exhaled smoke. And I couldn't believe who was standing with me.

I chugged up a knife and a half, giving the remainder of the second one to Jill. She exhaled for a long time, suddenly melancholy, and ran her hands through her hair. Then she turned and wandered out of the kitchen without me.

"Wait," I stammered. My sensory elevators were already plunging—it was incredibly potent hash.

She looked back. "What's up?"

"Don't you want to hang out? I . . . don't even know you."

She turned and scanned the room. "That's true. One dance would be fun."

"*One* dance!"

Jill shook her head. "I'm sorry—I mean *a* dance. I'm going on all sorts of different levels. Sorry. Come on."

I took her hand and we wove over to the dance area and found a spot. She had a long, thin hand that surprised me with its coldness. I tightened on it and was thrilled when it tightened back. Everything was beginning to mean too much as I approached the canyon's edge of the stone and prepared for the free fall. Jill turned quickly and began to dance, sweeping around in an unstructured order of spins and gesticulations. The music now was a popular funk song mixed through with some professor's taped response to a paper on Hegel. We heard two lines of a female vocalist and one line of mixer beat with a dry voice on a cheap cassette recording saying things like "Your comment about Absolute Knowledge comes prematurely." I was too nervous to find it funny.

As we danced, the aquamarine roses in Jill's shorts started lifting off and spinning. Space became foreshortened until those roses were the single object of my gaze. I wondered for a panicked second if I was going to take off all my clothes and run into a cold shower because my body was covered in piranha caterpillars made of pumice, as had happened the last time I smoked too much good hash.

"—your friends."

My head snapped up. I was drifting. "What?"

"I said I'm sorry if I dragged you away from your friends."

"That was just my roommate," I stammered. "And his girlfriend."

"Good," she said. "Great dope, n'est-ce pas?"

"Yeah. It was like Mercury back there."

She screwed up her eyes and bent close to my ear. "Come again?"

I laughed. I nearly couldn't stop. I was almost over the lip of the canyon. My lips were almost on hers. "I mean the heat, and the red . . . and the increasing depth."

"That's cute." Her teeth were bright white, like wet ivory. "I wonder how big the sun is on Mercury."

Cute. "Hey," I began, "I wondered too . . . did you dye your hair like that on a bet?"

Jill picked at a tuft of it. "A bet? No, I didn't, actually. Does it bother you?"

"No!" I shouted. "I like it a lot. I just remember my whole high school girls' tennis team dyed a blond spot in their hair for graduation. My friend bet them fifty bucks they wouldn't do it."

"Sounds like a terrific school."

"Wait, one other thing—you're Jill Lanigan, but you don't know my name, do you?"

"I don't. Do you plan to tell me?"

"Of course! It's Alex MacDonald. I like your name a lot. It's cool."

"Hi there, Alex," she said. "Are you enjoying yourself tonight?"

I bumped into someone dancing behind me and stepped closer. "Sure. The decorations are wonderful. Will they smash the stereo and hang that up for the next party?"

"Jiffy's roommate," Jill said knowingly. "I call it Western material culture chewing off its own arm. But tell me what you're about, Alex, since my name is so cool."

"What I'm about?" I looked at my feet and considered. "I don't know. I just got here. I am glad we met."

"Yes," she said ambiguously. "Here we are."

Jill was about to elaborate, but something behind me caught her eye. "Alex, I've really got to go, but thank you. Really."

She waved to someone over my shoulder and excused herself,

patting my forearm as she went. I immediately started to feel
abandoned, and on her social-phaser-shield-destroying hash I
certainly couldn't hide it.

"Wait, Jill! Can we meet for dinner, or a meal? I'd love to see
you for more than ten minutes."

She continued to walk away. Then I heard her voice—I
thought it was her voice—saying, "Sure, call me for a lunch
sometime."

Jill disappeared into a group of Eurochic people near the bar,
about eight of them, and instantly left with that whole group by
the front door. The space she vacated in front of me quickly filled
with more bodies. Now I felt myself falling back into a dark,
alienating corner of the stone, and my head swirled with white
paint drops over a black field. I walked forward unsteadily and
anchored myself against a short table strewn with the soggy remains of an hors d'oeuvre spread. My eyes squeezed shut at this
sight, and to my amazement Jill appeared in my mind's eye like a
floating afterimage of the sun. She was drifting in and out of
focus, at first alone, then accompanied by the blurred face of a
second woman I didn't recognize. I knew Jill, but who was the
second woman? She reminded me so much of somebody.

Yes, I realized, it was Katharine—as if my mind needed to run
that film again now.

I opened my eyes, saw a moving wall of strangers all in black,
and made a beeline for the bathroom.

6

Jill Lanigan was true to her word and penciled me in for
lunch at Commons, the freshman dining hall, seven days after
Jiffy's party. I knew that the odds of her canceling, rescheduling
or standing me up were high, so I told no one of our plans. No

one if you didn't count my mother. Luckily I was alone in the suite when she called.

"You have a date already?" she said. "I thought you might be mourning your losses a little longer."

"It's only a lunch, Mom. Lunch is like a date with training wheels."

"My first date with your father was a lunch," she said, then: "Do you need me to telegraph you any money?"

"Absolutely not," I said. I had a vision of my father running next door to borrow from our neighbors again. "We're going to Commons. Lunch is free."

"You're taking a date to the dining hall? Won't all your room-mates be sitting around watching?"

"You don't understand," I snapped. "There's no reason to go out; she doesn't really like me yet."

"I see." My mother laughed triumphantly. "She sounds like a great improvement over Katharine."

"I knew you wouldn't understand," I said. "Just don't send money, okay?"

I arrived at Commons six minutes late, already sweating through my boxers in the swampy heat. I scanned the scorching white acre of Beinecke Plaza several times before wandering back through the entry doors and checking for her at the College Street entrance.

"Hi." Jill tapped my shoulder as if I might explode should she tap too hard. She was leaning against a statue of the goddess Providence, her arms loosely folded.

"Hi!" I shouted, before I could mask my relief. "Sorry I'm late."

"No, I'm late, Alex, and it's very rude of me." Jill brushed her hand over my arm in greeting, and goose flesh sprang up where she touched.

"It's rude of me too," I said. I could smell Polo.

"We are a couple of incredibly rude people," Jill said. "No wonder we're reduced to having lunch together."

With the blame equally laid, we walked up two short flights of steps to the Commons antechamber. Okay, I thought, we're acting. Tomorrow or on the next date we might be real but today we're acting. Jill sauntered along with her palms pressed to the small of her back as if she'd just come in from a long run. She wore a white T-shirt tucked into a pair of torn jeans rolled up almost to the knees, a thick black leather belt and black Keds high tops. From her right ear a small blue wooden kangaroo on a pair of skis swung up and back. I looked down at my own clothing combination and immediately felt as if I'd been dressed by my mother.

We paused at the inner glass and walnut doors to the dining room. Jill gave me an amused once-over.

"Wild shorts."

I fingered one of the pockets. "I buy direct from this designer in Maine. L. L. Bean?"

"I should have guessed."

"You should have."

I pulled one of the massive doors open. Jill took a step back when she saw my doorman's stance.

"Aren't you coming too?"

I looked at her and looked at the door and realized that I was holding it for her. "Right. Let's do that again." I allowed the door to swing shut, walked up to it, pulled it open a crack and wedged my way through with my hands behind my back. The heavy weight of the wood and glass bumped threateningly against my forehead. Jill swept the door open from her side.

"Smart ass. Come on." She nudged past me and flashed her I.D. to the checker. "We've got to beat the one-fifteen rush."

I looked after Jill with wonder. Somehow she'd gotten past the notoriously sharp-eyed Commons checker without showing a meal card. I ran to her side, and we hurried across the enormous marble room to the kitchens.

Jill arranged a bowl of tomato bisque and a glass of water on her tray, while I loaded a burger, fries, a large piece of fresh challah, two root beers and an ice cream sandwich onto mine. She nudged me with an elbow at the condiments bar.

"Here, take these." She slipped two notebooks under my arm and looked out into the dining area. "There's a table about thirty feet behind you, on your right. You'll have to beat someone to it."

I followed her eyes out. For a minute the booming garble of a thousand people lunching and chattering made it too loud to see clearly. Every heavy walnut table and chair appeared occupied. Then through a break in the crowd I spotted the table that she meant.

"Good eye," I said. "Where are you going?"

She pulled at her red and blond hair with her free hand. Her tray tilted to one side and she righted it.

"I'm going to get a salad, or some fruit. Otherwise I'd be stealing from you when I finished."

I nodded dumbly. Say something.

"I'll be back there."

I beat two crew coxswains I knew slightly to the seats Jill described and put down my tray. My eye landed on a passage from something called *Male Fantasies* that was written out in tiny block letters on the back cover of one of Jill's notebooks.

The most urgent task of the man of steel is to pursue, to dam in and to subdue any force that threatens to transform him back into the horribly disorganized jumble of flesh, hair, skin, bones, intestines, and feelings that calls itself human.

I laid the notebooks down in the center of the table. I had been casting around in my mind for a conversation starter, but that wasn't it.

"Hi, thanks." Jill returned with a salad, settled in across the table from me and pulled her notebooks toward her as she shrugged her overfull book bag from her shoulder. "I'll get in gear in a minute here." She flicked a package of oyster crackers back and forth by one end and pulled it open over her bisque, then spread a napkin on her lap.

"You sound like you come from around here."

"What, Connecticut?" I shook my head. "Southern Maine."

She cut up her salad with broad strokes. "What do your parents do?"

I tried to think of an exciting euphemism, but none came to mind. "They run a small group of cottages on a beach."

"Is that so?" she said. "You rich?"

"No, we're barely middle class. Are you?"

Jill looked past me for a moment. "Rich denotes continuity. Dad's been bankrupt twice."

"Yikes."

"Oh, it fits. He's been divorced twice too. You have siblings?"

"A brother, twenty-six. He's an AP photographer."

"Interesting family. You love any of them?"

"Of course."

She raised her blondish-brown eyebrows. "Really?"

"Well, you know," I said, trying to seem sophisticated and postnuclear, "the way people love their families."

"Horribly, right." She bit into half a cherry tomato and washed it down with water. "But I can see that you miss them. You walk around looking kind of lost."

"I'm *always* lost," I said. "My old girlfriend used to say that ten minutes after I was born I was blindfolded and sent out to pick up a pizza."

"I can imagine. You should have seen yourself when you walked past me in the rotunda."

"Well," I said, "I'm not complaining now."

Jill balled up her oyster cracker package and looked disappointed. "If we're not going to complain this isn't going to be much fun."

"I just mean," I said, "that I'm glad you showed."

"I never stand up a lunch date," Jill said, as if this were the one thing she did not do. She tasted her soup and grimaced, puckering her lips. When I looked up again she was staring at me. "Alex, are you okay? You look sort of depressed."

"I'm fine," I said. I'm obsessed with you, can't you see that? "Or, I don't know, I guess I was just thinking a little while ago in the language lab. Don't you think it's weird to start a freshman French class with *Huis clos* by Sartre? I mean, the theme of the thing is 'Hell is other people.' "

She smiled almost reminiscently. "So it is."

"But when you've just arrived at a school and you're trying to fit into a new niche, that's sort of an alienating thing to have thrown at you, don't you think?"

Jill leaned toward me, her expectant eyes wide. "Have you ever considered not trying to fit into a niche so quickly? Maybe Sartre's trying to tell you something. You know, like literature relates to your life?"

"Like tell me what."

"Alex, my freshman roommate lost fifteen pounds in her first month because she was too scared to go to dinner alone. Now she's president of the Yale College Council."

"Fifteen pounds? Where were you?"

"Otherwise occupied, thank you. The point is that that month was what got her charged up. She got involved in politics for the first time and just went with it. I think you've got to go through a period of loneliness here, unless you're one of those horrible preppies with all the connections. Haven't you felt it already?"

"That's not really what I meant," I said. In fact I was thinking of several miserable lunches I'd already had at Commons, which opened with my frittering away several minutes cruising from one area of the dining room to another, telling myself that all the strangers who refused to invite me to join them were either phony, drab or impossibly intimidating, and ended with me land-ing on an empty table and throwing my books in front of the place across from my chair as if I were saving it for a friend who was still at the salad bar or in the serving line.

"Whether you go to dinner alone or not," Jill continued, pointing at me with her spoon, "it comes down to a question you've got to ask yourself when you're in a new place: 'Do I *find* myself excluded, or am I making a *conscious* decision to exclude myself? If so, why am I doing that?'"

"Maybe." I tilted back in my seat. "But who can just make the decision to exclude himself? Who would want to?"

"Why are you afraid of being alone?"

"I'm not." I looked down and moved my lunch around. How the hell had the conversation drifted into this stuff?

A long silence followed, one that felt increasingly difficult to break as the seconds ticked by. I felt as if Jill had just casually gripped the end of the window shade of my soul, pulled sharply and let it fly all the way up to the spring roller at the top. She had stopped acting and started being real without telling me, which was grossly unfair. I feared that I was boring her, and said the first thing that came to mind.

"Why the hell were you late, anyway?"

Jill sat back in her chair and laughed through her nose. "You really shouldn't get me started. I've just been shopping a couple of classes. Very bad."

I made a sympathetic sound. "Aren't course schedules due today though?"

"Have you passed yours in?"

"Not yet."

"Good, let's have a look."

"Oh . . . all right." I slid it from a notebook and handed it to Jill. She scanned it quickly, nodding approval twice, then paused.

"Westerbrook 'Postmodernism' Credit/Fail? That's such a cop-out."

"It is, but you don't know my section leader . . ." I watched, helpless, as Jill took a pen from her leather book bag, crossed out C/F next to the class and wrote in "grade." She tossed the form back over to me. A tip of it landed in my mustard.

"Alex, do you plan to go through *life* Credit/Fail? That class will change the way you look at the world if you put enough time into it."

"If you say so." I wiped off the mustard and put the form away. My eyes landed on Peter and Flavia at the salad bar behind Jill's head. Flavia was finger-noshing her way from the cherry tomatoes to the red onions, ignoring the sanitary tongs, and Peter was trying to press a pair of them into her hands. I didn't think I wanted them to join us.

"And you're working on your senior essay, isn't that right?"

Jill chewed a bit of celery. "Mm-hmm."

"And Julia Westerbrook is your adviser?"

"Right."

"What's it about?"

"Silence." Jill finished picking at her salad and continued on to my french fries. I laid the plate of them on her tray, above her protesting hand.

"Silence," I said, when I realized that Jill wasn't telling me to be quiet. "The silent treatment; I know what that's like. You must feel overwhelmed."

"It's not easy to talk about, as you might imagine. I'm trying to write about silence in women artists between 1850 and 1950, women who were injured or repressed by patriarchal society. So you've got Gertrude Stein, Angelina Grimké, even Duras. You start from a question like, if male writer X claims he can get inside a woman's head, an aware woman, then you have to wonder why the woman's voice is always subordinate or why it's just absent in their texts. Then you turn to the silence in a woman like Dickinson and see how it differs. Is silence an in joke, is it deliberately encoded, is it dying to be exploded, and so on. You know Wollstonecraft?"

"Uh . . . I think so."

Jill searched my eyes, then drew herself up resignedly. "To tell you the truth, I'm still not sure where it's going to go."

"I'm sure it'll be great," I said.

"Maybe. . . . Were we supposed to be discussing something here, Alex? I've got a lousy memory."

"Discussing?"

"Wait, now I remember. I left you at Jiffy's little housewarmer last week. She told me the next day you were sort of devastated when I took off."

"Did she?" I pretended to think back. The chicest party I'd ever attended was now a little housewarmer. "I don't remember saying a word to her."

She glanced at her watch. "Well, you certainly weren't the reason I left. You ought to be delighted to hear that, believe me."

I unwrapped my ice cream sandwich carefully. "I was bumming out, actually, but it was something else."

Jill took a cigarette from her bag, lit it and blew a long line of smoke straight up out of her mouth. "What was that?"

"Just a woman I saw my senior year. Named Katharine."

"Don't sweat it if it was just a *woman*. That's interesting, though, my mother's name is Katharine. I love that name, it's so strong. Tell me about your Katharine."

"Katharine . . ." I looked off and saw Peter approaching me with Flavia. He caught my eye and waved, but Flavia tapped him and whispered something, and they moved off through Commons in another direction.

"I grew up with her," I said; "we were always friends. But we were only really close for five or six months. If that."

Jill drew deeply on her cigarette. "You don't sound too sure."

I frowned. "I guess I'm surprised at how short the summer was. It's hard to remember specific things."

"That's nice for you. Most of my high school relationships stretched out to interminable length."

"I guess that's all this was," I said. *"Nice* for me. My attitude was like, hey, many people are nice."

"That's a great line." Jill rested her head on an upturned palm. "So is 'The Silent Treatment'; maybe I'll use that as my essay title."

"You have my permission."

"But you two aren't an item any more."

"Katharine and me? No, I screwed it up. I see that now."

"That's a shame. Nice girls are getting hard to come by. Me, for example, I have a lot of nasty turns in my personality. You probably wouldn't like me."

I tried to conceal my excitement. "Nice is all I've known."

"Well," Jill said expansively, and flung her cigarettes into her leather book bag, "I *never* talk about my personal life to strangers, but now that you've opened up to me, I should explain about Jiffy's too. I was really using you at the time to get back at my lover."

I had been watching the blue kangaroo on the skis swing up and back. Now I started.

"Your lover?"

For the first time in the meal, Jill looked into my eyes with complete candor. Maybe it was candor. She slipped her long cold hands over mine.

"It's all right. We talked and argued and talked, and Lauren's forgiven me. As usual. Except now I have to crash this party with her at a house she used to rent. The captain of the football team or something lives there. He threw out a couple of our friends on the night of Jiffy's thing, and you can imagine how everybody got their back up over that. About a dozen of us are going to stop by and see what happens. It ought to be *so* much fun."

"Wow," I said, "good luck." I sat up a little straighter. I hadn't been aware that it was possible to feel like such an utter fool.

Jill slid back in her chair and stretched to her feet. Then she wiped her lips on a napkin and smiled. "Thanks, Alex. And

thanks for lunch. I never dreamed I'd be meeting any more freshmen."

"There you go." I sounded numb.

"Would you mind busing my tray? I'm going to be late for my
session in Westville." She touched my shoulder lightly. "You
ought to come down and meet some of these women I counsel. I
think they'd find you refreshing. Thanks again. I really enjoyed
this. We should do it once more sometime."

"That sounds great. See ya." I pretended to be already attending to my French work sheets, or to penciling in a reminder to
call Jill three weeks from that day, but my whole face was burning and I really couldn't see anything. *Once* more, I was thinking.
We should do it *once* more.

When Jill was gone I sat awhile before going back to the language lab. With the exception of a small group of blue-aproned
women who worked at Commons and were clearing off the tables,
the enormous space was empty. In less than an hour Commons
had gone from a bustling food emporium to a luxury liner's dining
room after an Abandon Ship. In as much time, my hopes to be
with Jill had been pretty effectively dashed. At least she was up
front about it.

I smoked the last half of the cigarette she had left beside her
plate and watched the women clear tables and laugh together.
For a short space of time, probably no longer than ten seconds,
the movement of the women away from me began to seem not
only natural but inevitable. The fact that I had switched from
football to squash in prep school, had let my relationship with
Katharine go into the toilet, even the way I had become so
quickly accustomed to private study carrels at Sterling Library,
this and a flurry of personal characteristics fell into a frightening
pattern. Had I gradually been excluding myself all this time without realizing it, or was I being excluded? For almost a full minute
I was glued to my seat, too scared to move, and my life seemed to

crack open and let me look down at its lunar, insignificant surface.

Then the panic passed and, with it, my insight. I felt no conclusions and no solace in my solitude. I stared dully at the glass doors of Commons. No wonder my insight had passed: Jill had just slipped through my fingers and disappeared back into her gigantic life again.

1

At dinner Flavia, Peter, Brook and I closed down the Ezra Stiles dining hall, but rather than being allowed to lounge and procrastinate in our seats until seven-thirty, as we were used to doing, we received a pointed request from a large senior in a moussaka-stained apron to kindly bus our trays and go elsewhere. When we walked outside I saw that the sun had set but that the sky was still bright blue. This was usually my favorite time of day, and I loved to watch the light fade until the sky was transparent and seemingly without color. The effect didn't do much for me that night—it reminded me of my prospects with Jill.

Jill having a woman lover didn't really bother me; not in concept, anyway. We had had the same gay couple stay at our cottages for four years running in McMurtry, and no one but the older kids in town gave them any grief. Since McMurtry was overwhelmingly Protestant, the town didn't completely accept them, but there was never a problem with tolerance. I certainly had no problem with two people of the same sex getting together. On the day I headed off to my senior year at Hollier Prep (headed all the way across town with my dad in his truck—it was a strange departure for prep school), he took a long detour and explained to me, after condoms and drugs, which were no news, that everybody's sexuality was like an onion. Everybody was busy peeling away at their own layers and finding out what they liked and didn't like, so you had no right to dump on somebody else if their onion was different from yours. I squirmed with embarrassment hearing this from my father, but his advice stood me in good stead that summer, when Katharine and I came upon our veteran summer couple, Slade and Mark, as they were kissing on the beach. I had shuddered a little at this sight, but then I remembered Dad's sexuality onion and I was all right. What bugged me about Jill was that I hadn't sensed her sexuality earlier. Maybe I was bothered because something seemed to click between us. Using me to get back at her lover was a pretty lousy trick, but what did I know about how gay relationships worked? Maybe this Lauren woman wasn't appreciating Jill enough. What a soap opera. I wished that I could put all of it together and have it make sense. I had it bad, though. Jill was all I could think about.

While Brook brought me through the thrill and agony of his latest crew practice, Flavia and Peter walked on ahead of us and had a little tête-à-tête. Flavia wore a tight denim mini, a white polo and Italian leather flats. Her hair was pinned up into a chignon so that you could see her wide face and all the sun she had gotten lying out on the grass in Old Campus that afternoon, and how she was the focal point of our group. One minute she would look over at Peter and kiss his cheek, and the next she would look up the dirty, soda-stained block of Broadway and smile mysteriously, as if what she really had in mind was the handsome reptile clutch bag we had stopped to examine in a store window. I took great sensual delight in standing behind Flavia as she admired the clutch. Now she whirled around at me on the street, as if reading these thoughts.

"Alex," she said, "did you hear what happened with my roommate Tenley today?"

I snapped my fingers. "Must have missed it."

"Good. You tell me," she said, "did I grouse when she threw my grandmother's crocheted Kleenex house out the window be-

cause she thought it was gay? No. So today my other roommate
Cricket gets a package of Cloves from her brother with a beautiful card, and after a huge debate over what Tenley might do, we
light one up. With the windows open, and we practically cover
the chairs in newspapers. And Tenley hasn't shown her head in
the suite in three days, minimum."

"Didn't you worry about her?" I said.

She ignored the question, as I expected. "And then, of course,
we take two puffs and she's through the door. Two. And what do
we get? Hello, perhaps? How are you? *Right.* The first thing she
does is give me this withering look. I swear to God my watch
stopped. But before she can open her trap, Cricket stands up,
glares at her and says, 'I am *going* to smoke a Cloves cigarette in
my own living room, I am *going* to smoke a Cloves cigarette in
my own living room.'" Flavia laughed and clapped her hands
together, as if smashing a mosquito between them. "It was awesome. All Tenley could say was, 'We obviously line up on different sides of this issue.' Cricket says, 'Go divide something by
zero.' I was like, yaah."

Brook nodded. "That's telling her."

"Err-derr-derr," Flavia said. "Peter thinks I'm right, don't you,
Peter?"

Peter hissed out a belch and stepped over a fallen ice cream
cone. "Cloves make your lungs bleed."

"You're from hell," she concluded. "How can you stand him as
a roommate, Alex?"

"He's low-maintenance," I said. "Did I mention that I ran into
a guy from prep school in the Coop today?"

"Who is he?" Flavia asked.

"Lyon Gregg. He invited me out to a party at the yacht club in
Branford tonight. He invited all of us, indirectly."

"No kidding." Brook flicked his short hair back. "That sounds
excellent. You never told us you had any other friends at Yale."

"So," I said, "what's the big deal? Don't you have casual
friends from Andover here?"

"Sure, but . . ."

A smile grew on Peter's lips. "What he's trying to say is, isn't Hollier Prep the kind of place that advertises in the back of the *Times* magazine with Maryland Military Weight Loss Academy?"

"No shit," I said, and looked at Brook. "I know exactly what he's trying to say."

"I didn't say word fucking one," Brook said. "I was just going to ask you what kind of guy this Lyon is."

"He's okay," I said. "Anyway, it starts at ten-thirty."

"In that case, how does some ice cream at Thomas Sweet sound?" Peter said, running his hand up Flavia's white cotton back. "Since we all negged on dessert."

"Marvelous suggestion." Flavia flicked his hand away. "Why not tape it to my thighs and save me the trouble of swallowing."

"It's still a good idea, Flavia," I said. "You can get some decent coffee at least. And you'll be dancing it all off later."

"It's strange," she said. "I'm like not hungry, but I'm really hungry?"

Peter clapped once. "That's a yes."

We crossed Broadway and walked very slowly down York Street. Peter's foam thong sandals slapped on the sidewalk. At the door of the WaWa market I gave thirty-five cents to the Thirty-five Cents Lady, an obese woman in her mid-fifties who was formless under all her layers of clothing, and repeated her pitch over and over in a monotone. I wondered if the women Jill counseled were in as bad a state, and then realized that I probably would have ignored the Thirty-five Cents Lady had I not been thinking about Jill. Peter gave her money too, and observed that when he entered Yale summer school two years before she was only the Fifteen Cents Lady.

"That's nothing," Flavia said. "The guy who works my block at home asks for a hundred dollars now. He says he takes checks too."

Brook spoke up, eager to get off the topic of the homeless.

"Alex, how's Jill, isn't that her name? I heard she invited you to lunch today."

"Really?" I said. "Who told you that?"

Flavia slowed until we were all walking abreast. "You mean that radical-chic woman with the spiked hair took you to lunch?"

"Come on, Flavia," I said, "I saw you there, remember?"

Flavia made herself look as though she had swallowed a cherry pit. "He's right, Peter, we made complete eye contact."

"Whatever," Peter said. "How'd it go?"

"Isn't she the one who ditched you at Jiffy's place?" Brook put in.

"That's right." Peter nodded. "Just like a woman. They're such spiders."

Flavia nodded. "We are."

"They latch on and suck you dry."

"We do. Always." Flavia fell over onto Peter and embraced him. "I hate you."

He placed his fingertips over his lower lip. "You *so* don't."

"We had a good lunch anyway," I said firmly. I needed a cattle prod to keep anybody's attention for more than ten seconds.

"That's great," Flavia said. "She seems like such a totally person."

"Really?" Brook worked a toothpick between his molars. "She's got a harshatonic style, don't you think? I'd never have pegged her as your type."

"That's good, Brook," I said. "Just what is my type?"

"I don't know," he said. "Maybe more like Patti Kelly, that chick who does the film society announcements at the dining hall. She's pretty cool."

"Thanks," I said. "Great tip." From the two short conversations I'd had with Patti Kelly, I was sure that making film society announcements at Stiles was the most daring thing she could conceive of doing during her college career.

"Think of all those free movie passes," Peter said.

"Yeah," Brook continued, "and can you really see yourself taking Jill home to the 'rents for the weekend?"

I glanced at him. "Well, you can relax, I'm not going to disappoint anyone. She's already got a lover, okay?"

Flavia caught her breath. "Oh, we're sorry, Alex. Shit, I feel so inconsiderate."

"Bummer." Peter put his hand on my shoulder. "What, did you find out at lunch?"

"It's no big deal," I said. "It was silly to expect that somebody that attractive wouldn't already be in a relationship."

"Huh." Brook grimaced. "Attractive" might not have been his choice of words.

We fell into a short silence which Peter broke.

"So," he said, "who is he, that guy who falls all over her every day in Westerbrook?"

"Tony? No," I said, and added, as if an afterthought, "He's a she, actually."

There was a scraping of soft heels on asphalt. I was suddenly three steps farther down York Street than my friends, and turned to see Brook, Flavia and Peter staring at me. Brook spoke up first.

"No fucking way. She's a dyke?"

"Brook." Flavia turned and glared at him. "I'd appreciate it if you didn't use that word."

"Yeah, Brook," I said. "That's pretty insulting."

Brook paid Flavia and me all the courtesy he would a lesbian. "Jesus, I can't believe a dyke would lead you on that way. She must really have it in for men."

"Brook, she didn't exactly lead me on." I let them catch up. "Like you said, it never would have worked."

Peter shook his head. "I'm really sorry."

"That sucks, Alex," Flavia echoed. "I'm sure you'll meet somebody else nice."

Nice. Katharine in her hiking boots flashed like a recurring toothache. "Come on," I said, "she certainly *likes* me, she's just not interested in a relationship. And she gave me the impression that she's just not into men at the moment, that's all. I've only known her for two weeks."

"Goddamn it," Brook concluded. "I'm nauseated."

"*Brook,*" Flavia warned. "Chill out."

He looked up at the reddened sky and mused. "I thought her butt was a little wide."

"Brook!" Flavia swung Peter's arm up in hers angrily. "Ninety percent of the world is attracted in some way to both sexes. Anybody in touch with himself will admit it." Her tone made it clear that Brook was excluded from this latter group.

"Anyway," I said, "she never said she's a lesbian. And why do we have to use labels like this anyway?"

"That's *so* true," Flavia said. "I hate them too."

Brook shut his mouth, sensing that he was outnumbered, and we crossed York Street to Chapel. We headed for the door of the Thomas Sweet ice cream boutique, a glass and brick building filled with potted ferns and ceiling fans. There was also an attached courtyard where you could eat your three-dollar waffle cone al fresco. I had a strange sensation standing on the corner that everyone was staring at me.

"Why don't we sit outside?" Peter suggested.

"That sounds cool." I followed Peter's eyes out to the courtyard and—how lovely!—there was *Jill,* as if I'd wished her into place. She wore the same T-shirt and jeans, and had her eyes closed in pleasure as a breeze meandered through tufts of her hair. A tall, black-haired woman in slim cut-off jeans and a black tank top walked through the store and outside, then directly to Jill's table. She had large dark eyes, pouty lips and a luxuriant stride which probably turned heads in any ice cream parlor you cared to mention. Jill and this woman talked for a moment, smiled and then broke into laughter. They put their feet up on the same wicker chair and fed sundae to each other from a single dish, touching each other's arms, oblivious to everything. Maybe if I stuck around for a while they'd blow bubbles in their milk.

"That must be Lauren," I said, and then started when I realized I'd said it aloud.

Peter executed a wicked one-hundred-eighty-degree turn and made an ugly face at me. "I just remembered that I had the worst ice cream here last time. What do you say we go up to Ashley's on College? That's never crowded, either."

"Fine." I nodded, unable to drag my eyes from the two women. I knew that nobody was going to mention them directly. Why did that make me feel so depressed?

"I'm flex," Flavia said. "Come *on,* Brook. Their ice cream is better anyway."

"If that's what you want," he said, striding past us.

Peter stared at me. "Ashley's is better, don't you think, Alex?"

I tried to look off, but Jill was tickling her girlfriend below her ear, and blowing cool ice cream breath onto her skin. I wondered if she had put on a new cologne since lunch.

"Yeah," I said at last, with a hole in my throat. "It's much better there."

8

Brook picked us up in his Wagoneer at eleven-thirty in front of Old Campus, so we arrived out at the Corinthian Yacht Club in Branford, Connecticut, a few towns over, in time to see some kind of midnight dive a bunch of people took from the far end of the dock. We were in a suburban beach-town area with no streetlights that was much less New Haven and much more standard Connecticut. The yacht club was a peeling split-level barn with a dark, stained deck on the second floor and room for windsurfers, small boats and sails underneath. It was about as Corinthian as Lynwood Place was Parisian, but there was still something attractive about it. Thirty cars were parked at crazy angles on and off the grass, and even the cars looked happy that they had made the trip and found the party. We parked down on the road and walked up a windswept bluff full of cattails and weeds toward the building. Automatically, or because of the sharp incline, or because of the protection of the dark, the four of us held hands. I held Flavia's and Peter's hands, feeling against my arms the short bands of braided leather they had made for each other and looped around their wrists, while Flavia's other hand held Brook's. None of us mentioned it, but I knew that we were all smiling.

The regular wash of the sound so close by, and its fresh, salty smell, brought Katharine to my mind. Every night after I got off from work during the summer we would take walks up a short stretch of beach near my house, a grayish, pebbly beach very much like the one I walked above now. There were nights in July when her car was in the shop and we had nothing else to do than to walk that beach, in fact could not have wished for anything else. I would grip Katharine's hand and say with amazement, "What were we *doing* all those years?" and she would say something like, "Oh, just fun and games." Now I swallowed past an ache in my chest and a kind of highly strung tenderness that made the ache sharper. The warm night wind blew over my face and I felt as if I was suspended in one spot, missing something so much that I could have cried but with no idea what it was I was missing. I didn't really miss Katharine. Maybe I just missed feeling that way about someone.

Flavia squeezed my hand and released it as we went over the top of the bluff together, and the feeling dropped away. Music and light drifted out to us from across the sandy yard. I think we may have run the last few feet, we were so excited.

The inside of the yacht club reminded me of a ski condo or even an old sawmill. The building was unfinished except for a row of lofts enclosed up in the beams on the second floor. The ceiling for both floors was the roof. I saw a garage band with a bongo player against the wall in the main first-floor room. About fifty people were dancing. There were pretty women in polos and shorts, crew jocks, Beautiful People and a fair number of freshmen in Exeter and Andover and Hotchkiss shirts who looked like they badly wanted to be invited into one of these groups. Flavia's polo turned an unearthly chalk color in the row of black-purple lights hanging from electrical cords at the door, and when she smiled her mouth was full of pure white.

I had to admit that this was a better party than Jiffy's. If everybody was a clone of everybody else, at least they weren't being obnoxious about it. The band started playing "Brown-Eyed Girl" as we found a live keg and got oriented. A couple of unspeakably rich-looking women were dancing with their hands held up in front of their shoulders, much closer to the band than anyone else. Unspeakably rich to everyone but Dalton School Flavia, of course.

"You see the one in the windbreaker there? Geneva Voigt. I'm gonna toss. Every exam week she'd walk around Dalton going, 'I could really concentrate if I had a gram.' Her father used to own the Midwest."

Peter handed around plastic cups of keg beer. "Who'd he sell it to?"

"I think it went back to the shareholders."

I watched the rich women dance. Their angular haircuts, slim, tanned bodies and frighteningly sharp noses made me think of coastal towns in northern Massachusetts. In a way they were so far removed from me that I could only see them as finely bred greyhounds. They were dancing with a couple of guys who were a cross between forty and eighteen, one gangly and balding in tweed, the other a portly golfer jock in a deep red cotton sweater. Red was fixated on his partner, and I observed that the four of them looked strangely together. Obviously they did, Flavia said; the guys were rich as shit-all too.

I couldn't find Lyon anywhere. There were two stoned-looking blond guys in St. Paul's shirts near one of the speakers who seemed to be presiding over the party, so I walked up to them and shouted:

"How's it going?"

"Great, dude," one guy drawled out. "Aren't you in my Swahili class?"

"Afraid not. You see Lyon Gregg any place?"

"Haven't seen him."

"Thanks." The other guy looked more than stoned, up close. "Have you seen Lyon Gregg?"

"Sailor guy, about medium height?"

"Yeah, exactly."

"That's half the people in this place."

I stared at him. "You shouldn't be smoking those Anacin caplets, you know."

His head tipped back dreamily. "That's funny."

"But you really haven't seen him?"

"Ask Geneva, she knows where everybody is."

"Thanks."

The band kicked into "Rock a Pony," and since I didn't know anyone, Flavia pulled me over to dance with Peter and her. Peter looked a little put out by this, but I hung around because I didn't want to stand on the sidelines. Soon Peter was trying to shut Flavia out of our threesome, and she laughed and tried to block him back. After a long medley of rockabilly songs the band took a slow number and I went to get another beer. I looked around the club some more, then I stood against a beam trying to spot Lyon. Time was whipping by and I still hadn't seen him.

A short woman with curly brown hair in a sailing team jacket walked over after a minute. She looked vaguely familiar.

"Hey, aren't you Alex?"

I did a double take. "How'd you know? Oh yeah, wait . . ."

"We talked about Faulkner in line for 129 English. I'm Beth Webb, remember?"

"Of course, hi. I guess I've blocked out that morning."

"You mean you didn't get into the class?"

"No, I mean you were really boring. Of course I mean I didn't get in."

Beth grabbed my wrist impulsively. Her laugh took off in a deep gallop and rose to a wheezy titter. It was the first true titter I'd ever heard, and it was wonderful.

"Hey, Beth," I said, "you must know. I'm looking for a sort of friend who was supposed to be here. Lyon Gregg, do you know him?"

The garage band was now thrashing through the bridge of one of their own songs, something called "You Can't Take My Love Credit/Fail," and Beth stared at me with her lips parted until the bridge ended. Then she spoke close to my ear.

"Lyon Gregg? He was busted in town tonight for buying coke —didn't you hear?"

"Are you serious?"

"Alex!" Flavia ran up to me with Peter following her. "Brook's gone!"

"No way."

"Yes way." Peter looked pissed. "One of my friends saw him leave with a couple of people from Andover ten minutes ago. They were all heading to a party at Dave Freitag's in New Haven."

"Wait, don't tell me," I said. "There's supposed to be tons of coke there, right?"

Flavia nodded sarcastically. "Shows you where the guy's heart is. We're only what, twenty miles from town?"

"Great," I said. "This is great."

"I'm heading downtown, Alex," Beth put in. "They're supposed to be doing an all-night cookout at that party. I think you'd all fit in my back seat, if you don't mind squeezing."

"Oh, my God," Flavia said to Beth, and brought her fingertips to her lower lip, "I don't even know you, but you're so awesome."

———

There's a way you can get driving, either behind the wheel or just sitting in a moving car, when you drift away from everybody and drift right out of yourself, as if your mind is a note attached to a helium balloon that is rising out of sight. Whether anyone else was in this mood I wasn't sure, but neither Peter, Flavia nor I said much of anything on the way back to New Haven. We were all crushed into the back seat of Beth's Fiat while Beth talked and laughed with her roommate Melissa in the front. Now that Flavia and Peter knew about Lyon, I intended to explain that he had never meant anything to me. Then I realized that this wouldn't do much good, and anyway people tend to become hurt if you tell them that they've got the story wrong after they've poured out their sympathy to you. I was thinking of the early morning hours following my graduation prom when Lyon had suddenly appeared at the edge of the woods with a couple of friends who had graduated with him. They scaled Hollier Prep's blue water tower with a life-size dummy dressed in a tux, and when they got three quarters of the way up, Lyon pretended to have an argument with the dummy and threw it off. About a hundred people went into hysterics, including Katharine, whose uncle had fallen off his roof that summer and shattered his leg. It was a typical Lyon stunt. Maybe a night in a New Haven jail would bring him to his senses.

There had just been a minor accident which closed the local entry ramp to I-95, so Beth had to construct a route back to New Haven using secondary roads and the Boston Post Road, which is a nightmare at any hour. Add to this two wrong turns which Melissa suggested on some beachside streets, and it took us nearly an hour and a half to get back to town. Eventually Beth hooked up with Edgewood Road, and we took that all the way into the Yale campus. Everyone applauded as Beth made the turn onto Lynwood Place. We had passed only two houses on the street, though, before Beth had to slam on her brakes again.

There was enough red and white light on Lynwood to stun a

small herd of deer, long streams of light dancing over the tops of cars and flashing up into the overhanging trees. We inched along toward a crowd of people scattered over the sidewalk in front of number 38. Many people looked unpleasantly surprised, and everyone was talking at once. Coming out of the suburban darkness, it took several minutes to get a grasp of what was happening.

"Jesus Christ." Peter sat straight up and Beth's roommate rolled down her window as we parked. Brook's Wagoneer was parked directly across the street. Climbing out of Beth's little Fiat, I saw several New Haven cops standing on the stairs of Dave Freitag's house. One of them was looking down at a couple of dark spots on a step. At that moment another crowd exited from the house. Lauren was in it. She had her left arm wrapped in a towel and she was crying. As we got closer I saw that she was mad about something too. Up at the door a bunch of big guys, football players mostly, were talking to two Yale cops. One guy had a bloody nose and another had some blood under his left eye.

"*What* is going on?" Flavia said. "Wait, Peter—there's Brook! Isn't that him?"

Brook had stormed onto the porch in his white polo and shorts. One of the cops said something but he ignored him and kept going. The cop tried to grab Brook by the back of the shirt, but Dave Freitag spoke to the cop and he stepped back. Brook looked as if someone had spun him around a hundred times in the dark and let him go. He nearly tripped on the stairs.

"Brook!" Peter called as we ran up to meet him. "What the hell's going on?"

We crowded around him as he met us in the street. There was a small trickle of blood flowing from under his left ear, and a darkish brown smudge of blood on his arm, but he paid no attention to either. Brook barely took any notice of us, in fact. If anyone expected an explanation, he didn't look in the mood to give one at that point.

"Party's over," he said. His voice was hoarse. "Let's cruise. You guys want a ride?"

Now I heard a shout in our direction from a small crowd near Jill's girlfriend. A woman made a megaphone of her cupped hands. "We know who you are, asshole!"

"You can't hide!" somebody else yelled.

Brook turned around and stared. "*I* didn't do anything! I was on her side, okay?"

"Just a little friendly teamwork, right?" a woman in an orange T-shirt yelled.

Brook pointed at the woman threateningly. "You'd better watch what you say, bitch."

"We know who you are!" she continued. Now more voices picked up the shouting in front of the house and the cops started rushing around again. Nobody had a clue who was in charge. Finally the New Haven cops yelled for us to get moving, and Brook fished out his keys, angry at having to break the woman's stare, and unlocked his car. Flavia and I slid into the back seat of the Wagoneer and I unlocked the front passenger door for Peter. The shouting lessened as we got in.

When we were all safely installed Brook roared up to Elm Street, turned right and floored it. The scene behind us instantly disappeared. Brook slowed down once we passed Park Street a block on, then pulled up to a stoplight at Elm and York. All the local nightspots at this intersection were hopping and flashing.

"What happened to you?" Peter said.

"Fuck it." Brook wiped his hand below his left ear and looked at it moodily. Then he closed his eyes and opened them again. "I should've stayed out at the Corinthian."

"Come on, Brook," Flavia said. "What was all that?"

He turned and glared at me. "Most of it was *your* wonderful friend. If she had a fucking grip on herself . . ." He trailed off.

I leaned forward. "Who do you mean—Jill? What did she do?"

"She crashed the party with a bunch of her dyke friends, for starters."

"Brook," Flavia said, "would you please stop using that word?"

"Was there an argument?" My heart started to race. I realized that Jill hadn't appeared once in the scene we'd just left behind.

Brook went back to watching the stoplight. "She started one just by showing up. Freitag only asked her to leave. It was getting really packed, and it's his place. But she said she was having a good time, and then they all started shouting about it. I went into the hallway to get a beer, and then this crazy bitch threw a bottle!"

"How do you know it was her?" I said.

Brook roared up Elm on a green light. "What a fucking picnic it turned into after that. I was standing there in the dark trying to pull people apart and these two lesbos jumped on my back, and I fell over, and then somebody kicked me right under the ear." He pointed to his head. "I'm goddamn lucky they missed my eyes."

"Who broke it up?" Peter said. "The cops?"

"No." Brook hit his steering wheel and pulled up to another red light at High and Elm. "This Jill got knocked out and they had to take her to the infirmary or something."

"God!" Flavia started angrily. "Can't you guys keep yourselves under control for one minute?"

Brook glanced at Flavia in the rearview mirror. "Be realistic, would you? A bunch of dykes should know that wasn't the place for them. Let them go to their own dyke parties."

"Stop that word!" Flavia kicked the back of Brook's seat and wrenched her door open. "Forget it, I'm out of here. I've heard enough of this bullshit."

Peter reached for her. "Flav, come on—"

She slammed her door hard and spoke to Peter through his window. "If you don't want to come with me, fine."

Peter sighed roughly as Flavia stormed to the curb. He hopped out to the street and slammed his door. "Way to go, guy."

"Go ahead!" Brook shouted after them. "Get some fresh air!"

"Make sure you stick with him, Alex!" Flavia called. "He might drop you somewhere and take off again!"

Brook pulled across two lanes as the light turned green, and a sports car narrowly avoided slamming into our backside. He floored it again and we went roaring off. Now everything was flying along at twice normal speed. I saw a receding flash of Flavia with Peter on High Street. She was screaming about something and Peter was trying to pin her arms down and hug her. In the Wagoneer Brook banged the hell out of his steering wheel and yelled. "Yeah, fuck *me!* Oh, right, fuck me! Sure, fuck *me!*" In the back seat I felt a sick dread rising in my throat. Why were Jill's friends yelling at Brook if he was just pulling people apart? And would Jill really start that kind of argument? Over and over again I imagined her being lifted, unconscious, into the back of someone's car, her head lolling and her long, thin arms hanging at her sides. Hers was the only face I saw as we roared through the busy nighttime city. I realized as the city became suburbs again that I had no idea where we were going.

2

9

Jill left Dave Freitag's party with a bruised rib, a black eye and a mild concussion, and spent the weekend at the infirmary. I had to call, posing as her panicked older brother from Williams, to get even that information, so I wasn't surprised when the rumors started. Within a few days I heard that someone had shoved (or tripped) Jill for the hell of it while she was crossing Dave's living room, that she started kicking (or punching) blindly when a couple of guys chanted the word "dyke," and that she had come to the aid of two women (or men) who were being tossed out of the party for hugging. Serious hugging, that is, and not to be confused with jock hugging. Regardless of which version was true, Jill took off her patch once she was released and put her bulging black-purple eyelid on permanent public exhibit. The immediate wound to the campus mood was just as ugly, and due to the constant pressure maintained by the Women's Center, it healed just as slowly. If not for them, I'm sure the whole thing would have been written off as a little error in judgment by one of Dave Freitag's friends and quickly forgotten. Instead, each article in the *Daily News* about misogynistic violence or gay rights was taped to the doors of nearly thirty people, most of them football players, within hours of its appearance. I knew this because our suite usually received copies, thanks to Brook.

Also thanks to Brook, Jill broke off almost all contact with me. I knew this because I usually got a "Hi" or a passing smile on the street when I was alone. When Jill saw me with Brook, though, she looked hurt and disappointed, and somehow I was seen with

Brook a lot, even grew to enjoy the phenomenon, despite the fact that my views were about as instinctively left as Brook's were right. If we had lived in different suites in Lawrance Hall I'm sure Brook would have barely acknowledged me in the entryways, but since we lived in the same suite he became a sort of shotgun buddy. Maybe he wanted to find out what made a lower-middle-class liberal tick. It got to the point where Brook was often the first thing I saw in the morning. He'd pound on my door and hand me the new editorial recommending castration as a viable option for the woman who found herself being date-raped, looking like he either wanted to laugh or throw something through my window. At least I was never in doubt as to where he stood. Peter, on the other hand, struck out on some kind of self-watering program to make himself bigger than life, and the results were bewildering. The more genuine he wanted to appear, the more plastic his poses felt. He even auditioned for a Beckett play and then turned down the director when she wanted to cast him. We were playing squash every day for a while too, but that dwindled to twice a week as September flew to a close and he spent more and more time with the Political Union or his self-important friends in the Directed Studies program. I wondered if the Peter I met on our first day at the Old Campus fence was the sincerest one I would know.

I left several messages on Jill's machine about the second lunch we were supposed to have, even a long, rambling speech about a feminist theory book I was reading and would be happy to lend her (I even quoted from it on her tape), all to no effect. I suspected that Lauren was intercepting these messages, but then Lauren stuck to Jill like a bodyguard for the rest of the month, so I couldn't exactly run up and accuse her. Meanwhile Jill kept walking around like the silent black eye of her storm, and a slew of people became two-day media celebrities for writing inflammatory editorials or speaking at rallies. It was a great time to be falling in love.

It wasn't long before the campus celebrity spotlight paused on Brook. While table-tenting for the Yale College Republicans on the first Monday of October, he leaned over a just deserted table in the natural food section of Commons with a handful of printed cards announcing their next meeting. He moved to tuck one of these cards between two water glasses and found a message written in red on a napkin: "We're watching you. Bash any women lately?"

Brook broke a glass—or maybe two, he didn't quite remember —and left Commons in what I imagine was a less than happy mood. When I walked into the weight room at the gym that night I found him pumping a 150-pound bar back and forth from his chest like one of those hardware store machines that shakes up cans of house paint. I got bits and pieces of his story at the gym but didn't get a coherent account together until we were walking along Broadway after our workout.

Brook scrubbed the last sweat out of his hair, which was now cut a shade longer than what I grew up calling a whiffle. His new girlfriend Pascale had requested the change, though Brook's lewd theories as to what she might need a bristly male head for contradicted the woman I'd met.

"I've been trying to stand clear of all this and be objective, Alex, but they're starting to push *really* hard."

"I wouldn't take it so personally," I said, trying to see the situation from Brook's side. "At this point I don't think they're looking at you as an individual, just part of some anonymous gang. It's like what happened at the party—whoever beat Jill up looked at her as a lesbian and not as a person."

"Yeah. Fucking morons."

"But you crashed the party too, remember?"

"It's not the same thing," he replied stubbornly. "I didn't go to cause trouble."

"No, just to score drugs."

We continued up Broadway past the cookie boutique that had

replaced the Greek restaurant where Lyon bought his three grams of coke from one of the owners. Brook was deep in thought and getting lead feet.

"Hey," I said, "how about letting me treat you to a bacon-Swiss at the Ed. Burgher? I've got to get some caffeine into my bloodstream for this paper."

"That sounds great." Brook gave a tremendous, shouting yawn and clenched at the dark sky with his wide hands. "I'm already ready to crash."

"After your paper."

He grabbed the copy of *Either/Or* under his arm and brought it up to my eyes.

"If you got as little of this stuff as I do, you'd want to crash too."

"I told you to pay attention when we did it in class." If I remembered correctly, during the two Kierkegaard lectures in our intro philosophy course Brook was busy negotiating with Dave Freitag for the purchase of a Xeroxed set of the professor's notes for Economics 150.

We walked under the faded blue awning of the Educated Burgher and I put my hand on the clear glass door.

"Crowded?" Brook said behind me. He meant, "Any Women's Center people inside?"

I scanned the back of the restaurant and shook my head. It was empty in front, and empty back in the seating area, which was arranged with thousands of dead books in overhead shelves to conjure up a sort of Reader's Digest Condensed academism. If the fat guy with two-day shadow behind the grill wasn't packing an Uzi and a handful of anti-jock editorials, we might be able to eat in peace. Brook bent at the water fountain inside the front door.

"Just get me a burger, fries and an o.j. I'll get a booth."

"Why not get a milkshake too?" I pulled out a ten that had to see me through the next eight days. "I'll run a tab on my bursar bill."

At the condiments bar on the way back to the booth I was less than delighted to see that we were being joined by John Harper and Brook's drinking buddy, Bob Talbot. Harper was a defensive running back from the freshman football team and Talbot was a tight end for the varsity Bulldogs. About a week before they had eaten with our suite at Stiles dining hall on an all-vegetarian night, and Talbot had started a raucous, tray-banging protest against meatless dishes. Harper was tossing Brook's Kierkegaard text into the booth across from ours while Talbot was giving Brook a big hug. Brook laughed and pushed him away.

"Get off me!"

When I arrived with napkins and ketchup I found the three of them in deep discussion. I won a quick ten-cent bet against myself that I wouldn't be let in on the conversation, and moved a dime from the left pocket of my sweatpants to the right.

"So you don't even remember if you got any play?" Talbot said, and poked Harper. Harper was a tall, clean-cut, stubborn-looking guy from Louisiana. He bulged forth from a T-shirt which said "Roadies' Credo: If it's wet, drink it. If it's dry, smoke it. If it moves, fuck it. If it doesn't move, throw it in the truck."

Harper rubbed his eye and grinned. "All I know is, when I woke up I was on my bed, and my jeans were done up except for the bottom button."

Talbot yelped. "As long as you didn't touch the meat, dude. You touch the meat on that woman and she calls you every night for a *week*."

"Alex, you know Talbot and Harper, right?" Brook indicated the two with a sweep of his big arm. There was very little room at our booth now that these two had spread themselves over the benches.

"Sure," I said flatly. "How's it going?"

"We're gonna review some Spanish verbs with Brook here," Talbot said. "Before he sticks his head back in phi*lo*sophy. You can hang out if you want."

"No," I said, "that's all right. I'm taking coffee to go. I'll see you back at the suite, Brook."

Brook handed me my book bag. "Talbot's willing to let us use his computer to print out our papers, if you want to wait."

Talbot looked at Brook with what could have been mistaken for tact. "Uh, we may only have time for you, dude. Julia has to deconstruct some shit for tomorrow."

"No problem," I said. "Have a good one, guys."

Brook raised his burger in salute but the others didn't answer. I got to the door quickly and stepped out onto Broadway. As I walked along and blew steam off my coffee I thought of something Katharine had said at a rock concert that summer, after several big men cut in front of us at the entrance.

"That jock cliché really is unfair, you know. Each one of them is a jerk in his own way."

The suite was dark when I returned to Lawrance Hall, but at the open door to my room I sensed that somebody was lying in the bed. I stood and breathed in the dimness, waiting for my eyes to adjust and my ugly mood to pass. A beam of yellow light from Old Campus fell through the window to my desk and bed, and after a minute of staring there I made out the shape of a woman's body in a dark dress, the hair drawn up from the nape of her neck, wispy over the ears.

The bedside light snapped on and Flavia rolled to her side, stretching sleepily.

"Alex, how thoughtful to bring coffee."

Flavia was spread out before me like a visionary partner, and I realized again what an incredible thing it was to have someone waiting for you in your room when you returned to it, or to have someone beside you in bed when you woke there. The fact that over a month and a dozen parties had passed without my finding anyone but Jill cut into me, and I had to mask my pain with surprise.

"I am thoughtful. Wow, you scared the—"

"Did I? Sorry!" Flavia rolled off the bed and stood, extending her arms. I came forward. A black cotton dress in a thin sweatshirt fabric crossed over her breasts in a V and fell to a point a few inches past her knees. She smelled of a muted, flowery perfume and my sheets, as if we had just climbed out of the bed together. I shook off the thought. But her browned skin was warm and fresh.

"This is wonderful," I said, holding her lightly. "Do you turn into a six-pack and large pizza at midnight?"

"Very nice." She pushed me to arm's length, scandalized, then just as quickly herself again. "How are you doing?"

"So-so, how's yourself?"

"I don't know. I'm like not hot, but I'm really hot?" She looked around my room as if I were at fault.

"What a coincidence; Peter was just saying that about you."

"Oh, please."

"I have to write a paper."

Flavia's eyes widened. "You and me both. I have nothing to show, can I tell you? Is yours due tomorrow?"

"As of today."

"All right, a fellow sufferer!" She raised a hand for a high five.

I looked beyond her to a pile of unfamiliar books scattered over my desk and onto the bed. "All the seats in the library taken, or were you just waiting to seduce me?"

This attempt at flirting glanced off Flavia without effect.

"No, I'm meeting Peter, but his room is a sty. I can't even construct a thought in there. He left a bunch of his father's newspaper stories for you to look at, by the way." She let her arms flop to her sides and shuffled back to the desk slowly, her head lolling, zombielike. "Peter is over at another one of his Directed Studies sections. He called me from Linsly-Chit during the break and said, 'Sorry, honey, this thing's just starting.' I said, 'That's okay, darling. All will be well when you have drafted the Revolution.' "

I threw down my books. The fact that people like Flavia could grow up in New York raised serious doubts about my theory that New York was the alienation capital of the Western world.

"Drafted the Revolution . . . Christ."

First Flavia and I discussed our days (Flavia's twenty-dollar black dress was her big purchase of the week), then Flavia selected a long, moody piece of Pat Metheny for my boombox. While she did I flipped through Mr. Cliffman's clips and glanced at two. I noticed that since he left Boston and went to New York Mr. Cliffman had picked up a middle initial in his byline. I couldn't say for sure when I'd asked Peter to see his father's clips, but I seemed to remember them figuring in a beer-guided discussion of how much further Peter planned to go in life than any of his ancestors, including Boynkin Cliffman, the eighteenth-century Boston rope manufacturer who provided the family's first, albeit modest, fortune. At Flavia's behest I put the clips away, and after positioning our books and ourselves—me at the desk in my oak veneer chair, Flavia on her stomach on my bed—we tried to get started with our work. I opened up my Sartre and prepared to plunge into it.

A good forty-five seconds crawled by.

"I need more coffee." Flavia rolled onto her back and yawned. "*Paradise Lost* is done for if I go sleepy-by. You need some?"

"No, I'm fine," I said. "Thanks anyway."

I was asleep—that is to say, busted—when Flavia returned. I woke up to find her head next to mine, mimicking someone on the very roof edge of sleep, slowly bobbing her chin up and down.

"Alexxx . . ." she whispered in my ear. "Time to get up for schoool . . ."

I turned my head slowly, up into her bushy dazzle of hair. I felt that I had just awakened with a dizzying but entirely pleasant head cold. We joked around and shared her cup of coffee and dawdled back to work, forty minutes after the study break had started. I had exactly fifteen hours left, including sleep, to finish my paper. How, I asked myself, had I let the thing slide so far?

Flavia made a couple of attempts at concentrating on her work, but every ten minutes or so a book would slam shut behind me. At last I turned around and caught her trying to screw a Bible into her copy of *Paradise Lost* like a drill bit. She was looking at me, her blond curls covering one eye, when I pushed back in my chair with a screech.

"Come on, Flavia. You're never going to get anywhere on my bed."

I looked at the bed and looked at her and we smiled. Then we stopped smiling but continued to look at each other. Three, five, ten seconds passed. My heart began to pound. Flavia slid from the bed and stood. She placed herself behind me, slid her warm hands down my chest and shook me lightly until my head lolled back. I saw her chin, then her lips, nose and eyes.

"Alex," she said, "don't be so obvious. You know I won't get anywhere till you're in it too."

Flavia's face lowered to meet mine, and she gave me a playful kiss, almost a tickle, on the lips. At the same second, the suite's front door opened in the common room and steps started down the hall. Instead of breaking away, as two rational people might have done, we brought the kiss in closer and deeper, daring whoever had just entered to find us. Maybe we would pull apart in time, maybe not.

I hadn't been kissed in at least a month, and had forgotten how it is the sweetest, most confidence-restoring touch. Flavia opened my mouth with hers and made a nest for my head with her hands. Our lips parted as a key slid into the bedroom door across the hall.

"There you are!"

Peter! Was he in the room? I blinked quickly. Flavia was six, then twelve, then eighteen inches from my face. Who had moaned like that? Was it me?

"Hi." I stared straight ahead to his dim reflection in my window. "I didn't even hear you come in."

"I'm light on my feet," Peter said. "How's it going?"

"He's enthralled with something on page one," Flavia said as she embraced him. "I caught him in the Rodin position." She half closed her eyes and leaned forward to demonstrate.

I turned in my seat. Peter was in his new gentleman scholar uniform, which consisted of an old tweed blazer, a wide-stripe blue oxford shirt, khakis, a brown basket-weave belt and a pair of his father's burgundy loafers. Like Brook, he had just gone in for a haircut, though he'd chosen the one with the close-clipped sides and the thick, tapering wedge at the back that was all the rage. Flavia called it the pigeon butt.

"Thanks for the clips," I said. "I enjoyed them."

"You're welcome. I guess you decided to get some exercise tonight after all."

"Come again?"

"You know, working out. If Brook was, then you certainly must have been with him."

"You mean my soul mate Brook Morehouse," I said with relief. "Where'd you see him?"

"Right outside of Linsley-Chit, about half an hour ago," Peter said. "He looked pretty hosed."

"Hosed?" I said. "Impossible. He's working on his philosophy paper. *Our* philosophy paper."

"Not when I saw him."

"Honey," Flavia said, "what's up?"

Peter looked at Flavia and then at me. "I was getting out of my section meeting, and I saw Brook and a couple of his buddies walking down near Vanderbilt Hall. One of them started calling to a woman in my section, Debby Bass. I'd just been talking to her inside Linsley-Chit. And maybe she didn't hear the guy, I don't know, but when she didn't answer all three of them started shouting. Like 'Hey, you stuck-up bitch, you dyke,' that type of thing. I walked out and heard the tail end of it."

"That's crazy!" Flavia sat down on the edge of the bed. "What kind of morons is Brook running around with?"

"I know," Peter said, "I couldn't believe it either. You should have heard this first guy's tone of voice, too—really ugly."

"I don't know about those other clowns," I said, "but Brook's probably blowing off steam. Did he tell you about the nasty note two women left him in Commons today?"

Peter contemplated this without answering. After a moment he shrugged and walked out toward the hall again.

"So what did you do?" Flavia said. "Where have you been for the last half hour?"

"Actually," Peter said, "I dropped over to the *Daily News* and wrote up something about it. It should be in there tomorrow."

"You're kidding," I said. "Was it that bad?"

Peter smiled. "Don't worry, Alex, I didn't name anybody. Anyway, I came up to get you two to join me for coffee at Debby's. I called her from the *News*, and she still feels kind of shaken up. She could probably use some company right now."

Flavia exploded out of my room, much the same way I had exploded out of it on the morning I met Jill. "The poor thing."

Peter gave me a sober look, and in a moment we followed Flavia. She led the way down the cool, brick-lined stairs of Lawrance Hall, sliding into the worn-out hollows in the center of each step in her rubber-soled shoes. With Flavia in front of me I momentarily forgot about my paper. I forgot about Brook, Peter and Debby, the latest additions to the campus celebrity list. I only knew that I would be replaying Flavia's kiss for the rest of the night.

10

Peter's editorial was published in the *News* the next morning, and the whole campus was buzzing by lunch. Copies appeared on doors, hastily taped up in hallways, even folded under the windshield wipers of parked cars along College Street. Peter got complimented on the piece wherever he went. Neighbors in Lawrance Hall, other Directed Studies freshmen, even our teaching assistant from "Postmodernism and Cultural Codes" spoke to him about it.

That night, after our squash game, Peter and I met at the Linonia and Brothers Room. The L&B is a Sterling study hall with bronze table lamps, green Naugahyde armchairs, a wrought-iron catwalk and a heavy contingent of Beautiful People. Within an hour the flow of Peter's praisers threatened to bury the reason he'd written the editorial in the first place: an innocent woman had been harassed by three men she didn't know. After getting a reference book from the shelves I approached Peter from behind and tapped his shoulder.

"May I have your autograph, Mr. Cliffman?"

Peter smiled and nudged me away. "Jump up my ass."

"You want coffee? Downstairs?"

"No, thanks." He turned his attention back to his Hegel. "You need electroshock after staying up to write that paper. Stick one of those metal tapes to your forehead and try to get past the security gate."

"That's an idea. Wanna come watch?"

"I'll pass. I'm cruising on this text."

"Aren't you always, though." I pulled the band of Peter's mock turtleneck back and deposited a ball of paper there, then gathered my books into my book bag and slung it over my shoulder.

I felt my head clear as I walked out into the cool stone cathedral-body of Sterling. Where the L&B buzzed with ostentatious midterm tension, in the library's nave it was comparatively quiet. The only noise came from the heavy wooden front door as it swung shut and the unoiled wheels of a portable desk carrel on which a graduate student was picking through a drawer of reference cards like a man tending to his garden. I headed down the long staircase cut into the center of the nave, and at the bottom walked straight through the glass doors and about five hundred years of architectural history into Machine City, the International Style cafeteria wedged between Cross Campus Library and Sterling. Machine City, built entirely of chrome, aluminum, plastic, Lucite and pressed fiberboard, looked like a fifty-seat port-o-potty. It was packed that night with people discussing academic horrors and which restaurants their parents would take them to for Parents' Weekend, which was coming in three days.

While I dug for a dollar at the change machine, I glanced back at a table of women playing the round-robin pattycake game called Categories, which was very much in fashion that fall. They were doing cities when I fished out my dollar, but a familiar voice quickly changed the topic to feminists.

"Feminists!"

Clap clap.

"Starting with!"

Clap clap.

"Virginia Woolf!"

Clap clap.

"Susie Bright!"

Clap clap.

"Catherine MacKinnon."

Clap clap.

"Hélène Cixous!"

Clap clap.

"My lover!"

The group broke into delighted laughter, and I turned to see who they were when I had my change. The last time I had played Categories was at my eleventh birthday party, when the most popular topic had been breakfast cereals. I should have guessed who would call out, "My lover!"

Jill sat in a slinky purple spaghetti-strap tank top with her arm around Lauren. Her left eye still looked like an illustration from a pathology book. It had developed an orbit of egg-yolk yellow around its purple-black nucleus. She glanced at me casually: sorry, no men allowed.

At the coffee machine at the other end of the room, where I prepared to drop money through the change slot, I heard another familiar voice.

"Alex!" Flavia waved from a round white table where she was talking to and passionately gesticulating at Brook's girlfriend, Pascale Trowbridge. Pascale looked over and waved too. She was a San Franciscan debutante who spoke flawless French, German and Italian, two facts which I never tired of trying to reconcile during the long dinners when she enthused about how much fun she'd had at Betsy's party and at Oxsana's party and how much better a place the world would be if everybody could go to everybody else's parties. A rose half-moon light glowed over her blond hair as Flavia went back to some sort of monologue about being "part of everything I've seen, heard and done, just like Odysseus," to which Pascale responded, "That's so excellent." I called out:

"Are you all sticking around?"

"I have a reserved table," Flavia called. "I'm holding court!"

"Good—on my way."

When I looked back at the machine I realized that someone had written "Out of Order" above the money slot.

"How's your nice girlfriend?"

I jumped at the almost whispered sound. Jill was standing at the broken machine beside me considering its choices and wearing—I sniffed—Vetiver, which my brother Marty had given my father for his last birthday. She stared at the machine with a knowing confidence that was unaffected by her black eye.

"I doubt we'll be getting back together," I said in the same low voice, though when I looked over my shoulder I saw that Jill's table had dispersed and that Lauren was nowhere in sight. "How's yours?"

"Great."

"How are your fingers?"

"What do you mean?"

I pushed a raised square of plastic with a paradigmatic bowl of café au lait printed on it, and turned to her as a six-ounce paper cup fell into place and was splashed full of gray liquid. "Haven't you been taping up *News* editorials all day?"

"I told you," she said. "I don't pimp any more."

"I forgot."

"No harm done."

I retrieved my coffee and stepped closer to her. "Look, Jill, I'm really too tired to stand. Can you join me for an expired sandwich and a cup of café au lait?"

"Thanks, but this drink I'm getting is for someone else."

"Right." I sipped at my coffee. "Well, I'll give you a call."

She smiled slyly. "You mean one call."

"That's right, one call."

She watched me as I stepped back. "Bye-bye."

I turned and headed for Flavia and Pascale's table, feeling carefree and elated. Why would Jill have stared at a vending machine with "Out of Order" scribbled on it and talked to me in a near whisper unless she really did feel something for me? Maybe her sexuality was just a stage, maybe all she needed was a man who would really care about her.

I paused in mid-step. Right, and all every lesbian needed was a good screw, and all gay men had cupboards full of Fiesta ware and strived to lisp. I was a walking cliché generator.

Flavia patted a chair beside her. She smiled at me as if I were exactly the person she wanted to see.

"Hello, Mr. Sunshine."

I dropped my book bag onto the floor, unsure of how I felt about a conversation with Flavia or Pascale now that my mind was on sex.

"What do you mean?"

She stuck out her lower lip. "Well, look at you—I mean, who

shat in your cornflakes?" She naturally put her feet up on my legs. "I think you'd be better off to stay away from that Jill. Every time you talk to her you get into the worst mood. *The* worst."

"I haven't talked to her in weeks, that's the problem. How are you, Pascale?"

Pascale fingered one of her gold teardrop earrings and searched through her purse. "Hey, Alex. Real good."

"That's real good. Did anyone shit in your cornflakes today?"

Pascale turned, and her perfect ponytail whipped around like a baton. "No, but I found a caterpillar in my salad at lunch." She touched her fingers to her temples and stood. "Anyway, I've got to fly. Is Brook upstairs?"

"He should be, by now. I'm sure he can't wait to see you."

"Good." She slipped her purse over her shoulder and picked up her coffee cup. "Ciao, you guys. Flav, you wanna have lunch tomorrow?"

"Call me," Flavia drawled. "Of course lunch."

"Great."

"Bye, sweetie." Flavia reached into the *New York Times* delivery bag Peter had given her and pulled out a packet of cigarettes. I looked around for Jill but she was gone.

"She's the best, don't you think?"

"Who?"

"Pascale, stupid. Care for one?"

I leaned forward in my seat as Pascale ran up the glass-walled stairwell to Sterling. "What the hell are you smoking for?"

Flavia lit up and blew out. "I'm nervous. Peter and I have got to do a presentation in Westerbrook tomorrow on alternative art, and I am of course just putting the finishing touches on it with plenty of time to spare." She spread her hands and displayed air. "And Peter's already three hours late."

"Late? He's upstairs buried in Hegel at the moment."

"No way." Flavia rubbed her free hand over her forehead. "And do you know what he's doing in that class now? Nonphenomenal events. I said, 'Peter, you're busting your butt about things that don't happen!' He said, 'Yeah, but I've *got* to deal with it.' " She waved her cigarette dangerously close to my face. "And we were supposed to go over to this happening ten minutes ago. He promised he wouldn't forget."

"Happening?" I squinted at her. "You mean an art happening? Didn't those things go out in the sixties?"

"Not here, apparently." Flavia stood and brushed herself off. "Tell you what. I've got a special invitation to this happening, and since I'm pissed at Peter you're going to come along as my guest."

I shook my head helplessly. "Flavia, I've got another paper to finish, then I've *got* to crash."

"It'll only be thirty minutes, I promise." She dug in her bag as if the matter were decided. "You'll be back at your desk by ten. And if I use any of the experience for our paper I'll give you third authorship."

"Flav, I haven't done anything but drool so far tonight. And I can't stand that happening stuff."

"Would you wait?" Flavia produced her saline solution and squirted a little clarity into each socket. Two alligator tears ran down her cheeks. "This is no mere bullshit. This is brilliant bullshit. I've actually gotten an invitation to Gore Heilbroner's senior essay!"

"Who?"

"Alex. What kind of social slug are you? This is the guy in Jonathan Edwards College who's calling himself a piece of art for a week. He's acting out his final project. I'm sure *Jill* probably knows him."

"Go on."

"Well? We can go watch him *be*. Pascale did half an hour yesterday and watched Gore argue on the phone with his mother and play with himself at the same time. He got a thousand dollars out of her. She said it was absolutely amazing."

I sputtered out a laugh. "You and Pascale must have dain bramage. That's the stupidest shit I've ever heard."

She grabbed my hands. "See, you're already having a reaction to art! I hear he's going to get either an A or an F, and probably an A. What a great tidbit for those letters home, hmm?"

I tried to release her hands. "If my parents knew I was spending my nights watching some guy play with himself and beg for a bigger allowance they'd yank me up to U. Maine Orono in two seconds flat."

She pulled harder. "But, Alex, you may not see me for two or three whole *days* once Parents' Weekend starts. I'll even throw in a free sundae at Ashley's."

I mulled this over. "Large?"

"You're such a bum. Come on."

We used the Sterling exit. Outside it was drizzling. Flavia grabbed my arm and snuggled up to it. Her flats made beautifully precise tapping sounds on the wet pavement. Through some twisted reasoning I felt sure that I would bump into Jill at the happening.

"Alex?"

I nodded unsurely at a guy passing us, someone whom Peter had introduced to me after a squash game. He was carrying a Hegel book too, and heading for the library.

"Yes, darling."

"Are your parents coming for the big weekend?"

I raised my hand to press for a walk signal, but withdrew it as one came up. "Uh-uh."

"How come?"

We crossed Elm Street and continued up High. "They're out in Arizona now that the big tourist season is over. The last thing they need now is more of New England."

She adjusted my sweater collar. "Would I like them?"

"God, no."

She nudged against me. "Why not?"

"They're not good with strangers unless they want to know what to do in McMurtry."

"That's ridiculous," she said decidedly. "You're such a great talker, Alex."

"Am I?"

"Absolutely. So talk to Peter, would you?"

We slowed our pace and approached College Walk, a dark, flagstoned path between Branford and Jonathan Edwards colleges. "I always talk to Peter," I said.

"No, I mean about this little problem we're having, you know."

"I'm afraid not."

She looked at me in disbelief. "Isn't it obvious, the way he's been kissing me off for his work—and for *your* squash, I might add?"

"I need four more years of practice if I'm going to make the team, Flavia."

"Oh, right," she shot back. "You haven't lost a game to him in two weeks. Am I right?"

"I should have known there was a guilt component in this deal."

She squeezed my cheek firmly. "Be serious. I feel like I'm in this arranged marriage all of a sudden. I'm at his goddamn beck and call. 'Meet me at eleven here, I'll be busy until two, I can't sleep over tonight, and *this,* and *this,* and *this.*' Jesus, I'm not even coming any more."

There was a short silence. I slid my eyes toward her tentatively.

"Uh . . ."

"Coming, you know. When Peter and I started sleeping together during the first week of September I still wasn't sure about breaking it off with my old boyfriend Jonno in New York, and I wasn't coming. I just told Peter I was. The problem is that now I'm *supposed* to be, and I'm . . . just not. I'm faking. Jonno called me yesterday, and he seems to know the end is near. I just want to be sure it is, you know?"

"Seems to know!" I said. "Flavia, you can't just leave boyfriends hanging in cities like old bank accounts. What if he decides to come to New Haven for a visit?"

"You'd be amazed at how well I can make up a last-minute crisis. It's not really an intense thing anyway. But I don't know about Peter."

"What's to know?"

"I've never dated a goy before, for one thing."

"So? Neither of you are religious."

"I know . . ." She laid her arms lazily over my shoulders. "That's not all."

I dropped my book bag onto the small flagstones in front of Jonathan Edwards. "Go on."

She became serious again. "Alex, he won't see all of me. He tells me it doesn't matter that I'm Jewish and he really means, 'I don't care that you are, but just don't go around letting it *slip.*' When I went away to grade school in Massachusetts I was the only Jewish girl in my whole goddamn class. The kids used to drop pennies behind them in the hallway for me. That's a lot of pain, all right, and now Peter's more interested in yappin' about Nazis like Heidegger. What is that?"

"Heidegger wasn't a Nazi."

"You haven't talked to my father."

We walked up to the J.E. gate. "Fine. What do you want me to tell him?"

She tilted her head and considered. "Just *suggest* to him that I seem dissatisfied. He respects your opinion. If he's not spending time with me, say, later tonight, be totally surprised about it. You ought to know how much attention I deserve."

She tickled me softly in the side, and I pulled her to me as someone walked up behind us and produced a gate key.

"Flavia, you're a complete opportunist."

She slid her arm across my back. "No, I'm what you call a pragmatist."

11

Gore Heilbroner lived on the second floor of an entryway that gave on to the shadiest section of College Walk between Branford and Jonathan Edwards, the two coolest residential colleges at Yale. According to Brook, Branford was where they put the Beautiful People, and J.E. was where they put the mentally unstable Beautiful People. Flavia knocked twice on the heavy walnut door that led to Gore's hallway while a light scent of fabric softener over a deeper stink of floor wax wafted into my nose. A short—a tiny—woman answered the door, and Flavia started.

"Marissa!"

The woman's eyes bulged. "*Oh*. Flavia, right? How are you? How good to see you!" Marissa wore a leopard-skin pillbox over her black hair, and a kind of fisherman's overall in bumblebee yellow.

"This is Alex MacDonald, Marissa. He's my guest."

"Fabulous." Marissa touched each of us on the arm to indicate that we were welcome. "Make sure one of you signs the guest book. You should only have a short wait. The last pair just left, and we're running in half-hour shifts tonight."

I brushed a few droplets of mist from my shoulders while Flavia signed in for us. "Are you getting credit for this too?"

"No, I'm just a friend of Gore's." Marissa seemed to shun being placed in the same category. "He's a brilliant sculptor, I really admire him. Please help yourself to a snack. There's some great Nicaraguan coffee on the table. I'll go tell Gore you're expecting him. Or . . . whatever. You know what I mean!"

She slipped through a door marked 778 with great care and shut it slowly. I made a cartoon happy face at Flavia.

"She's nifty."

"Peter's friend. Get a grip." Flavia gave her a limp-wristed dismissal. "Here, have a food thingie." She laid a plastic-wrapped egg-white cookie in my palm and poured half a cup of coffee for herself. The cookie package had Swiss written all over, and Japanese.

"What is this?"

Flavia shrugged. "Eat it, it's chic. Oh, my God, this coffee tastes like *wa-ter.*"

"Did you see Jill's name in the guest book? Maybe she does know Gore."

Flavia shook her head. "I didn't. Maybe you should check yourself."

At that moment Marissa reappeared. She leaned into a grave half bow like a new altar girl unsure if she is standing before something particularly holy, and we went in.

The main room of Gore Heilbroner's suite was furnished with blue and gold Navajo rugs, dark mahogany and cherry furniture with red upholstery and a framed eight-by-ten photograph of a guy I supposed to be Gore squatting on his knees, naked, before a large tray of frozen Vaseline. As far as I could tell, Gore was making wave patterns in the Vaseline with his mouth and tongue. If this was what Marissa meant by brilliance in sculpture, I had some news for her. The door in the opposite wall of this room led into another. Flavia laid her book bag on one of the rugs, grabbed my hand and let me take her through. I picked up Brian Eno airport music playing on a stereo.

The second room was much smaller and nearly dark, but as my eyes adjusted I began to make out the shape of a thin man in a red candy-stripe shirt and a tall naked woman who was moving over the sheeted surface of a double bed with him. The fun, I saw, had already started. Gore was blond, patrician, and slightly built, his girlfriend beautiful and underfed-looking, with long bright red hair and a wild, exhilarated expression. Any existing sexual charge in the room was due purely to the woman. Her small breasts came into full relief as they slid toward a softly glowing table lamp and began to kiss. Gore cupped the woman's head in his hands and she slid her hand in and out of his boxer shorts. Neither of them took any notice of us. They were Art, after all. Flavia and I eased our way to seats in the dim light, and I picked up the sharp tang of pot smoke.

Minutes passed and the foreplay built. The woman loosened one button of Gore's shirt and kissed him deeply, loosened another button and kissed him again. Eventually he was naked too. I wanted to leave but I couldn't bring myself to do it. That would be like looking at Duchamp's *Nude Descending a Staircase* at the 1917 Armory Show and getting all riled up over it. The redhead squatted over and then sat on Gore's surprisingly large penis. Flavia was nonchalantly craning her neck from side to side and she seemed to be scribbling notes.

I whispered to her, once they had been at it for a few minutes, "What are we going to do?"

Flavia put her lips on top of my ear. "I don't know, Alex. I don't see another bed."

Now I was sure I wanted to leave. I had a raging hard-on, but since the only light in the room burned near the bed I didn't think that Flavia noticed. She found my ear again and said: "Don't worry if you're erect, Alex. I'm totally blushing."

This changed the picture considerably. I held a trembling hand to her shoulder. "Do you want to go?"

She shook her head slightly. "No . . . let's stick around. It should only last another twelve minutes or so. I just read that in *Cosmo.*"

I started to giggle and then couldn't stop. It was pure church-pew giggling, the kind that even the weekly reenactment of the crucifixion of Christ can't stanch. In direct violation of the manifesto posted on the outer door, Gore looked up, his brow slick with sweat, and stared into our corner of the room. I thought of his senior essay mark dropping from an A to a B— to a flat C and giggled harder. Now that Flavia and I had been subjectified, the whole event started to trouble me. I realized that I was not on a road that would lead to any significant aesthetic revelations. And since my summer with Katharine I already knew what to do in bed with a woman. It would be wiser, I felt, to leave before the climax: mine, Gore's, his girlfriend's or Flavia's. I leaned down to her ear.

"I'm pulling out."

To my horror, Flavia dropped her notebook, clapped her hands and produced a murderous shriek of laughter. The red-haired woman scrambled off of Gore, grabbed a pillow and fell back against the bed's headboard, screaming. From the way she began to light into her boyfriend, I was pretty sure she thought visiting hours for the night were already over. Flavia and I scrambled for the exit like frenzied ants, ran past Marissa in the sitting room, doubled back for our books, took the stairs in blurs of two and three, and tumbled out into the wet J.E. courtyard, laughing until I thought we would puke. I tried to jump over a low section of fence around a small green and ended up falling flat on my back. A sky of fat gray clouds catapulted away as I gasped for air. Flavia stumbled into view, clapping her hands and squealing. Naturally, inevitably, I held up my arms.

" 'Art Gets a Boner!' How's that for a title?"

"How about 'Performance Art Goes Flaccid!' "

Flavia landed more or less on my body, and before I could enclose her in a hug I was covering her face with kisses in the wet darkness. She rolled me over to my side and slid her arms around my back. The grass and drizzle tickled my face as I pulled her into a full embrace and kissed her more deeply. Only after several minutes of this randy play did she finally push me off.

I had somehow unbuttoned Flavia's flannel shirt, so that her breasts, sheathed in a silk negligee top, were within hand's reach. I was drunk on her.

"Flavia," I gasped, "let's go back to your room, please!"

I believe that she would have had the entryway door across from us not opened. A short, shadowy figure in bumblebee yellow stepped out—Marissa. She walked up to the edge of the green's fence, not fifteen feet away from us, and tilted her tiny head on its long ivory neck and thin, curved shoulders. She smiled with amusement, or pity perhaps. Flavia clutched at my arm and stared as if a Council of Mothers had caught us conjugating the verb.

Marissa let her eyes rest on us for another moment, then she laughed brightly.

"Well, I guess life really does imitate art!"

Flavia braced her arms on my shoulders and stood to brush off the grass. She glared at Marissa as we walked away.

Flavia's friend Deb, a junior, lived in a house on Dwight Street near the edge of campus. Flavia had called ahead on the J.E. Common Room pay phone and had a fast, unintelligible exchange with her about our situation. I guessed that this was where we were going. After hanging up she brushed her tangled hair and added a little lip gloss, then slipped brush and gloss back into her *New York Times* bag and gave me a quick wink. We walked hand in hand to the locked gate and waited.

"I have half an hour, isn't that hysterical? I'm supposed to be meeting Peter"—she checked her watch—"at ten-thirty." Her finger traced a little circle in the palm of my hand. The drizzle that had been falling when we entered had just stopped. Though there were several people walking through the college behind us, I felt snuggled into a thick cone of silence with her. Suddenly something occurred to me.

"Flavia," I began.

She gripped my hand. "What is it, sweetie?"

"If we go back to your friend's house, are you going to hold back on me too?"

"What?" Flavia squinted until her eyes almost disappeared. "What do you mean?"

My heart dropped. "I mean, what are we going to Deb's for?"

She looked me over again, as if the body I had crushed to mine ten minutes before was owned by another woman. "Weren't you listening, sweetheart? I'm going to call Jonno in New York and break off our thing."

I felt sure that I had never blushed so fiercely in my life. "Of course. You couldn't exactly have Peter walk in."

"My God, I'd kill myself." She stepped forward as someone entered the college from outside and held the heavy gate for us. "Are you ready?"

"Sure," I said. "And I'll make sure to talk to Peter."

"Would you?" She let the gate slam shut and kissed my cheek.

I looked away as we walked back up to High Street, arms platonically hooked around each other. Super, I said to myself: if this is all your sexual allure promises for the year, you might as well rent yourself out as Art too.

12

The seasons changed, and I continued to think about Jill. I thought of her most when I got back to my room late at night and heard Peter's creaking bedsprings and Flavia's laughter from across the hall. I tried to blot her out after she stopped auditing Julia Westerbrook's lectures, but then I'd see her sweeping through the yellow and red leaves on the Old Campus in her vintage-store overcoat, giving a big wave to someone across the quad, and she'd be on my mind for the rest of the day. She had a finer grasp of how to move through space than other people. She always walked with intent expectation on her face, as if she knew the most stimulating place to go at any hour. The friends who walked with Jill must have felt this too, because whenever she tilted her head back and laughed they looked around for someone they knew. People wanted to be seen with her.

Meanwhile work assignments had started to pour from my professors' mouths and the first set of midterms had hit our suite like a hurricane against a coastal town, leaving it bleary-eyed and badly shaken. I caught cold. I screwed up my courage and played a match with the squash coach and was told to try back at the end of the month. Peter joined the *Daily News* and I lost my squash partner. I went on dates with two women of my "type" from Lawrance Hall and found both more interested in the idea of dating than the specific escort. I slept through four Sunday Masses and kissed my immortal soul goodbye. I sat with Brook in Machine City and took two-hour study breaks and whined. Had everyone else I knew not followed my lead, I might have felt left out. My journal contains two entries from that October, one beginning with and the other closing with the sentence, "I have to make a new start."

The general picture improved when the Yale administration decided to throw a number of parties for its students. The parties, which were scheduled at each residential college and at Commons for the twelve hundred freshmen, were to commemorate some anniversary of the residential college system. They also kicked off an experimental long weekend which the College Council pushed through, a three-day break which granted a breather from twelve uninterrupted weeks of classes between the first day of September and Thanksgiving. The whole event was kept under administration wraps, but a week beforehand people started buzzing about five-figure budgets for each party underwritten by alumni donors, haute cuisine meals and dance bands hired from New York for the evening. I said a prayer of thanks to Jill's old roommate, the anorexic College Council president, and called Jill to ask if she was free. Lauren answered and said she'd give her the message. This is what October was like.

Brook and Peter declared the Commons party a black-tie must, and left me to fend for myself while they reverently lifted shawl-collar tux jackets and spotless trousers from their closets. I could see it in Brook's eyes whenever the topic of the parties came up: at last, a chance to prove that not all Yalies were created equal. I had made up my mind to rent a tux, but after much hemming and hawing over budget I decided to prowl through some vintage clothing stores along State Street and buy one. The likelihood was strong that I would be obliged to dress black tie at least once more before death.

By the afternoon of the party, which was on the twenty-fifth, the campus was as deserted as my tiny town in Maine in the last few hours before Halloween night. It was an overcast, raw day that hinted at rain. I handed in a paper at four-thirty, borrowed thirty bucks from Brook, milked my cash machine to the last five-dollar drop and sped off on Peter's Japanese racing bike. It was almost two miles straight downhill to State Street, a long strip of underground boutiques and abandoned auto repair yards. After I found a tux there I was in charge of buying the champagne that Peter, Flavia, Brook, Pascale and I had chipped in for. According to Peter, there was a liquor store on the way back to campus that served you if you could reach the counter.

It was a few minutes to six when I had put together a jacket, trousers, cummerbund and real bow tie that landed somewhere in the black family. The stooping, white-haired man at the antique clothing shop threw in a mothbally tux shirt for paying in cash and let me change from my jeans and sweatshirt while he wrote a receipt. His tiny wife came out of the back with her lips puckered around two straight pins, wheezing, and tied the tie for me. We took a long, critical look in the mirror together.

"A little threadbare in the elbows, maybe, but wonderful," she ventriloquized over the pins. "You would like me to tuck in that waist?"

"No, thanks." I stuffed my shirt and jeans into a plastic bag. "I need a little margin for error on the bike seat."

"You're not riding a bicycle?" The woman tisked. "It's just started to rain now, darling. Better to get a cab. My husband will call one for you."

I looked past a pair of mannequins in the front window and shook my head. "No, it's just a little drizzle. Anyway, all the cash I've got is for our champagne."

"All right then, dear, happy evening!" The man and woman held the doors and I scooted between them with Peter's bike.

It was growing dark and much colder as I rode along State under the orange-rusted expressway bridges. A light wind began to pick up the drizzle and angle it into my face. The drops grew in size quickly. At the corner of Ogden and State I picked up some late rush-hour traffic and started sticking to the sidewalks until I made it up to Chapel Street. By some miracle I didn't get lost.

Near the corner of Chapel and George, in front of the local mall, I paused to tie my shoelace and secure my plastic bag of clothing to the handlebars. Now it was raining by anybody's definition. Half a block away, I saw Jill step out of New Haven's only Ann Taylor shop with a small bag of clothing of her own. I wish that I had a videotape of the unconsciously sexy way she accessed the street with a quick glance to the left and the right. She wore a black fisherman's sweater—I'd never heard of nihilist fishermen, so she must have dyed it—and black jeans with black gladiator sandals. As I approached she was scanning the street for a break in the traffic to cross to the opposite side.

"Jill!" I pedaled furiously up Chapel Street, letting a looping snake of water from my back tire soak whoever got in the way. "Hey, it's Alex!"

Jill paused and gave a little wave. "Hello, Alex."

I turned and pulled up alongside her, on the curb side, so that she continued walking down Chapel next to me. I could tell from the pointedness of her walk that she was in an ugly mood. Strolling with a straight white male in a tuxedo wasn't likely to make this better, so I broke the silence quickly.

"Your eye's almost healed."

"Yes." She looked at her watch and walked faster. "Isn't it something, the way our bodies rejuvenate?"

"You need a ride somewhere?"

"Thanks, no," she said. "I'm just on the way to my apartment."

I glided along with my weight on the right pedal. "You live

fifteen minutes away, don't you? Come on, you're going to get that pretentious bag soaked."

Jill fixed her green eyes on me. I broke in before she could speak.

"I know, I know. But it's just a friendly gesture. There's absolutely no obligation."

She stopped walking, turned her head and looked into a store window. Then she looked back at me with her hands on her hips, blinking as the rain hit her eyelashes.

"What'd you do, lose your limousine?"

"I can still provide a wet bar," I said. "It beats walking."

"Jesus, all right." Jill let her arms sag and flung one of her long legs over the tiny padded seat. "I'm warning you, though, I've got a splitting headache. You're sure you want to do this?"

"Of course. If I didn't want to meet you I would have tried to cross the street."

She smiled as we got into shaky motion. "So witty for a freshman. Where are you headed dressed like this?"

We gained speed, and I had to shout over the traffic and the hiss of windy rain. "This party at Commons for all the freshmen. It commemorates something."

"Of course." She tapped my right shoulder and I turned right at the corner. "An event obviously cooked up to take everybody's attention off other matters."

"No kidding. I think everybody needs a long weekend now too." I said this like some jerk being quoted by the *Daily News*.

"Think so?" She jabbed my left shoulder blade and I steeled myself away from a parked car. "I just got off my shift at Commons, Alex. You ought to try explaining what a long weekend is down there today."

I looked back over my shoulder at her wet, spiky hair. "They'll be getting overtime, won't they?"

She snorted. "You sound like our dear president. Buying stock in South Africa means *jobs* for the poor, can't you get the picture?"

I made no answer to this and let New Haven's buildings and pedestrians fly by on either side. There isn't much of a downtown to the city once you get outside of campus, just some greasy spoons, bus stations, banks and a couple of streets of pre-mall stores. With Jill's hands close at my waist, though, the dark sprawl looked strangely exciting. After a few minutes we left the business district and got onto Audubon Street, where cars were parked along both gutters and the available asphalt narrowed to the width of a bowling lane.

"I meant to ask you," I called, "do you always blow your check at Ann Taylor?"

I knew at once that this was a major faux pas, for Jill let her bag slide over a car's wet roof and slapped it against my back. I got control of the handlebars just before we sailed head on into a mailbox.

"Whoa! Are you crazy?"

"As a matter of fact," Jill said hotly, "this fifty-percent-off blouse is a gift for a woman I counsel at a welfare hotel in Westville. She was saving money to buy herself some new clothes, but her husband found her hiding place and beat her up. It's my money. I earned it icing a five-foot-high Eiffel Tower of cheese for your party tonight. I'll get off here, please."

We were on the fringe of the old Italian part of New Haven, where the mafioso landlords kept the tight streets and triple-deckers safe for God and democracy. I braked sharply at the corner of a small side street and Jill fell against my back.

"Alex!" Her voice shook as she swung her long legs off of the bike. "Did you go to all this trouble for a little *frottage?*"

In one swift motion I jumped off the bike and pushed it away. It sprawled onto the oily asphalt in a crash of gears and metal tubing. "Jill, tell me what I'm doing wrong." I was so exasperated that my voice was shaking too. "I'm so tired of trying to get through to you."

"You're standing there in *black tie* asking me that and you can't figure it out?"

"All right, fine." I dug wildly in my new trouser pockets. "How much did the blouse cost?"

She took a step back. "Look, Alex—"

"How much? How much!" I ran for her between two cars. She pushed a palm into my chest on the sidewalk as if I were a mugger she was trying to talk down.

"It was only twenty-five dollars. It didn't break my savings, trust me."

"Great. Well, I'm not one of those cheap-ass rich kids either." I found two tens and a five and thrust them into her hand. "Here, give my best to the woman. I'll send along a pound of flesh after I gorge myself at Commons."

Jill held the money out in her hand. "Twenty-five dollars will not buy you good politics."

I dragged the bike to its wheels and climbed on. I was soaked through to my boxers already, and there was a long grease stain on my right trouser leg. "You're welcome for the fucking ride."

"Alex." Her voice became concerned as I turned the bike around and pedaled away. "It's getting dark. Are you sure you can get back to campus all right?"

"I'm already in the dark, wouldn't you say?"

Jill's response floated up out of the rain to me as I turned the corner.

"Then follow the yellow brick road, asshole!"

I changed from my Topsiders into dress shoes back at the empty suite, which was tinged with the excitement of a theatrical first night. I brought my own excitement under control by discovering that someone had borrowed my umbrella, so for all my precautions I still got my feet soaked again before I arrived at dinner. I carried with me two eleven-dollar bottles of Chardonnay, since the contribution for the blouse combined with the tux made two bottles of champagne an impossibility. Being so centered on Jill during our bike ride, I hadn't thought out the implications of spending Brook's and Peter's money, not to mention Flavia's and

Pascale's. It was going to be a pretty tense scene unless I thought of a good alibi. Could I have left a twenty in the pocket of a tux I tried on? Could I have lost some money on the bike? The truth seemed to be the only reasonable way to go but, knowing how highly Brook thought of Jill, that was out of the question. I could already hear him bellowing: "What! You gave twenty-five bucks of our money to a *dyke?*"

As I approached Commons I saw that the line of freshmen for dinner stretched out of the columned entrance to Woolsey, around the three-footed Calder mobile on Beinecke Plaza and ended in front of the president's office at Woodbridge Hall. A roof of umbrellas twitched and twirled over the crowd. I must have looked pretty forlorn by that point, because a few people from Lawrance didn't even recognize me, or maybe felt it wiser to ignore me. It felt like the first day again.

All the way along the plaza, up the steps and through the marble rotunda, I found strangers. Inside Woolsey the high domed ceilings amplified the excited conversation into a nearly deafening chatter. I was ready to turn back and start searching again when I saw Brook's aquiline face just outside the door to the dining hall antechamber. He was taking a last look back at the unlucky hundreds in line behind him.

"Alex!" He seemed more angry than relieved to see me, and when he stared at the wet bags in my hands I blanched. The rest of the group turned as I jogged up, and it took me a moment to recognize them as my friends. Pascale floated on Brook's arm in a chocolate-brown knee-length wool dress with a thin leather and gold belt cinching her in at the waist, while Flavia had Peter's arm in a scoop-neck black velvet number and heels. The latter two were dopey-gaga that night, and stared at each other as if they'd been coated in love glaze or Spanish flypaper.

"Hiya!" I said. I felt that I was both rain-wet and sweating. "Who's the nasty person who took my umbrella?"

Everyone squinted slightly, as had the other people farther back in line. Peter whistled as if I had a huge shiner.

"Alex! Did you steal that tux off somebody's clothesline?"

I bared my teeth and blushed. "No, I just got splashed for three blocks. This truck in front of me looked for potholes. And yes, I did wipe your bike off."

He grinned. The whitish roots of his hair seemed to grin. "Cheer up, man. You're going to be out of place with that long scowl."

I brushed myself off and stepped along with my friends, feeling the remark grind a wider opening in my chest than the one already there. "I sure wish someone had told me we were going as official couples to this."

"It was sort of last-minute," Brook said. "You got the bubbly?"

"Yeah." I held up the two sagging brown bags. "Right here."

"Oh, *great.*" Pascale stepped through the doors into Commons and gasped. "Everyone, come look!" I caught the door from Brook and stepped into the hall.

Since lunch that day, Commons had been transformed into a luxury dining room suitable for the *Lusitania.* Blue and white balloon arches were strung between the chandeliers; new painting lights had been installed above the gallery of portraits that hung high along the wall opposite the kitchens; the marble floors were polished to a dazzling sparkle; the seventy tables were set in bright blue and white linen, fine china and silverware; and twenty-foot-long buffet tables were laid out with hams, whole turkeys, racks of lamb, breads, cheeses, fruits, pitchers of juice, sparkling water and eggnog. Waiters in white tie and tails distributed plates, and even the mean woman at the I.D. desk wore a starched white blouse with a ruff collar. To top it off, at least half of the freshmen were dressed in black tie. The word had certainly gone around. The enormous room was pounding with loud voices, excited screams and the pop of champagne corks. Everyone was taking flash pictures of each other. It was an extraordinary sight, and one I'd looked forward to for days, but when I thought of the dining-hall staff underneath us sending extra turkeys and desserts up in butlers' elevators, and Jill's words, it became strangely repulsive to me.

As we inched forward, a long procession of food began to flow from the kitchen door to my far right. On rolling tables bedecked with blue and white linen tablecloths, two smiling employees of Commons brought forth a scale model of the university baked in gingerbread and decorated with jellied candies. Behind them came four chefs in high white hats, supporting on their shoulders a wide metal tray decorated with blue and white crepe paper. In the center of the tray was a lobster trap made of painted breads that spewed out from its door two fiery-shelled lobsters on a bed of oysters. Behind them two women in white middy blouses pushed along a five-foot-high model of the Eiffel Tower executed entirely in custard and cheese, with a gelatin Y at its peak. There was wild applause. Next came a javelin of a baguette and a black and white frosted cake shaped roughly like Old Campus. Peter grabbed someone by his jacket sleeve and pulled him into our midst.

"Everybody! This is Price, my old roommate from school. We're racing to see who makes *News* Board first. Price McManus, these are my suitemates."

Price was a very tall, slight blond who wore a white rose in his lapel. He shook hands briskly.

"Price wrote the article on the party in today's paper." Peter slapped his back.

"Terrific," Brook said. "That was one of the funniest pieces I've ever read in that rag, man. Congratulations."

"Absolutely," Pascale sang out. "All those statistics, six thousand eggs and everything. What fun."

Price folded his arms. "Actually, it was a pretty tough assignment." He proceeded to tell us how tough. While he did I scanned the crowd sitting down at table. It was a habit of mine that, when someone pointed out that I was in a bad mood, the mood intensified. Peter was right, though: there wasn't a glum face in the bunch. Even George Grabowski, the redheaded guy from Providence who seemed destined for membership in the Stiles dweeb elite, the guy who was at that moment scanning our side of Commons for his roommates, looked merry. As I watched George he met my eyes and started toward me.

"Alex, how are you?"

I walked back a few steps and leaned over the edge of the burgundy velvet rope that separated the tables from the line of people waiting. "At this point I feel like I'm about two generations late. Where's your party?"

When George put forth his hand I could see the anxious set of his eyes. "I wish I knew," he said. "I'm almost finished eating. They're around."

George wore a mismatched gray blazer and white duck trousers which made his jumble of red hair stand out in the wrong way—not casually disheveled, just unkempt. The velvet cord between us made me aware of a division between inside and outside.

"I'm surprised you didn't just oversleep a circus like this," I said.

"It really is a circus, isn't it?"

"Though it is free." I glanced back at my group and saw Peter staring at me strangely. He looked at George and beckoned to me with his index finger: no, no, Alex; not him!

George gripped one of the velvet rope's upright supports, not taking his eyes away. "You're right, circus seems to be the message. The serving people were saying, 'Come on, don't you want any more? I don't want to see any white space on that plate.' "

"That's a switch." I took another step back. "I'd better get out of the way of this gingerbread house."

George looked past me to the break in the line. "You better."

"Alex!" Brook's voice boomed. "Hand me over one of those bottles. I want to toast this aspiring writer."

"What's the big rush?" I handed over a bag and cradled the

other one against my stomach, dreading what was coming. George's eyes were still glued to me, waiting for an invitation.

"Listen, George," I said, "I'll see you at Amy's next study break, okay?" As the words exited my mouth I realized that I sounded just like Peter kissing off some non-Beautiful Person in the L&B room: "Let's have coffee sometime! Say, middle of the next century?"

"You know," George said, "if you guys want, I'll save you my table."

"No, don't go to the trouble. I'm sure Peter will want to sit under some ancestor's portrait."

"Okay, man." George shook my hand again. "But stop over and have dessert. By that time I may have found my suite!"

"Alex!"

"I'll look for you," I said. "I may see you in a bit."

"Great."

I walked back up to our place in line, relieved that I had stopped dripping. Brook immediately brought the bottle of wine up to my face. He spoke evenly.

"Listen, guy, what is this?"

I scanned the label carefully. "Looks like the '81 vintage to me. I was told it's pretty crisp."

"Very funny." Brook looked like a country club director who had discovered that my application had never been in order all these years. "Where's the champagne?"

"Didn't I say? I couldn't get champagne."

"Say what?"

"Everyone sold out?" Flavia gripped Peter's arm. "I feel guilt. You poor thing—you shouldn't have run around everywhere in the rain."

"That's impossible," Price put in, looking at me as if his taste buds were prepared for nothing less. "I was just at Quality half an hour ago, and we got a bunch of Mumm's."

"No," I said flatly. Everyone's attention turned to me. "I mean, there was champagne, but there wouldn't have been enough for all of us if I'd bought it."

Peter did mental arithmetic. "How can that be, buddy? Didn't we count out the cash before you took the bike?"

"Yes." I laughed as new beads of sweat rolled down my back. "I had a hundred dollars with me, the tux was fifty . . . and seventy-five with the shirt, so I had twenty-five left over. And the wine was eleven-fifty a bottle."

Peter counted on his hands. "But we all chucked in ten each for the champagne. So you had fifty, right?"

"Exactly," Brook said. His face was red. "Couldn't you have chosen a cheaper jacket or something?"

"Come *on*, guys, you'll get it back when I get paid Thursday." My voice seemed to boom and shrink at the same time. "Would you rather I'd come without a shirt?"

"*Al*ex," Pascale insisted, so that I instantly knew that money issues were for her issues where there was no gray area, "that's . . . kind of bad, isn't it? Shouldn't you have put the champagne money in one pocket and the tux money in the other?"

I smiled helplessly. Here it came. They could have decided it didn't matter, but instead they decided that it would. I was finally being put in my place.

"Well, Christ, I was in such a rush, I really didn't have time to haggle the people down . . ."

"That's all right," Peter said quietly, "you've got to toss thirty a bottle to get decent champagne anyway."

"It's horribly overpriced," Flavia said. "Don't worry about it, sweetie. We're glad you got here."

This seemed to placate almost everyone. Price certainly wasn't going to offer any of his Mumm's. Brook, unsurprisingly, went on.

"It is not horribly overpriced. A bottle of Moët White Star is like twenty-one seventy-five. Come on, Alex, what's going on?"

"Come on, yourself," I said angrily. "Look, I rode through the pouring rain to this ghetto liquor store you sent me to and got the best wine I could. I even had to carry Peter's bike inside with me so it wouldn't get stolen. I don't want to stand here on trial arguing about carbonation!"

By my own calculations I had another ten or fifteen seconds left before I self-destructed. I also saw out of my right eye that the Eiffel Tower of cheese and the rumba line of chefs and applauding people behind it were almost upon us. It would take a miracle to steel myself and wait for its passage.

As the crowd stepped back to the wall and made room for the procession, I brought the second bottle of Chardonnay up in my hand and shoved it at Brook.

"Wait, I have the perfect solution! Just shake this real hard, and use a little fucking imagination."

I turned, held my breath tightly and pushed through a wall of festive, exhilarated faces toward the doors.

13

I heard my cheap postderegulation telephone begin to screech as I trudged up the dank brick stairwell of Lawrance Hall, but I ignored it. The *last* thing I was going to do was take a message for anybody. When I got to the third floor the phone was still ringing, and even though I knew that rushing the thing would immediately stop it, it rang again, and then again, so that I found myself flying up the last few stairs, daring it to stop, then crashing through the door and over the woolly white arm of Brook's couch to snatch it up.

"Hello?" My voice remained stubbornly even. "Hello?"

Silence.

"Have you hung up?" The run on the stairs caught up with me and I began to pant.

There was a bit of throat clearing, then: "Hi. May I please—"

"This is Alex, Jill. What a surprise. How are you?"

"I'm fine. Why aren't you dining with the swells?"

I fell with all my weight onto the couch and strained the springs to their breaking point. "It's too embarrassing to talk about. I didn't have enough money left to buy the champagne. Everybody is so pissed."

"No champagne? In that case you hang up and I'll call Reuters and the *Times.*"

A sob surfaced in my chest and began pushing up to my throat. "Look, Jill, there's only one thing I can't *stand*, okay, and that's having people angry at me, and almost everybody I know is furious at me at this moment. So if you just called to bullshit I'd rather not."

"No, I didn't," she said in a softer tone. "I wanted to thank you for the ride and for paying for the blouse. I know this woman is going to be thrilled. Otherwise this has been Day from Hell."

"Yeah, tell me about it." I put my feet up on our coffee table, kicked off Brook's "I Like Ike" ashtrays and heeled off both shoes. "How is your headache?"

"It's resting for a while." Jill blew what I guessed was cigarette smoke into her mouthpiece. "But I should have burned my mood off at dance class instead of being a bitch to you and then bringing it all back to the apartment. Lauren couldn't get away fast enough."

"Where'd she go?"

"New York."

"All the way to New York?"

"No, Alex, she was already planning to go to New York. It's her parents' twenty-fifth anniversary."

"I get it." I peeled off my wet socks, which clung to the shape of each foot. "So what are you up to?"

Jill hesitated. "Well, I'm calling to see if you were free for a party tonight. There's no way I can get out of it, but I don't feel like going stag and having a hundred people talking at me."

"One social disaster per evening is usually my limit. What kind of party?"

"It's a new group, the Alliance for Sexual Progress. Don't worry, though, it's not gay or lesbian, just liberal."

"Jill, I—"

"Great, you can come?" she said expectantly.

I leaned back in the couch and looked at the receiver. Having waited so long for Jill to ask me this kind of question, it took me a minute to realize that it was happening. "Should I change first?"

"Are you still wearing the tux?"

"Yes."

"That'll be perfect. It's some kind of a formal. I'll get Lauren's brother's tux from the closet; we're still storing some of his clothes. We'll be a pair! A couple of something."

"All right." I sat up. "Where should we meet? Can I pick you up at your place?"

"No," she said abruptly. She tapped a fingernail on the phone. "The Dramat. Outside the back office. Or no, no, meet me inside. At ten."

"Ten it is." I started snatching newspapers from the floor near the couch, trying to find an order-in dinner menu. The *Daily News,* I saw, was in the middle of a six-part exposé called "Sex at Yale: The Big Lie." I dropped the pile of papers and sat back. "I'll see you then."

"Good. Just come to the Dramat and look for yourself."

I hung up, lay the phone on the table and addressed the common room. "Unbelievable."

The Dramat is an enormous Gothic ark on York Street with a canopied stone porch covered in thick trees. The rain and cold that night made it look especially lifeless and foreboding, but the single light burning in the offices along the side was all the assurance I needed.

I came upon Jill drinking coffee at a card table in a cramped, poster-covered room whose floor was littered with stage spotlights. She was dressed exactly like me except for her tux shirt, which was black, and she had dyed her hair black too. She glared straight ahead at the opposite wall, her thin face drawn tight with concentration, her right hand massaging a spot on her forehead in small counterclockwise circles.

I shook off the rain and knocked on the screen door. Jill looked up and smiled.

"It's open. You're only a little late."

I brought a bottle from behind my back and laid it on the table. "I had to let this chill."

Jill examined the bottle. "A '78 Veuve Clicquot? I thought you had no money for champagne."

"It's old," I said. "I forgot I had it."

"That's sweet of you." She rose halfway in her seat and pecked my cheek. She smelled strongly of peppermint and very faintly of dry-cleaning chemicals and mothballs.

"We'd better start moving. Uncork that and I'll get us a mirror."

"A mirror?" I pulled out a paint-splattered folding chair. I was so nervous that I could hardly get it open. "You mean we're going to get coked too? I should have brought Brook along."

She gave me a discomforting look and walked into a small adjoining closet. "No, we're doing makeup."

I popped the cork of the champagne. "We?"

Jill returned to the table with a small black vanity case, which she emptied over its surface. She glanced at me while she herded the rolls and tubes together. "This is cool. I love champagne."

"I knew you had a soft spot. Do we have glasses, or . . . ?"

"Just take a swig." She picked up a tiny compact with a mirror and a tube of mascara. "You drink my half and I'll drink yours."

"Awesome." I took a long, gradual swallow from the bottle. The champagne seemed to explode into life as it hit my mouth. I put the bottle down for a second and breathed heavily, reading the label. Jill reached across, took a long, deep drink and went back to her mirror.

"Mmm . . . Oh, *look,*" she said excitedly. She leaned forward with one eyelash daubed in black. "See my wrinkle?"

"Where?" I met her halfway across the table. "What, on your forehead there? I can barely see that."

"Don't qualify your sensory perceptions. Wrinkles are either visible or not visible."

I took another gulp of champagne, but this time it blossomed out of my lips and dribbled down my chin. Jill didn't seem to notice. "It's probably just the day you've been having. This stuff'll iron you right out."

She paused, searching my eyes for something I don't think she found, and opened a tiny jar of white cream. She began to daub this over her cheeks and nose.

"I suppose it doesn't matter. My youth is over anyway. Seven more months and I'll be jettisoned back into the nightmare of the real world as an adult."

"Nightmare?" I said. "That's ridiculous. I've just come from there."

"You call Maine real?"

"Don't start."

Jill's teeth flashed at me, now the same color as her whole face. "Really, it's not so bad passing into old age. Virtue kicks in, it gets easier to deal with options. When I was eight I wasted three nights a week dreaming about when I was going to become a world-class gymnast. Now I have dreams about sequoia trees crashing down over a rose garden."

"Jill, there are tons of things you can do." I paused over a gaseous belch. "You could write almost anywhere. You could work for an editor, or get into journalism."

"Journalism!" She groaned. "Presstitution. Here, bring your chair over. The hierarchy in journalism is more conservative than the hierarchy in banking."

I placed my chair beside hers and dragged the champagne across the table. "Try banking, then. I can see you in a silk foulard and a navy skirt."

"Try sitting still for five minutes." She pushed the tip of my nose up so that it was shaped like hers. "You just reminded me of the moment I knew I was a feminist. It was in eighth grade, I was at the Lycée Français in New York. One of the rare years when Dad's fortunes were up. On the second day of class they gave us the first computer career test ever done in the City. I answered a hundred and fifteen ridiculous questions, and two weeks later a little slip of paper came back telling me that I should become a florist."

"A *florist?*"

Jill lifted a considering finger to her lips. I wanted to lick it. "Exactly. Then it hit me that when I filled in 'Female' on the second question, the computer probably cut my possible jobs in half. I screamed at Monsieur Laurent, 'Just *try* and make me a florist!' I broke a desk that day, I think. . . . Look, are you going to give me some champagne or not?"

"I think there may be a little backwash left."

"Thanks." She took another long drink and reached for the silver mascara tube. She began to unroll it slowly, and a smile of genuine, mischievous pleasure grew on her lips. I suspected that Jill had no intention of letting me out of the Dramat unmade-up, but I knew there would be no arguing with her either. As long as she touched me it was fine.

"I feel like we're in Berlin," I said. "Isn't that the transvestite capital?"

She laid her mirror down and came at me with a long nib that resembled a pipe cleaner dipped in crude oil. "Just hold still, and we'll be out of here in a jiff."

I breathed through my nose and thought of becoming a statue as Jill's fingertips slid over my cheek.

"And you." She applied mascara just this side of carelessly. "You had a bad day too?"

"I don't know . . . I mean yeah."

"Did you like my Eiffel Tower?"

"Actually, I found it sort of revolting."

"Alex, s'il vous *plait*. Do you have any idea how long it took for the copyright permission to come through from Paris?" She penciled under my eyes as if I were a casual telephone conversation she was having while writing out a check.

"Come on," I said, "stop toying with me."

"Sorry." She looked me over and cracked up.

"What's so funny?" My head swam with champagne and Jill's strong peppermint smell. "Do I look that ridiculous?"

"Of course not." She held her head two or three inches from mine. "I'm only amused that you're not running around deranged because I'm putting you in a little makeup. Did you do this when you were a kid?"

"Only war paint, I'm afraid." I grimaced as she moved on to the face cream. I closed my eyes and listened to the rain and to Jill's breathing. At last she leaned back and pushed out of her chair. I rose to meet her. With her hair parted and combed over like mine we were almost equal in height. I wanted to plunge my face into a sink of warm water.

"Good," I said nervously, "how do I look?"

"How do I look, how do I look?" She clattered chairs and gathered tubes together. "You're even beginning to sound like a slag."

"That's not very specific." We walked to the door, slowed by the first effects of the champagne.

"Damn, look at this rain." Jill fished out a set of keys and held the door open onto the dark, wet alley. "Don't worry, Alex, you look just like me, and I look just like you."

I stepped up beside her. "Great. I want to look just like you. Want to finish this bottle?"

Jill took it from my hands and let the last three or four ounces swirl down her throat as I flicked off the overhead lights. She reached around a shelf and laid the bottle on it, then turned without any warning and pushed her face into mine. She pressed my mouth open and gave me one short, deep kiss, her tongue dancing over the inside of my left cheek and then withdrawing, plugging me in and then yanking out the cord.

"Sorry," she said glibly, and tweaked my nose with her thumb and index finger. "It's a custom in my family to kiss the person beside you when you finish a bottle of champagne."

"Great." I stumbled out into the night on the firm push of Jill's hand at my back. "As long as it's custom."

The first annual Alliance for Sexual Progress party was held in the basement of a large graduate student bar and eatery on the outer edge of campus. Jill and I got so many unbelieving stares that I tripped on the steps going into the bar.

The first thing I saw when we ducked our heads into the small entry room was Brad Lee, from my "Great American Novels" class. He was smoking a Benson & Hedges Ultra Light 100 and wearing a full-length dinner gown made of a shimmering silver fabric. With his free hand he waved a large red fan. Brad was originally from Seoul but had spent most of his life in Paris with his diplomat father and now called himself Eurasian. To look at him in the reflected light that flashed up the long stairway from the basement was to know the difference between putting on makeup and putting on a face. Then again, in a spectacularly strange way, he looked rather attractive.

Jill handed over tickets and we walked up to him.

"Jill!" Brad grinned and marked her right hand as paid with a swipe of his lipstick. "You look oh oh so so very *very!* But who's the lucky girl? Could I know her?"

I stuck a fist out for lipstick and deepened my voice. The effect was ludicrous. "We did a presentation on *Moby Dick,* remember?"

"Alex Macsomething!" Brad flicked his fan shut in mild shock and revealed a row of huge wet white teeth. "I just cannot believe. It's so nice of you to intro*duce* him, Jill."

"We've got to go downstairs and get dry," she said. "You can talk about Moby's dick later."

"I hope we can, Alex." Brad winked at me.

"Yeah, I'll see you in class." When we got out of earshot I grabbed Jill's arm.

"What did he mean, introduce me?"

"Don't worry about that itch," Jill said delightedly. "He meant that I'm your in. Don't you know what an introduction is? I guess you and Brook have been seen together too much."

"Oh, right. Why don't I get to spend more time with you, then?"

The stairway down to the party was thick with people and the smell of colognes. Most of the people were dressed way up, many were dressed for the other gender, some dressed higher up than the other gender might have taken the trouble to go. I glared at the back of Jill's head—"some kind of a formal," my ass. The chic women looked one bite away from vampirism and the bohemian ones on the verge of consumption. The men seemed indolent with conceit and checked me out with a sort of bored, momentary fascination. Jill, on the other hand, looked like Jill in makeup. Maybe it was my familiarity with her; probably it was my terror of losing a point of reference. She turned and drew me through a clear shower curtain with Duchamp's *The Bride Stripped Bare by Her Bachelors, Even* decaled on it, and we entered the main dance room. In the center of this black-walled space someone had assembled a fully sheeted mattress and box spring crowned with a hot pink cardboard banner that said, THE ALLIANCE! A package of condoms and a circular plastic container of birth control pills sat on individual, heart-shaped pillows.

"This is very strange," I said. "Am I going to know anybody here?"

"Don't fret," Jill said. "The jocks are at the townie gay bars where they won't be recognized."

"Great."

"Come on." She tugged at my sleeves. "You look pretty strange yourself. Let's dance."

"How about *one* dance?"

She smiled and kissed me again on the mouth. "This way, my clone."

In opposite proportion to the parties I usually attended, all but a handful of people were dancing. The music was loud enough to make my flesh thump in time to it, but I didn't recognize the bands and I didn't like the high-energy sound. I found my feet falling back into the old junior high two-step.

"Loosen *up*," Jill admonished me, "you're among friends!" She shook me by the shoulders. "Everyone'll think I brought some old queen."

"The music's weird." As I said this a Grace Jones track started playing, definitely her pre-James Bond period. Everyone hollered and screeched and the dance floor fused into an orgiastic pod of dangling jewelry and unshaved armpits. I maneuvered Jill to a corner, where my attention was caught by two guys up on a small stage dancing between the speakers. One guy was thin and red-haired, in a black string vest, the other one was big-muscled, bare-chested and, as Flavia would say, butt-ugly. Flavia! What would she say if she knew I was down in this basement? Compared to this scene, my friends over at Commons were playing shuffleboard and drinking prune juice. They certainly weren't drinking champagne.

"Jill—"

Jill was gone. I realized with a shock that I was dancing by myself. I wasn't the only one doing this, but I made for the sidelines as fast as I could push through. Once out, I headed for the bar at the other end of the room. A guy in black jeans and a white T-shirt stared at me from inside a coat check hole in the wall. It was obvious that men in makeup were not his personal turn-on. I felt my pockets.

"Got any champagne?"

He shook his head. "Wine's all gone. There's beer at your feet. Unless you want to go to the bar upstairs."

"Think I'll pass on upstairs." I looked down at a small aluminum barrel full of bottles on ice. A coffee can attached to it said, "Beer $1.00. Honor System. Protect Your Karma." I dropped in the two singles I had left over from buying the wine and got a pair of Miller Lites. Grace Jones was still herding in all the misfits and freaks from the edge of the night. From across the room I saw Brad sashaying toward me with his fan, looking intent on being herded. I glanced around in panic and stepped up to the first woman I saw, a tall, long-haired blond in a man's couture suit and high heels.

"Excuse me."

"Yes?" The woman had an upper-class British accent. It figured.

"Hi. Can I please offer you a beer so the transvestite behind me will leave me alone?"

The woman looked me over and her face lit up. "Oh, the *other* transvestite. Of course. I'll take the Miller."

I twisted off the cap. "You're an angel."

"I'm told." She drank.

"Hey, you!" Brad put his hand on my elbow. "Come on, Alex, we're in the same class, you've got to dance with me!"

I unhooked myself. "Are you sure we've met, madame?"

"Absolutely sure. You *will* come to dance, won't you?" He blinked his false eyelashes at me several times. I shuddered and looked away.

"Thanks, but I don't think so. My date wouldn't like it."

"Oh—pussywoof." Brad sneered and walked off.

"I was having this conversation!" I called after him.

The woman clicked my beer in a toast. "Here's to you, pussywoof."

"It's Alex Pussywoof."

"Annunziata," the woman said. "I hope that you're showing Jill a good time. Everyone's been saying, 'I didn't know she had a brother.' "

"I'm flattered," I said. "How do you know her?"

"We shared a hice."

"Oh . . . oh, a house! Which year?"

Annunziata drank from her bottle daintily and winced. "We go farther back, I'm afraid. To Choate."

I stopped with my beer halfway to my mouth. "You and Jill went to *Choate?*"

"Yes, don't you fancy it?"

"Sure," I said. "She sort of left that out of her history, that's all."

"That doesn't surprise me at all. There are lots of things she's probably never told."

"Really?" I said. "Such as?"

Annunziata's eyes played over me. "Oh," she said absently, "just a little thing here and a little there. What's a personal history but a little thing here and a little thing there?"

She winked to someone over my shoulder. "She can fill you in now, actually. Thanks so much for the drink." She turned away and I felt a hand on my arm.

Jill's face was light pink and her hair was damply matted around her ears. I had never seen her look so relaxed, and I kissed her impulsively. "You're sweating!"

She poked my chest. "And you're not."

"You abandoned me!"

"Can't you find a boy to dance with?" She walked back to the floor, pulling at my sleeve with one hand and sipping a cup of wine with the other.

"No one even spoke to me."

She shook her head and started gyrating to a piece of African music. Juju, she called it. "You look repressed and condescending; I wouldn't ask you for a dance either."

"You just did."

She began to drift away. "I only brought you back into the fold."

"Okay, wait!" I lunged for her. "Watch me relax." I started to mime Jill's dancing, and in a few minutes we were hopping forward to meet, shoulder to shoulder and hip front to hip front as the intensity of drums built. I tried to meet her eyes and hold them without being frightened off, and she kept eye contact up and back, back and forth, for almost a minute. The people around us started to dissolve, and for the first time Jill let me into her private space without fighting me. Then I had to open my mouth.

"I met Annunziata!"

Jill frowned and did a quick 360-degree turn on the floor. The intimate minute was history. "How is she?"

"She seems nice," I shouted over the music. "A little prim, maybe."

"Prim!" She threw back her head and laughed. "Annunziata makes every nymphomaniac bisexual I've ever met look like a nun."

"No way."

"She's also a pathological liar, but then again she knows lots of beautiful lesbians. Other than that, I can do without her."

"I see." My eyes landed on the two kissing men again. "Did you first realize you were a lesbian at Choate?"

She gave me a shocked look and took another sip of her wine. "Who told you I was a lesbian?"

"Didn't you?"

"Didn't you?" she mocked.

"Come on, be straight with me."

"I never said that either."

I danced on, trying to keep my mouth shut, but the prying stares I was now receiving as Jill's satellite were too much.

"When you dance with Lauren, who leads?"

She fluttered her eyelashes like a sex kitten. "Depends on who's got the whip."

"Jill, I only asked a question."

"Try putting yourself in her place."

I looked around slowly, touching my chest. "Isn't that where you've put me?"

"I think not."

"That's not a very satisfying answer."

"Then stop pigeonholing me." She spun around twice, swallowing wine and letting her head loll on her neck.

"I'd be happy to tell you when I first realized I was straight," I said. "I thought we were supposed to make sexual progress here."

Jill bopped up to me. When she got close enough to kiss she said, in a deep voice, "You want to make some sexual progress, go jump onto that bed and mas-tur-bate. You'd be a hit."

The music changed to some old Prince, and another cheer went up. The skinny guy and his muscular friend were now ecstatically grinding crotch to ass beside one of the speakers.

"I don't mean to pigeonhole you," I said.

"Tell that to your John Birch Society roommate and his buddies."

"Come on." I put my hand out. "Now you're being closeminded."

She slapped me away. "Alex, I don't want to be rude and blow you off, but I don't necessarily need a penis to have a good time tonight, okay?"

I stopped dancing. "Screw you. Why didn't you just bring a mannequin from the Dramat then?"

She took my arm with her free hand. "That's not what I mean. I just want you to stop being so morbidly fascinated with me. I don't live on some inner groove and I don't live on a pedestal, all right? I'm an outsider. I had to define my own space, and it's still crashing in around me all the time. Your worldview happens to correspond with normalcy."

"Oh, Jill," I said, "let me apologize. I knew somebody had the monopoly on suffering around here."

Without missing a beat, Jill flicked the last few swallows of her wine into my face. I wrenched the cup out of her hand and threw it on the floor, then clutched at my eyes as they began to sting.

Jill stepped back and kicked the cup aside. "You don't know anything about suffering."

I laughed and blinked and rubbed my eyes. "Christ, it sounds like you live on a pedestal to me!"

"Maybe this was a bad idea. Maybe you should go."

I glared at her. "I was planning to. I'm not about to apologize for being normal."

"You shouldn't. But you shouldn't expect everybody else to be normal either."

"Would I be here if I did?" I said loudly. "I came because I like you. I'm not trying to pigeonhole you, I'm just trying to get to know you. And if you call me up and invite me to a party—"

"I wouldn't have been thinking of you if you hadn't forced me onto that crazy bicycle in the rain."

"Wait a second," I said, "let me finish. If you invite me to a party and then don't let me get any closer, of course it's going to look like morbid fascination. I'm only asking you to be honest. If you're just interested in a friendship, then tell me that. I don't know how to read all these signals."

She folded her arms and looked up at the ceiling. "Please, Alex, not here. I'm going to have to think this through."

"Good, do that. Give me a call when you decide."

Outside the rain hadn't let up. With no other direction to go in, I started toward home, looking down at the wet sidewalks. I was sweating. I couldn't help remembering Jill's kiss at the Dramat: underwhelming, too sudden and casually intimate, debased, weighty like despair. I stumbled and rubbed my eye and it came back black. The cold air and rain brought me to my senses pretty quickly.

Up ahead a clump of shadows under the dark trees in front of the Dramat resolved themselves into four large men in blue team jackets walking with their collars up. Each one was carrying a bottle. They were definitely coming in my direction. I was determined not to cross the street for them, but I picked up my steps in the hope of slipping under the shade of an elm tree before they got a full view of Mr. Alex Pussywoof. As we approached each other, two of the guys started horsing around and ran forward. One of them struck me as familiar from the porch at Dave Freitag's house. I had just come up with his name and passed the group when they broke into laughter together.

"Hey, buddy," one of them called, "lose the beauty contest?"

"What was that?" another added.

A pause, and then: "That's a fuckin' faggot."

I stopped, stunned, and turned around, but the four men had taken a sharp right down the alley next to the Drama School and were already gone from sight. I wanted to run after them to smash their heads with their own bottles. I also wanted to run away.

"Assholes." I kicked hard against one of the elm trees, and my shoe came back with silty bark on its tip. I was a boy in makeup for one night, wasn't that obvious? What the hell was the matter with people, were they brought up in vacuums? We were all Yalies, weren't we?

"Exactly," I imagined Jill saying. "Now do you know how it feels?"

I hesitated in the wet, open air. The empty spot in my chest was widening again. If it widened another inch everything would fall in. Ahead lay the bright lights of the York-Elm Street intersection, far behind me the bars at the corner of York and Chapel. I breathed deeply. I would do it, I decided, I'm going to keep going right down the street to Elm and then right through the center of campus, just as I am.

Yes, I said, as my feet suddenly disobeyed me and crossed York Street to College Walk, which was shorter and dimly lit, I am going to walk right out into the light and stride home. I wasn't scared by a little misplaced homophobia. Here I go, shouldering the weight of the issue. The world of theory will stand up to the world of practice.

Another group of people approached, and I hurried into the darkness toward the open steel arms of the Old Campus gate, dodging the puddles in the flagstones and looking straight ahead at my goal. Three quarters of the way down the walk I heard heavy steps splashing up behind me. Great, I thought, now we'll see some action. I whirled around with my fists raised.

"Okay, asshole, come on!"

To my astonishment, Jill ran up in the rain, breathless and soaked, and grabbed my hands in hers. Her makeup was a mess too.

14

Jill lived on the third floor of a battleship-gray tripledecker house that was slipping off its foundations into the blacktopped lot behind it. Her porch slanted out at a precarious angle and was in bad need of paint and new wood. In her kitchen a rainbow of candle wax dripped over two champagne bottles which sat in the center of a small round table set with rattan and bamboo chairs. I sat in one, fearful to test my full weight against the back, while Jill shed her wet clothing in the next room. I could see flashes of her through the half-closed door as she walked back and forth and hung things up to dry. Neither of us had the money for a cab, so we had walked in the rain for twenty-five minutes. I, at least, was on the verge of passing out. Occasionally Jill paused at the door and glanced out at me with concern. She hadn't really explained why she ran after me, but it was obvious that she needed somebody whom she trusted to walk with her and be with her. I just hoped that I could stay awake.

"You'll have to wait for me while I shower," she called. I heard her step out of Lauren's brother's tux pants. "Or you'll wake up covered in black dye."

Was I sleeping over? I tried not to stare through into the next room, but I was too tired to willfully direct my eyes away. "Where do I—"

"Just plunk down on the bed in here. It's hard to miss."

I stood and pulled at my jacket. "Should I take off my face first?"

"You should. There's cream in the bathroom."

"Thanks." I tried to get a last glimpse of Jill through the door, but she was standing somewhere behind it.

The tiny bathroom was surprisingly free of feminine cosmetics. One overnight stay of Flavia's produced more clutter in our Lawrance Hall bathroom. I backed a bar of facial soap out of its green plastic garage and went to work.

Jill walked into the bathroom behind me and tapped my shoulder while I was doing the tenth rinse. I grabbed a towel and wiped my face clean.

I started. She was completely naked. She was slighter than I imagined, but much more shapely. I was surprised when she let me kiss her. This kiss was gentle and warm. I was impressed that I could still speak.

"Hi. What's up?"

"Nothing." She rubbed my cheek with one hand and smiled. "I feel better having you here. I really couldn't have taken being alone tonight. So thanks."

"Hey, thank you." I didn't realize how ridiculous this would sound, and we slipped into exhausted laughter together.

"You know what I mean."

She pulled back the shower curtain and turned on the water in the tub. "What?"

"You know . . ." I stared at her white, sloping back and the graceful, concave ridge that ran below it to her ass. "I've just wanted to see what you looked like since I met you, and there you are."

She turned up to me while testing the water, her face red. "And how do I look?"

"You look beautiful. You must know my opinion by now."

Jill left the water running and hugged me tightly, then let her head drop to my shoulder. "Lauren would slip a knife between your ribs if she found you here, you know."

"But you invited me, didn't you?" I tried to lift Jill's head with my hands, but she pushed me away, suddenly uncomfortable.

"I've got to take a shower, okay? Meet me inside."

" 'Nuf said." I backed out of the bathroom obediently. It would be better in bed.

I wandered around the small apartment festively while Jill splashed and sang in the shower. The floors of the bedroom and living room were polished hardwood, strewn with nubbly cotton throw rugs, the moldings were painted white, and books covered every other surface that had once been recognizable as interior furnishing. Books covered the tables, the couch in the living room which faced the street, the stereo rack and the open closet, the top of the wardrobe, the vanity table, a sewing machine and two desks. Literary theory, feminist theory, medieval history, lots of Virginia Woolf and Shoshana Felman. On the wall above the bed there was an enormous framed poster of a messy yellow, red, pink and blue abstract painting called *When Alexander the Great Wept by the River Bank Because There Were No More Worlds to Conquer, His Distress Rested on Nothing More Substantial Than the Ignorance of His Map Maker.*

"Not too many photographs of the loving couple!" I called from the hallway.

There was a jangle of shower curtain rings. "We don't do public appearances lately!"

"Yeah, right."

"Why don't you undress? It's too cold out there to be wet."

I fingered my new trousers. "I'm bare-ass naked."

"Then stop snooping around!"

"Wow—somebody's paranoid!"

"Just lie there and wait like a good bitch, okay?"

I started unbuttoning my shirt. "Don't you be rough."

The rush of water had become a rapid drip. I stripped every-thing off, laid it in a neat pile over a chair and slid into the double bed under a down comforter. It felt exquisite. I was faint with anticipation. The woman I had lain awake fantasizing about, a woman impossibly distant, was about to join me in bed.

Jill walked into the room after a moment in a red kimono robe with a towel turbaned over her hair, holding a glass of water in one hand and several pills in the other. She swallowed these, went directly to the mirror on her vanity table and slid her finger-tips over her nose and cheeks. Even in this gesture I responded to her unflappable self-confidence. My heart dropped.

"I'm falling in love with you, Jill," I blurted out.

She unwrapped the towel, smiling as if I were a disobedient but amusing corgi, and scrubbed her now blond and red hair. "You're just drunk."

I slid my feet farther down the sheets. "You know, I have this feeling nobody's taking me seriously tonight."

"You're the first man I've allowed to sleep in my bed for nearly a year," she said over her shoulder. "Believe me, I'm taking you seriously."

When Jill finished brushing out her hair she stood, stepped out of her kimono and spread it over a book-covered chair. She left the room and walked around the apartment turning out lights with the air of an efficient parent. At last she came to the bed and, gripping the base of a fat table lamp for balance, slid in beside me. This last lamp she left burning. Her breasts, small but large-nippled, leaned toward me and begged to be touched. Her flesh was firm, warm and fragrant there, but she tensed and pulled back when I brushed my hands along her flat stomach.

"Hey," I said softly, "what's wrong?"

She slid out of reach in the big bed. "I don't know, Alex, maybe this isn't such a good idea. I like having you here, and I

feel connected to you even though I've only known you for whatever, two months. But I really don't want to have sex. I don't want
you to be crushed either, because you're an attractive guy, but I
just have this commitment to Lauren. That's really the truth."

"Jill." I moved toward her again. "Come on, don't shut me
out."

Her hands shot forward to meet mine. Our eyes met too. "Alex,
no more, please. I'm not trying to shut you out."

I stared at her for a minute, then broke away. I swung my legs
out of the bed and banged my feet on the floor. "Fine, I'll sleep
on the couch. You can chain me to the radiator if you want."

"Stop that." Jill pulled me back toward her. "Don't short-
change yourself. I can't help how I feel right now. Let's just get
some sleep, okay?" She reached over to flick the table lamp off,
but waited for my answer.

"Okay?"

I searched her eyes again. Would I ever be able to tell when
she wasn't wearing a mask?

"Alex, okay?"

"Okay, good night!"

She flicked off the light and darkness rushed in. I leaned down
and found her mouth. All I got was a friendly kiss, a very definite
withdrawal of tongue and a hug.

"Mmm, good night." Now she sighed and snuggled up to me. It
was torture. "You have a nice body, Alex. I guess all you Wasps
do."

"Please stop," I groaned, "you're too fuckin' hilarious."

She rested her head on my chest again. "Sorry. Sleep well."
She began to doze almost on impact.

I encircled Jill and let my hard-on jut against her thigh. Warm
water from her spiky hair dripped across my arms and onto the
sheets. I lay holding her for a few minutes with her light breath
against my shoulder. There was a sharp ache all through me.
Maybe she did have a commitment, but I was still a lightweight,
that's what it came down to.

Jill's elbow nudged me in the stomach, so I thought, from sleep.

"Alex. Would you relax? I promise, it's not you."

"Got it." I closed my eyes and breathed Jill in. I fell into an oblivious sleep before I could reflect any further.

Voices woke me in the morning, all of them mixing and rising from one or two rooms' remove. I shifted in bed, and my sore back instantly told me that the mattress under me wasn't mine. I was about to open my eyes and investigate when a deep male voice approached the doorway.

"Honey?" it whispered in a polished Irish accent. "Who is this?"

Jill's voice called from the kitchen. "That's just Alex, Daddy. You'll meet him later."

"Yes, darling," a woman's voice added. Was it German? "Let's hurry. We have a reservation at eleven."

The man sighed and moved away. It would have taken a ninety-degree turn of my head to get a look at him. "You never tell us about any of the men in your life," he said. "I would like to meet them sometime. All at once."

"You ought to get up here more than once a year," Jill responded. There was an edge in her voice that she probably softened after a look from her mother. "Alex is a late sleeper. I promise we'll bring back a danish and surprise him."

"All right." There was the sound of a light kiss. "Although it looks to me like you're housing a minor."

"Archie!" the woman's voice called. "We're on a tight schedule."

The trio washed out some cups, opened and closed the refrigerator, put on coats and pulled the back door of the apartment shut quietly. A short push of cold air ran over the bed about half a minute later. I waited with my eyes open on the white plaster ceiling for the sound of their car engine and sat up when they had driven away.

My hair was stuck up on end, and the blood in my head felt like strawberry jam. I was smiling, though. It really was too hilarious. She had been plotting this from the minute she invited me to the party. Now I could imagine Lauren's departure for New York. "Look, lover, the parents are on their way into town and you've just become inconvenient." I rubbed my face with my hands and considered my next move, unable yet to nudge the hard fact of what had just taken place, a fact that was currently lodged like a ball of phlegm in my chest. One thing was clear. Little sleepover Alex wasn't going to be there for his little danish when the Lanigans zipped back to their precious daughter's apartment.

I stood shakily, my feet cracking on the cold wooden floor as if the heels were made of filo dough. The bedroom glowed with a pale yellow Saturday morning light. It was essential that I leave a note for Jill. I scanned the room slowly but found only a stub of pencil on the dresser. Although the idea of a few lines in lipstick on a mirror was appealing, I gave that up and searched for a scrap of paper.

In a drawer of the bedside table I found two pens and a notebook with some clean sheets. Underneath the notebook were four framed photographs of Jill and Lauren. I went through them.

"You coward! You fucking coward!"

The first photograph was a bucolic portrait of the pair, a prep school pose. Another highlighted shenanigans of a costume party where Jill and Lauren were dressed as men. The third picture showed a happy embrace with both parties in earlier hair colors and styles, but the fourth and most incriminating featured Lauren lying with her head upturned on Jill's bare lap, a shot taken by an artiste friend, from the bombed-out look of the room beyond. Separately the photographs were harmless enough, but together they left little doubt as to what was going on between these two women. Together in a drawer, they also left little doubt as to the fact that I had been worked as one works makeup over a wrinkle.

After I put my damp, cold tux back on, I spread the photo-

graphs over the bed, two to a pillow, and pulled the comforter up
to nestle against them gently. A note wouldn't be necessary now.
I felt in my pocket for my room keys and went into the bathroom
to spit out the gunk that was hanging in my chest. As hard as I
tried, though, I couldn't get anything to come up.

15

I walked directly back to my Old Campus room in the
cold, clear morning air. If anyone looked at me I stared them
down. In my room I undressed, balled up my tux, threw it in a
corner of the closet and slid into my yellow oak bed. I didn't
sleep much that day but I didn't leave the bed for any reason.
The shame I felt was like a fever. Every time I blinked Jill was
there, running up to me in the rain and asking me to go home
with her. When I tried to shut my eyes I heard the conversation
with her parents on an endless tape loop. I supposed, in her
defense, that Brad Lee in her bed wouldn't have been nearly as
impressive. "Darling, you're sleeping with a transvestite, how
nice for you." Mr. and Mrs. Lanigan sounded like the kind of jet-
set parents whose children were fucked up until at least the age
of twenty-eight.

Brook eventually found me and got me to unlock my door. He
was on his way back from a late dinner and wondered why I still
hadn't shown my head. He sat on the edge of my bed and said
that I shouldn't be hiding out because of the champagne incident
since everybody—especially Flavia—had yelled at him. I was
pleased about that, but I was too embarrassed to tell him anything beyond a story about being up most of the night comforting
a friend from Maine on the phone, a friend who'd had his heart
broken. Brook seemed to accept this in the full knowledge that I
was lying, and wished that he could stay with me, but as it was he

was in a rush to get over to Vanderbilt and help out with a party at Price's dump. I told him to send my best to Price and rolled over onto my face.

"Come on, dude." Brook leaned forward on the bed and rubbed my shoulder. "Don't put on a bummer on a Saturday night. It's bad enough during the week."

"You suck!" I shouted into my pillow. After a minute I rolled over. "You suck."

"No, I don't." He stood and walked to the door. "You made a mistake, but it's no big deal. Everybody still loves you."

"Price too?"

He laughed and pulled the door open. "Especially Price."

By midnight the shame over Jill had become a fever. I woke to find myself covered in sweat, my sheets wrapped around me like huge unrinsed dishrags. When I tried to climb out of bed to get to the bathroom my legs crumpled under me and I fell right on my forehead. I tensed and closed my mouth over a wave of that WOOMB sound that goes off in your brain when you get smacked hard in the skull, but luckily nobody in the suite woke up. While I was down on the floor with the dust balls I decided to hang out for a minute and concentrate on getting enough energy together to get over to the door and down the hall to the bathroom. I could hear my breath in my ears and all through my head, and watched light and dust drift in under the door from the lighted hallway. I sang my favorite blues tune under my breath several times and tried to draw energy from that. Soon I got tired of strategies and put off moving for a few minutes. Every time I swallowed I got stabbed in the throat, and my lungs felt like they were ready to surge out of my windpipe. I had chills too, the kind that make your back teeth chatter involuntarily. I refused to think about any of it, especially my forehead. The world around me became very small.

When Brook got back from his party at sunrise he found me in the same position on the floor, dried blood covering half of my face from the cut on my head. He claimed that he hardly recognized me. Apparently I wanted to know where my tux was so that I could trade it in for champagne. Brook dressed me, threw his long wool overcoat over my shoulders and supported me on his arm all the way to the infirmary. I could see my breath billowing in the air as we walked past the church spires on College Street. The sun felt cold.

Later that day my eyes opened on a large nurse with red hair and a wide Irish face who was padding up to me on Naturalizer earth shoes. I was lying in an orange hospital room several stories off the ground. From where my bed sat I could look out a picture window that took in the gentle slope of Hillhouse Avenue to the point where it intersected with Grove Street. The arts buildings and the heart of the campus were several blocks away, but with a stretch I could see one square, granite slice of Silliman College.

"Good afternoon," the nurse said. "I'm Mrs. Greene. You look a little more sensible than you did this morning."

I ran my fingers up to the top of my forehead, which had a small bandage on it, and grimaced past a swallow. "Thanks. I wonder why I feel like I've been run over."

"You've been under sedatives, that may be why. Now you're all caught up on your sleep, though." The nurse waited for me to lift my head and fluffed the pillows. Then she worked her hands under my mattress, sliding all the excess sheets and blanket in until I was saran-wrapped into place. She rose with a flush in her cheeks.

I wriggled out some breathing room. "What's wrong with me?"

"What's wrong with you?" she said expansively. "Physically you've got nothing to worry about. A mild concussion, I believe, and a little case of the flu."

I felt my jaw, which was sore and thudded painfully against my fingers. "Stitches?"

"I think you may have been awarded one."

I watched Nurse Greene lay a pitcher of water on the night table. "Did I get any cards?"

She flung the curtains all the way back on their aluminum rings. "In six hours? You've got high hopes. Your friend . . . Flavia, is that right—?"

"Flavia."

"Yes. Flavia called about an hour ago and wanted me to tell you that she would try to get over later on. She didn't sound too well herself."

I felt around the bandage again. "Has someone called my parents, by the way?"

Nurse Greene rubbed her wide hands over her hips and looked askance at me from the windows. Another brat from the undergraduate college. "I don't think that sort of thing is in someone else's hands any more, young man."

"My other question is, when are visitors' hours? And when do I get out of here?"

She handed along a color-coded menu for Infants, Children and Patients With Sensitive Stomachs.

"That's two questions, I'm afraid, but just to humor you"— Nurse Greene leaned close and felt my forehead with the back of her hand—"two to five for visitors on Sundays. And I'm afraid that the doctor will have to speak to you about when you may leave. As soon as two days, possibly."

"Two days—great! How am I supposed to make my squash tryouts tomorrow? And do you know how far behind I am in my work?"

"I assume that these are rhetorical questions," she said. "But I suggest that you get back into a piece before turning to the sports. You don't want to lose what's left of the good head you've got."

She padded out of the room.

An hour droned by and my mind drifted into the recent past. If anyone had told me in August that I would be running from men in gowns, kissing lesbians and giving myself a concussion after a night spent in makeup I would have shown *them* to an infirmary. Truncated from my friends in a foreign, antiseptic space, though, I was amazed at how quickly the exhilarating effect of Yale was replaced by a longing to be with my family, my father especially, and even to see Katharine the Nice again, if only to talk. I didn't know whether to fight this impulse or give in to it, but when no one showed their visiting face at my door by four-fifteen I walked out into the hallway in my johnny shirt and picked up a pay phone.

My parents were away on a fishing trip (Mom loving every minute of that, no doubt) so I left a message on their machine. My brother, according to his machine, was still "away on a shoot." Following this, I failed to reach two friends from Hollier Prep who had gone on to Dartmouth, and was finally rebuked by Katharine's seven-year-old sister Jane, who had been left instructions not to give out Katharine's number to anyone unless they got Katharine's personal approval. How one was to get directly in touch with Katharine to ask permission to get her number was beyond Jane's mental stretch, but I left a message in case she called in from Orono. Then I made a sixth call. The motion was too spontaneous for me to rethink it. There had to be someone around who would be interested to hear about my concussion.

"I'm not calling her," I said, as I punched in the numbers. "I am not calling her."

Jill's machine kicked in on the first ring with a new message. The "Hi, I'm not home right now" spiel was on the tape, but it was spoken by at least fifteen women simultaneously, and ended with them bursting into hysterical laughter together. Oh, that Jill, always having fun with somebody.

I received a tone. "Hi . . ." I coughed and found the ball of phlegmy resentment back in my chest. "Hi, this is the other person in the tuxedo. He too has been struck low by a blow to the head, and can be reached at the University Health Services building, Room 518, until further notice. Black tie visiting hours run around the clock."

I hung up and walked back to my bed to start in on my Sensitive Stomachs dinner. The ball was in everyone else's court.

16

Flavia didn't get around to visiting me until Monday afternoon; the hours before this I spent popping my medicine and concentrating on getting well. This concentration produced the opposite result somehow, and by Monday morning my fever was up over 101 and my whole head throbbed and proved incapable of holding a thought for more than a few seconds. The staff at the infirmary rubbed the backs of their knuckles along my eyebrows and pronounced me on the heal, while Nurse Greene promised to tie several sheets end to end should I decide on an early escape.

After lunch, bored beyond words, I finagled a double dose of Mr. Codeine out of one of the nurses and settled back for the ride. Several minutes later I spied Flavia in the corridor, crouched and unbelieving, perhaps hoping to rush in all at once and scare me. From where I lay it looked like she had placed her head squarely on top of my night table. She had a blue cashmere scarf twisted up in her hands, and the lower half of her nose was a deep red.

"Oh. My. God," she began, tiptoeing over the carpet. "I have such guilt for not visiting, how are you?"

"Hi, Falvia," I said, then: "Wait, I mean Flavia. The doctor said I was going to be a little dyslexic for the first few months."

Flavia's mouth widened in horror, then she frowned knowingly and began to lash me with her scarf.

"You are so full of shit, Alex MacDonald. We're all *really* worried about you."

"Thanks."

"I'm serious. Pascale is meeting me here in about two seconds. We feel awful about what happened in Commons. That Brook is such a goddamn snob."

I followed her with my eyes as she slid out of her overcoat, threw it on a chair at the opposite wall and gave the large space a once-over. The codeine swelled and receded in my head.

"I really will pay all of you back," I said. "Where's Peter?"

"He's doing a story," Flavia replied sulkily. "That's all I hear these days. 'Sorry, Flav, gotta do a story.' He told me to meet him for dinner at the *News* building last night, which is colder than a barn, I might add, and when I got there he said all the editors had gone to dinner and he couldn't leave until one of them came back. Is that quintessential Peter Cliffman or what? I said, 'Peter, what news story is going to break on a Sunday afternoon at five o'clock in New Haven? If Giamatti chokes on his lamb chop it'll happen in the dining halls!' There was no arguing with him, of course. We dined on the cold remains of the pizza they get free from that greasy pit on York. Pizza from Thursday! I had T-zone" —she moved her index finger in a cross from left cheek to right, and from the tip of her nose to her forehead—"all night."

"Tell him that I demand he play squash this week."

Flavia poked about and didn't respond. "This is a pretty nice room, you know. A double all to yourself, private bath, plus a color TV. I didn't even have this at Mount Sinai."

I rubbed my finger up and down my nose. "Why were you at Mount Sinai?"

She smiled sarcastically. "Never you mind. I was just kvelling over your nice room."

I glanced at the TV, which I hadn't yet turned on. The sharp definitions of its plastic corners were softening and slipping.

"I guess you're right. I've got the highest ratio of luxury to income of anyone I know."

"Al-ex—"

"Alex!" Pascale called. She stood at the door, waiting for me to acknowledge her. While I sat in bed with dirty hair and a johnny shirt, Pascale stood, superbly, in a black linen blazer over an off-white cotton fatigue sweater; pricey, loose-fitting jeans held with one of Brook's black leather belts; a pair of pointy-toed black leather boots; two silver-dollar-sized gold hoops in her ears and Brook's Ray Bans wedged over the top of her shimmering blond hair. She frowned, empathic with my condition, then took Flavia's guiding hand and came to the bedside.

"How *are* you?" she purred. "We all lost our appetites at brunch yesterday when Brook told us."

"I'm fine," I said through a yawn, "I just need some rest."

"You were right to hold out for good champagne," she added. "I had a hangover from the mouth of hell all Saturday. I went to Price's party and slept in his bed there for *four* hours."

"Everyone wondered where the hell she was," Flavia said. "And did Brook give her shit . . ."

"Endless shit." Pascale shook her head tragically.

"Wow. I hope you're feeling all right."

Pascale reached down and squeezed my hand. "I'm much better, thanks."

"Wait!" Flavia exclaimed. "Alex, we have to do this joke for you. We have this awesome joke to cheer you up."

Pascale became embarrassed. "Flav, do you really think so? Alex doesn't look so hot."

"Thanks—"

"No, he'll love it." Flavia was already pulling Pascale back from the bed. Her perfume was making my Sensitive Stomach turn.

"Okay, Alex? Watch closely." Flavia lined herself up next to Pascale. "We have to do this quickly or we're gonna spaz out and screw it up."

"Good." My eyelids were beginning to droop, though I felt that my body was rising quickly.

"Alex," Pascale said, "over here! You have to guess what we are, okay? What are we . . . oh, my God." She bit down a smile, took a deep breath and exhaled, tongue extended, into a loud, wet raspberry. On inhaling she slid her tongue back and stood with her mouth in a fat, round O. Seeing Pascale do such a thing jerked me aware momentarily.

"Now watch," Flavia said. She leaned forward and drew the thumb-and-forefinger end of her half-open fist back and forth over Pascale's lips. "Okay, guess!"

I concentrated on both women but could only shake my head.

"You see, I knew he wouldn't know." Pascale clicked her heels together and pointed to her chest. "I'm an asshole . . ."

Flavia framed her face with her open hands and raised her eyebrows. "And *I'm* an asswipe!"

"Alex, isn't that hysterical?"

"Alex . . ."

"Come on, Alex, at least a titter."

"Thanks, it was great." I could hardly keep my eyes from falling shut. "Are you sure you've got the right room?"

"Should we go, honey?"

I made a feeble wave and rolled over to face the window. Did you apologize to someone for humiliating him by humiliating yourself around here? Very strange. Within a few seconds I was out.

"Alex." A hand flicked wet into my eyes, a hand attached to a full, shapely voice of concern. Just this moment, I thought: save it. I felt myself blushing. I was aware of a long pull back from the fall into water, another pull that assured wakefulness if I could just sit still and think about getting awake for another second, and not worry if I nodded on and off, until I slid past the last conscious instant which, flipped round and read backward . . .

"Alex."

Now a testy voice. I blinked and blinked and kept looking. This time I got nearly a whole handful of cold wet in the face. The sounds and shapes began to rush back toward me like a house strapped onto a flatbed truck, roaring down a highway to be slammed over a man sitting in a field in an easy chair reading a—

A hand touched my chest and my eyes flew open. Jill was sitting as close to me on the edge of my bed as the mattress permitted. Her vintage-store overcoat and gloves were thrown on a chair. Outside it was almost dark again.

"You were tossing around."

"Hi." I tried to smooth down my hair. "It was this dream."

She leaned forward expectantly. "Was I in it?"

"Sure. You, and Auntie Em. . . ."

"I must have come in when you started flinging your arms up and down."

"That makes sense." It struck me that Jill's slicked, moist hair was all platinum. I wondered if a confrontation with her parents had prompted the switch, or if her hair now changed colors without her doing, like a tree. She looked softer and somehow purified without the rusty red.

"Are you getting enough drugs in here?" She tilted her head toward the drawer of the night table. I wondered if I had left the drawer open, then thought of Jill's open night table drawer. Had she done that deliberately, just to set the scene?

"Plenty," I said. "Codeine, antibiotics, penicillin, the whole workup. Actually, I'm stoned on codeine right now."

"They must be shooting you up with more than that," Jill said. "You look like you're doing a methadone program. And where's your telephone? How are you going to leave messages for me and Lauren?"

"It's in the hallway." I pulled myself forward, despite her protests. "I think it's there, isn't it?"

She laughed and ran her fingers up through my hair. "At what time did you break into the diluadid?"

"No, no shit like that. The stitch goes tomorrow morning and then I go. I've got no time for a relapse."

"Still, give a call if you arrive on death's door. I know a couple of good hymns."

"Thanks a bunch."

Jill checked out the room's décor. There was a long, uncomfortable silence, and neither of us brought up the subject which we were both thinking of. No one was running forward with an apology, certainly.

"My mother was on her back for six months once," she said at last.

"That's rough. Did your mother find the pictures?"

"That was my stepmother."

I folded my arms behind my head. "She didn't, did she? Or you found some way to bluff it."

"Alex, my life at college is *mine*. I don't have to justify anything to occasional visitors who aren't going to understand."

"So in control of her life," I said groggily, "but still closeted to the people who brought her into the world."

"That woman did *not* bring me into the world." Jill walked to the foot of the bed and leaned forward over the guardrail. "But you, Mr. Disturbed Apple Pie Face, tell me what tragedy's befallen you? You mentioned a blow to the head."

"It's like this. I was dared to go to this all-dyke party—"

She shoved. "That's not funny."

"You're right. Actually, I picked up a nasty cold after I walked a friend home in the rain, and then I seem to have collided with the floor of my room."

"Sounds pretty unpleasant."

"Unpleasant . . . I remember an unpleasant disclaimer. 'That's just Alex, Daddy. We'll bring him back a danish.' "

"I've still got the danish if you want it."

"Give it to Lauren," I said. "How could you deliberately set me up like that?"

"It wasn't premeditated or deliberate," Jill said calmly. "Their visit was a complete surprise."

"If it wasn't deliberate why were those pictures hidden?"

She stared down at my sheets. "I warned you not to give me that bike ride, Alex. You're always insisting your way into things."

"Me?" I laughed. "You're the one who asked me to chef for you at Jiffy's. And you didn't have to visit me."

"You invited me."

"That's right, I did," I said. "I guess we're even now."

"I'd hardly call it even," she said. "What happened to me was pure intolerance. What happened to you was amateur masochism."

"If I were a masochist I'd go to a party thrown by people who openly hated me."

Jill broke off from the bed and surged away. "Here we go again! My God, can't you understand?" She paused, about to take another step, for a second that over the course of several breaths became a whole minute. I watched her lift her hands to her temples as if she were putting on a pair of glasses. I assumed that she was still gathering her thoughts when I heard a sob. She slid one hand around her stomach and bent forward. Her green sweater slid up to reveal her white, white lower back.

"*Damn* it . . ."

My anger and wooziness evaporated. "What's wrong?"

Jill rolled her head back, and one tear ran from the corner of each eye straight down into her ears. I reached for the call button, which I remembered was on the fritz.

"Hey! We need help!"

"No, shh . . ." Jill held a silencing finger up to me, the lines around her half-shut eyes a progression of tight, radiating furrows. "Wait a minute. Just don't talk." She produced a blue pill from the pocket of her jeans and drank it off with water from the sink in the bathroom. Then she started to inhale and exhale deeply and massage her scalp from front to back and back to front. While I watched her our breaths fell into unison. I concentrated on passing calm to her, whatever health I had, everything I felt for her, though I only succeeded in getting a headache myself.

After a few minutes she walked back through the room and sat on the edge of the bed again. Her shoulders were slumped. I reached out and touched her folded hands, and she let me take one back to my lap. She slid her four fingers through mine and we made a loose fist.

"You ought to be in here, Jill, not me."

She leaned forward until her forehead was resting in her right palm. "A pressure headache is no reason to commit yourself, especially here."

"What do you mean?" I thought of the bandaged bump on the front of my skull.

"God, if you only knew the number of women who come in here with urinary tract infections and get sent home with a prescription for cranberry juice and Tylenol. You should be grateful to be a man just for that reason. Men only get sport injuries and colds."

"Right, me and my harmless concussion. Is this the same headache you had on Friday night?"

"No, this one's even better. I'll be fine."

We listened to a rubber-wheeled cart move down the corridor and pause at my door. A nurse I didn't recognize was pushing it. She glanced into the room but ventured no farther.

"Did you come by just before I woke up?" I said.

"No. I was here for ten minutes or so. You look like a *child* in bed, did you know that? Your face goes completely blank. I remember watching you on Saturday morning."

I let my eyes close for a moment. "Yeah, I slept like a rock that night."

"Not only exhaustion, though. It's like a death mask."

"You sound like Brook."

"Did he beat me here?"

"He walked me over yesterday. He forced them to take me

without an appointment. Of course it was six o'clock in the morning."

"Another merit badge for Brook."

Jill's fingers slipped out of mine, and I opened my eyes.

"Hey."

"What?"

"I'm sorry I left those pictures out on your bed."

"Don't sweat it. I've got to go."

"Already? You're the first good visitor I've had today."

She stood slowly, stretching her arms up. "I'll come back after my appointment."

"Who with?"

"Never *mind*. But I'll come back, okay?"

I stared down at my lumpy feet under the blanket. Having Jill in my room was like having a loaded gun in my hands but not knowing how to shoot it. "Maybe I should stop insisting my way into your life, like you say. Maybe you shouldn't bother."

After a minute I heard Jill sweep her coat over her shoulder and walk to the door.

"I understand."

"I don't want to see you until I've got this straightened out," I said, my heart thumping. "But I think I know why you really invited me back to your house."

We stared at each other, immobile, for a good ten seconds. Jill put on her coat and buttoned it.

"Like I said, I have a commitment to Lauren. And you have your girlfriend."

"Ex-girlfriend, and I wish you wouldn't pigeonhole yourself. You're too good for it."

Jill twisted the doorknob and released it. She walked to the bed, leaned over me and let her lips rest on mine, softly, as if kissing a handful of new snow. It was as unlike her other kisses as I could have dreamed possible, and when she lifted away from me it was to resolve into a face surprisingly unsure of itself. It was in this momentary hesitation and a flutter of deep emotion I saw in her eyes that I realized how fully open our possibilities still were.

"There," she said. "Compromise, you see? It's the basis of good politics."

One more electrifying smile and she was gone.

17

After dinner I started a letter to Katharine. I got to the second page of throat-clearing before I tore it up and started another. I tore the second letter up halfway through the first page and, since my pen was on the point of drying out, began to outline a third:

—I'm in the hospital.

—I'm thinking of you all of a sudden.

—I feel like shit for insulting you.

—Can I see you sometime before Christmas?

I stared at this for a while, added a "Dear Katharine" and a "Love, Alex" and put it away until I could mail it. I would send it care of U. Maine Orono and see what happened. Then I picked up a book by Wallace Stevens which Brook had brought along when he dumped me at the infirmary. Katharine had given me the book for my birthday in July and inscribed it "To another mind ahead of its time." It was hard to pick up anything I had come into contact with during the summer and not call up an image of Katharine and me together, or the two of us wanting to be. I was sure that I loved Jill at that moment, and yet I trusted Jill's judgment so completely that I started to wonder if the door to Katharine really was shut. Why had she just said "your girl-friend" instead of "your ex"? It was like subliminal emotional advertising.

Later, it bothered me that I couldn't find the short poem I'd hit upon in my reading. Both ground and sky were sharply figured in it, but only as coordinates that pointed to an almost unknowable horizon. The key to knowing this horizon was a woman. I thought for a long time about such a horizon, tinged just green like a Stevens sky, and as I lay there thinking about Stevens and thinking about Katharine (and occasionally nodding off), a sort of horizon began to open in my own mind. Since I didn't have another pen or a pencil I was forced to try to embed all of my revived thoughts about Katharine, her reality and her qualities, between this poem's lines for future reference. Katharine was a Stevens fan too, and I imagined as I turned pages in the book that she was approving of my efforts.

That was the irony, for as I laid the book aside and closed the pages with the pleasant aesthetic ache of one whose spiritual strings have been plucked, only five stories below—almost directly below me, in fact—just outside the University Health Services building, Jill was seized by an epidural hematoma brought on (or perhaps not brought on) by the seven-week-old head injuries and the tension of our argument, and she was dancing crazily on the pavement. By the time she was found and placed on a stretcher, blood was flowing exclusively to the burst blood vessels and had stopped flowing to her brain. By the time she was lifted into the back of an ambulance to be rushed to Yale-New Haven Hospital, she was already suffering the irreversible smudge of brain damage. By the time she arrived at the hospital, delayed by the traffic from a Peter Gabriel concert happening in town, she was legally dead, and by the time she reached a resuscitator in the Yale-New Haven Emergency Room, she was dead beyond anyone's rules.

Jill had bumped into her counselor, Dr. Christy Moran, while waiting for a new painkiller prescription at the infirmary drugstore. Since she mentioned our visit, Dr. Moran brought me the news after leaving a message for Jill's parents. For the half hour she was able to sit at my bedside, I held all my thoughts in like a murderer refusing to confess. Behind the sober silence I knew that I might lose my mind if I started to talk. Later, of course, when I could have used such words, there weren't many to go back to.

That night was probably the longest one of my life. I was too shocked by the news to get back to sleep and too groggy from the codeine to think straight. I wanted the whole semester to run before my eyes in microscopic exactness, but nothing got me out of seeing that orange room. Even after Dr. Moran arrived I was terrified to do anything. My bladder was throbbing but I couldn't get out of bed. It was like sitting on the threads of a spider web; if I budged, I might not get the opportunity to move again. When my feet hit the floor I might sink through it. All of this seemed possible.

Dr. Moran was a tall, wiry Australian woman with tight brown curls and huge brown-gray eyes. I felt that her eyes could see more and see deeper, because of their size.

"How do you feel?" she said, massaging my hand. "You've barely said anything."

I stared ahead at the opposite wall. "I can't understand. Isn't there any chance of getting her back?"

"No, no chance."

My hands shook a little, and I balled them into fists. I was remembering the contours of Jill's body in the dark and the fragrant water in her hair that ran down my chest. It wasn't possible that this would be the extent of it. Six kisses—I'd had more than that on a single date.

"I'm not prepared to believe any of this."

Dr. Moran unballed one of my fists. Her hand was extraordinarily long. "I'm sorry, Alex, I'm very sorry."

"Forget it, it's okay." I pulled back my hand and started biting off the skin around my cuticles. I wondered if counselors now trained in voice control; I'd never heard such heartfelt empathy from someone I'd known for twenty-five minutes.

"I know that you had to work hard to get through to Jill," she said. "I know I did. And I certainly got the impression that you left each other on good terms. Isn't that right?"

I looked at her. How could she have ingested this already? "Jill and I? Oh, sure. We talked some things out. I guess you could say we parted on good terms. As good as they could be."

"She thought a lot of you. She was in a very peaceful mood when I saw her."

"Good." I tore a long strip of skin from my pinkie cuticle, too long, and red leaped up underneath. I slipped this hand under the sheets and we sat for a minute. I heard steps out in the corridor and a soft knock at the door.

Dr. Moran stood up. "What am I going to tell her parents?"

There was another knock, and Nurse Greene entered. She was just beginning a graveyard shift and looked fresh from sleep. Dr. Moran went out.

Neither of us spoke beyond a simple greeting, but when Nurse Greene slid the alcohol-dipped thermometer into my mouth, the tip of my nose and the back of my throat began to sting. I winced, and water slid out of my eyes. I had to breathe very quickly through my nose to keep the thermometer in. I didn't think the time would ever be over. We sat silently, and the room did not change, and the lights did not flicker or go out. We were things above the earth, and Jill had become a thing of the earth. I would never be able to get my mind around it.

The nurse removed the thermometer and recorded the results. I could see that she was trying not to look at me. When she finished with my pulse she wrote that down.

"How are you, Mrs. Greene?" I said at last.

"Alex." She wiped under my eyes with a tissue. "Are you okay, darlin'?"

I shook my head. "I'm afraid."

She gripped my hand and looked down. "That's all right too."

My headache seemed to cave in all at once, and then I closed my eyes and fell into a deep, almost immediate sleep where I did not dream. All I remember, slipping down, was a sensation of inclining, magnetically almost, toward Jill: poor, lovely, blue-shifted Jill, who was already thousands of miles ahead of me in the past tense.

18

An abrupt doctor pulled the stitch from my skull and I earned my discharge from the infirmary on a deeply cold Tuesday morning. All I had to put on were the black jeans and yellow oxford shirt Brook had found for me in my room after the fall. My fever was gone and my new headache had nothing to do with the concussion.

On the first-floor concourse I was saying goodbye to Nurse Greene outside the elevator when I felt a hand on my shoulder.

"Dr. Moran!" Her face was pale, and the lines under her eyes sooty gray, as if she hadn't slept all night.

"Christy," Nurse Greene said. Her voice, tired too after her long shift, was like a sponge drawing up anxiety.

"Good morning, Alex, I'm glad I caught you." She spoke strangely high and breathless. "I'm just coming from a rally that's gathering outside the president's office."

This seemed like a non sequitur to me. "Why is that?"

"It's about Jill. You'll have to walk over and see some of the signs. Lauren Bozorgi is announcing that she wants every football player on a lie detector machine by the end of the week or she'll sue the university. I think you should see. And if you feel comfortable, I think you ought to get up on the soapbox and say a few words. You're probably the last person to have a meaningful conversation with her."

My chest started aching again. "Of course, Doctor."

"Christy, Alex, please."

She slipped a Kenya bag from her shoulder, dug through it and brought out two blue plastic diskettes. They were labeled "Essay Draft 1" and "Essay Draft 2."

"I have to ask you to do me a favor and take these disks to Jill's senior essay adviser. I checked the schedule book that was in her purse, and she's got an eleven-thirty meeting. I don't know if it'll be of any use, but could you?"

I nodded quickly, though I was actually outside, watching myself respond. I wanted more codeine, any sort of buffer. "Sure, I'd be happy to. What's the adviser's name?"

"Julia Westerbrook, from the Literature Major."

"I knew that," I said. "I owe her a paper anyway. Thanks. And thanks for your help." I tossed the diskettes into my duffel bag and walked off through the bright lobby without looking back. Outside there were long patches of ice under my feet, perfect for sliding down the hill to central campus, but I was afraid to test them.

Sixty or seventy people were grouped around two chairs and a folding table outside the president's office at Woodbridge Hall. It was now the beginning of a class change, so hundreds of people cutting across the plaza were pausing to see what was going on. I stood under the branches of a potted tree, my knuckles light purple in the cold, my lungs slowly becoming accustomed to breathing unfiltered air.

"Fucking gays are up in arms again," a voice behind me said.

"Thhh thhh thh thhh," another voice lisped. I turned around.

It was Michael Wagnall, a roommate of George Grabowski's, and a friend of Michael's I didn't know. From a few conversations we'd had in the Lawrance Hall stairwell I thought Michael might be gay himself. I moved forward. Lauren was standing on the table with a bullhorn, clearing her throat. Her face was blotched dark pink and she was dressed in black from head to toe.

"Can't any of you hear me?" she began again into the bullhorn. "Jill Lanigan died at Yale-New Haven Hospital last night! The woman who was beaten at the Bulldogs party in September died last night! What is Yale prepared to do to find the people responsible? If she were a straight white male, would we have to be standing here?"

"No way!" A chorus of screams rang out.

Lauren repeated more or less the same line until her throat gave out. Then the crowd around the table started a chant, "We want action! We want action!" over and over.

In less than five minutes there were too many people on the plaza to count. In the common shock even moving seemed out of the question. People leaned out of classrooms in Harkness Hall across the street and from dorm windows in the south court of Berkeley College. Gray was how I remember the faces, open-mouthed and gray. Whether they knew Jill or not, everyone was stilled. Jill's close friends were easy to spot; they were the ones bawling.

I ran, followed by curious stares. I might have my say, but not so close to the event. I ran until I hit Elm Street and crossed in a half jog. Peter was crossing in the opposite direction and called to me, but I didn't stop. I tried to make it through to Old Campus without crying, but I hardly got inside the gate. Somehow that was all right.

Julia Westerbrook's office was on the second floor of McClellan Hall, at the end of a shady corridor. A schedule of office hours hung under her name tag on a sheet of yellow legal paper. Jill's name was signed in for the eleven-thirty to twelve-thirty slot. I stared at this signature for several seconds and fought off the urge to go. I couldn't see light coming from under the door, but I knocked.

"Jill?"

"I'm here for Jill," I said. "This is Alex MacDonald, from your postmodernism class?"

"Hold on." A chair scraped, a few steps crossed a floor, and the door opened.

Julia Westerbrook wore a dark brown wool turtleneck, a tan

vest and baggy brown checked wool trousers. Her loosely curled
blond hair spiraled down, vinelike, over her retro Dior glasses. A
lighted cigarette twitched between her right forefinger and middle finger. She looked very tired.

"Alex, what can I do for you?"

"This is about Jill Lanigan. She's a friend of mine."

"Yes?"

"Can we step inside for a minute? It's sort of personal."

Again, she looked around.

"Sure. Do you mind if I keep the door ajar so I don't miss
Jill?"

I glanced past her. On the desk there were three piles of
papers, a photo of her with her husband, I supposed, and a small
black-on-white sign that said, REMAIN DETACHED AND IMMANENT. How
the hell was I going to tell this woman?

"Jill's not coming, Professor. That's why I'm here."

She met my eyes. "This is something. Take a seat."

"Thanks."

She flowed around to her chair, snuffed out her cigarette in an
ashtray and sat with her elbows spread apart over the desk top,
her head far forward, as if in a yoga stretch.

"What's up?"

I rifled through my duffel bag and brought out the two diskettes. On second thought I dropped the "Essay Draft 1" disk back
into my bag and handed over the new one.

"This is from Jill."

"Great." She took the disk from my hand and sprang back in
her seat to examine it. "I see Draft 1 is now a thing of the past.
That's extraordinary. I'm still waiting for some of my senior essay
people to fix on their topics. You know what they'll be doing on
December 20 at 4 A.M."

"Yes."

"You must be a good friend if Jill asked you to bring this over.
She's a Scrooge with her work."

I nodded dumbly. I was experiencing the same block I'd had

trying to talk to Jill for the first time, perhaps because I had the distinct premonition that Julia Westerbrook was going to snub me. "Well, I haven't really read any of it."

Her look changed to mild suspicion. "I'm surprised you haven't if you've got this."

I stood up sharply. The chair shrieked over the stone floor.

"Professor, it's never going to be more finished than it is."

Now she looked almost amused. "What do you mean?"

"Jill visited me in the infirmary yesterday where I was sick," I said, "up on Hillhouse Avenue, but as she was leaving she had some kind of brain seizure. No one knows why, but nobody discovered her for about ten minutes, since it was dark, and so her brain stopped functioning, and then she didn't get revived in time. I'm sorry to break it to you so quickly, but she's dead."

A wave of color dropped out of Julia Westerbrook's face. I saw the struggle to grasp a moment of $X = 0$.

When she spoke again I heard a low anger in her voice. "Are you joking?"

"No. I've been in the infirmary since Sunday morning, and she visited me last night. Her doctor came up and told me."

Julia Westerbrook put her hands on her ears and rocked back in her chair, staring up at me and then down at the disk. The third time she stopped, her eyes dead on mine. The shock of this sudden intimacy was too much for either of us. I blushed and she pushed back out of her chair.

"Excuse me for a moment. Sit down, please." She rushed out of the room and slammed the heavy wooden door behind her. Several minutes passed. My hands felt icy and turned light purple between the knuckles again as I waited. I started to drowse off while I watched the detached/immanent sign on the desk. In the middle of a yawn I caught myself, stood and picked up Jill's disk from the desk top. It felt weightless and cold in my hands, like a poker chip. As I laid it down again Professor Westerbrook returned with a small paper cone of water. She walked around her desk and sat down heavily. She placed her head in her hands and spoke through spread fingers.

"I feel as though you've just presented me with her remains."

We watched each other for a second. "What can I tell you?" I said. "I'm sorry."

She removed her glasses and rubbed her temples. "Yes. What can you tell me? . . . I lost my mother last year, and some of that feeling is coming back. What you think is solitude is a joke until your favorite parent goes."

"Jill spoke highly of you."

This seemed to annoy her. "You don't have to tell me that."

I made a move for the door. "There's a rally going on at Beinecke Plaza, in case you're interested."

"Yes. It looks like I've got a free hour."

"I'll have a dean's excuse to go with my paper when it's done."

"Thank you, Alex. I hope you feel better." She looked at me for the first time with concern. "And thank you for letting me know."

"Okay, no problem."

I closed the door, walked two steps down the hall and stood. In the perfect silence I imagined Julia Westerbrook, reigning Yale Queen of Who Manipulates and Why, sitting and staring, maybe scribbling out a note or two. I wondered if it would be an immanent note or a detached one.

I leaned against the cool stone wall in the corridor and caught my breath. I could feel blood thudding against my cheek in a way that made me push off from the wall, horrified at this awareness. My breath began to speed up again, and then I found that I couldn't catch it. The more I concentrated, the faster it came: I seemed to be choking from too much air. Finally a professor rounded a corner of the hallway and said something to me. I shouldered past him without looking and ran all the way back to Lawrance Hall to shower off the suffocating smell of the infirmary.

19

A memorial service for Jill was held at Battell Chapel on the Old Campus a week later, without any official announcement or advertisement, and three hundred people came. From four-thirty to five I sat on the altar of the chapel in a suit borrowed from Peter and oversaw the gathering of the assemblage for her. Next to me, a half dozen other students were sitting and waiting to make remarks. I looked up at the brightly patterned ceiling details of the chapel, feeling proud that I'd been chosen to deliver a statement in Jill's memory, and then I looked down at the friends Jill had known for three, five or ten years, and felt ridiculously out of place.

At ten minutes to five I saw Brook slip in, fresh from practice in his blue and white crew anorak. He stood at the back, rubbing his stiff, wet black hair, and scanned the rows for me. He'd said that he probably couldn't make it to the service, but here he was. I could see when he finally took a seat in the crowd that I was blocked from his view by the podium. He certainly couldn't have known that I was going to speak, because I didn't know it until that morning when Jill's father and stepmother had called. They still assumed that I was her last boyfriend.

"Alex," Mr. Lanigan had said, "it would mean a lot to us. We both travel so much, we hardly got to see her at all this year."

"You probably knew her better than we did, recently," Mrs. Lanigan added, on another phone. "We'd appreciate it so much."

I was sitting on the couch feeling my hot face. "Is Lauren going to speak?"

"Her roommate? I believe so," Mr. Lanigan said.

"Won't she mind?"

"Why would she mind?"

I realized what I'd said and closed my eyes. "Of course I'll speak. I'd be honored to."

———

The chapel bell began to strike five and I sat up. The chaplain walked unannounced to the podium and read one sentence of Thomas Bernhard.

"For Jill Sonja Lanigan: 'We can exist at the highest degree of intensity for as long as we live.' "

A string quartet of four women in tuxedos walked to the center of the altar with chairs, sat down, tuned up and started playing the fifth part of Beethoven's Fourteenth Quartet. This was a strange choice for a memorial service, particularly the fifth part, a *presto,* which is played with the alto violin sawing away like a mind that can't stop processing, the two violins all dulcet sweet and puckered, and the cello scrabbling along like a German shepherd sticking its face into a snowbank and sneezing. For one second the melody is joyous, then it's almost nightmarish, then the music stops as if it has lost track of itself.

I don't think that anyone took notice of the carved jade jar sitting in the middle of the altar until the music started and eyes began to wander. From where I was sitting I was close enough to reach this jar in two steps, but when I realized it was there, a chill swept through me. Jill had been cremated. Her final shocker was simply not to exist before three hundred people.

Lauren had shaken my hand in welcome, as she had the other six speakers, but there wasn't much conviction in her grip. At the beginning of the Beethoven she spoke in low tones to a woman beside her, then she leaned back in her seat. Her eyes were dry, and her skin, under the altar's spotlights, was flaking down both cheeks in very fine patches of white. She wore a simple black wool skirt and sweater and stared straight ahead, legs crossed, her right foot occasionally rising and falling as if to some inner rhythm.

The speakers followed the quartet and went quickly. Each told one or two short anecdotes, probably in deference to Lauren. Maura, one of Jill's sophomore roommates, spoke in the slot just before me about introducing Jill to the Westville welfare hotel program. During Jill's first week, a couple who had been in the hotel for two months had a big blowout. After the man beat his wife, he tore off her wedding ring and flung it out the window of their room. Jill had not only talked the situation through with the wife to get her moved out—she had been beaten by and reconciled with her husband six times, which was about average—but on the morning of the wife's move into safer housing Jill rented a metal detector and combed the field beside the hotel for two hours until she found the wedding ring.

"That way, Mrs. Shipley could put it in an envelope and leave it taped to her husband's door," Maura said. She stepped down and began to walk back toward a seat on my left.

Everyone smiled because Jill was so present there, but when the smiles disappeared I noticed other people who were crying. Again, Jill had mentioned her work in Westville to me in passing, but as soon as I heard a substantive account of the experience I felt so tangential to her life that I wanted to run down into the crowd and disappear. Jill had known scores of people like me in her four years in New Haven, and they each had as legitimate a claim to her affections as I did. And they, at least, could read her affections in the right light; I had gone off the deep end on a couple of parties and a lunch. It was obscene, I thought, that I was sitting there, like some talking head in the street being swept into public office on the strength of one comment. But now, with Maura done and back in her place, the attention gradually shifted to the space my body occupied. The weight of common attention was falling over me, and I was expected to rise and speak eloquently too.

I stood, and felt every eye on me, including Brook's; he shifted in his seat and looked down. I steadied my hands on either side of the podium and cleared my throat. It hit me as I did that no one had addressed Jill's sexuality. What was I going to say with Lauren behind me? Jill's parents were right in front of me, though. I decided to defer to Lauren too.

"My name is Alex MacDonald," I began, "and I'm afraid that I don't have a lot to say. I've known Jill as long as I've been at

Yale, which is only about two and a half months. I met her through an anti-Apartheid petition she was circulating for the Women's Center, and then at a party. I have to say that I lost my head pretty quickly over her. I remember closing down the dining hall after one lunch we had." I mentally edited out the contents of that lunch and took a long breath.

"I didn't see much of Jill after she was beaten up at the party in September, but it was almost like she knew that we had to wait for some time to pass. I mean, in order for me to understand her position on the whole thing. She had every right to be furious about it, and she was.

"I'd been in the infirmary for a couple of days for an injury, and Jill appeared out of nowhere to visit me. In fact she was my favorite visitor. As usual, though, when we saw each other we got into an argument within two minutes."

A few polite laughs echoed from the vaulted ceiling as a finger of hot sweat slid down my back. I cleared my throat too close to the mike and a woman in the front pew jumped.

"This was last Monday." I paused, hoping that this would at least justify why I was up there. "Jill had had headaches since the week after that party, so she was actually stopping by to get some new painkillers. She didn't have to go out of her way to see me, but it was like her to do that. Anyway, we had our argument, some of it still about the party, and as usual she was right. I think that the most important thing she's taught me is that the space between tolerance and acceptance of anything can be enormous. Even at Yale, apparently."

A distant sob came from the balcony, and more stifled sobs followed it. Brook was staring directly at me, without expression.

"I guess I'm here because I was the last friend to see Jill. I was reading Wallace Stevens after she left me, so I'll close with one of my favorite lines, for Jill: 'The vivid transparence that you bring is peace.' She taught me a lot and I'll miss her very much. Thank you."

I stepped down and glanced at Lauren. When our eyes met she

looked at me in a way that was half dismissing and half amused, as if I were more an annoyance than a rival. By the time I got back to my seat I was drenched in sweat, and Lauren had taken my place at the podium.

"Hi," she said simply. "I guess I'm last. Or least." She stood with her arms folded, a step back from the podium, not even bothering to adjust the mike. Her voice was clear and strong, though it wandered off once she had everyone's undivided attention.

She let her eyes sweep the large chapel. "I don't know what I should tell you because I know you all want to hear something different. And I can't see that what I say will make any difference —any *difference*, and tolerance and acceptance certainly aren't news. I was sitting up in bed this morning, wondering what I was going to say . . ." She trailed off and swept her thick black hair away from her neck with one hand. "But this is what I was thinking.

"When I was ten, my parents moved to New York. I just made the cut to fourth grade because of my birthday, and on my first day of school in PS 92 I sat down next to this girl. She was very pretty, Spanish, a foot taller than me, and her name tag said she was Betsy Mendez. But before I said a word to Betsy Mendez, Betsy Mendez leaned over to me, very close to my ear, and whispered something. I was a Berkeley brat, so I was expecting a wonderful secret, or expecting that Betsy would ask me to play with her at recess, but instead, what Betsy said was, 'If I stick my pencil in your ear, it'll burst your equilibrium and you'll die.' "

A tall man in his late twenties in a black T-shirt sitting about ten rows back in the chapel started to laugh. The people in his row blanched and stared, and the discomfort rippled around the space from one section to another. The man nodded at Lauren as if he'd heard this story before. When the movement died down Lauren continued, in a strong, clear voice again.

"I thought, Well, I'm going to cry now, but instead I decided to become Betsy's friend, and after that day Betsy and I turned our animosity toward Amy Johnson. Amy was one of those perfect girls. Later that week, in exchange for my California pencil case, Betsy got me elected as head of our class's Scholastic Book Club, over Amy. She had to make a few threats, but everyone voted in conscience. Betsy got me fired up, is what I'm saying, and once I got past her exterior I loved her. It was very easy to love Betsy Mendez.

"But. One of the perks of this club was that, with every ten book orders you got as president, you got a free book yourself. This was the year that this one particular book was very hot, called *The Magnet Book*. Anybody remember that?"

A few people nodded. Lauren slid her folded arms over the surface of the podium.

"The trouble started when Amy Johnson brought in her *Magnet Book* one day and everybody was her friend. The best thing about the book was that taped to the inside back cover was this little black bar magnet. You not only had the book with all the neat experiments, you had the magnet too. Then Betsy let it be known to the class that they could order copies of this book from me, and that it would cost twenty-five cents less than in the stores, and nobody would even have to pay sales tax. I think our homeroom teacher decided to pick up sales tax, actually.

"I'm sorry this is taking so long." She slid her hands around until her open palms were resting on her lower back. I thought of Jill walking that way as we went into Commons for lunch. I wondered who got it from whom.

"But I got ten orders." Lauren sighed into a smile. "In fact I got thirteen orders. Like all young New Yorkers, we were faddish. And I'd get my free copy. About three weeks later the box came back from Scholastic Books. Blood ran strong that afternoon, I can tell you. Our homeroom teacher tore off the tape and started passing around the books. Betsy got one, my boyfriend Larry got one, everybody except Amy, who had already moved on to Nancy

Drew, but screw Amy Johnson. The last person to get a book was me. That struck me as fair, since I was getting the complimentary copy.

"You've probably guessed it by now. Every book had a magnet in it but mine. I opened the back and there was a black rectangle, like a charcoal smudge, even a piece of tape there, but no magnet. It was the first time I think I ever experienced real loss. And I just couldn't get it through my skull either, you know? I pretended like I was too cool to play with my *Magnet Book* that day, but on the bus I got the book out of my Flintstones briefcase and flipped open the back, like the magnet would be there now? And I kept looking and looking for it, like it would spontaneously generate? Pavlov would have written an article about me, you know?"

I wondered why every sentence Lauren spoke was becoming a question, but when she turned slightly from the podium to look at her tall friend, I saw that her face was wet.

"And it's been the same way with Jill, right?" Her voice began to expand and break, and heads in the crowd looked down or looked away. "She was like Betsy, she was so kind past her surface, and she was very easy to love. And I'm still going back and going back to see if she's there even though I know she's not. There's just an indentation inside me right now, and a little black outline . . . That's all I think I can say. Thanks."

When Lauren stepped down there was a collective release of breath. As she took her seat silence settled over the crowd, a silence so complete that I heard the early evening traffic passing on College Street and the shouts from an Ultimate Frisbee game on the Old Campus quadrangle. There was nothing left on the program, not even a closing hymn, so we sat together, three hundred people and Jill. Some people wept, some people leaned forward and rested their chins on their folded hands and stared off into space. There had been one common realization upon seeing the jar, and here was the other side of that loss.

Without any announcement, people eventually began to get up

and leave. I was one of the first to do so. I didn't want to go until I could think of a moment when Jill and I were laughing together and I could hold it in my mind. I thought of us hugging in her bathroom as she got ready to shower off the rain and sweat and hair dye. I thought of us laughing then and held onto it and stood up. I took the side aisle so that Jill's parents couldn't catch me. I don't think I could have stood being thanked.

At the carved back door of the chapel I buttoned Peter's suit and pushed out into the vestibule, then eased the door shut behind me. I stepped out into the surprising dusk of College Street and walked around the corner to Elm. New Haven's evening commuters were roaring along with headlights burning, racing to get home and do whatever New Haveners did when they got there. As I turned up Elm Street I thought I saw Brook turn from Elm onto High, a block distant.

I tried, but I couldn't get myself to walk fast enough. All at once there was thick, viscous cement in my legs, and I felt trapped within a wide-angle movie shot where the blip at the vanishing point walks and walks toward dead center but makes no perceptible progress. I got so exhausted that my eyesight blurred out, and then I walked blindly, by routine, and somehow crossed a street or perhaps two. Then I slowed and ran my hand along a familiar railing of stone that tucked into a swan curve. It was the granite wall of a college moat. I stood here shivering with anticipation. Jill was just about to clatter down the street behind me and put her hand on my shoulder. We would approach the street and step down off the curb at exactly the same time.

As the dusk deepened and the minutes passed, I gradually dropped back down to reality and found myself almost at the library, hanging onto the stone railing of the Trumbull moat wall. I was at a point just past the lozenged windows of the dining hall, and decided to continue on to Sterling. While I walked along beside the facade a metal gate swung open and a car suddenly backed out of a garage which was recessed beyond the edge of the moat in a small brick cul-de-sac. Though the dark body inside the car flagged me forward, I stood at the edge of the small curve of brick and waited. While I did my eyes fell on something I had never seen before.

Just to the left of the gate, at waist level, the car headlights picked out a tiny Gothic niche with a carved stone chalice tucked inside. When the car had cleared the drive I walked up to the niche and stared in. The chalice had petals like a daisy's on its border, tarnished green with age, and a tiny water valve like the hollow tip of a straw at its cobwebbed center. I frowned and stepped closer. A tiny plaque read, "In Memory of John Christopher Schwab, 1886 B.A." Behind it I found, nearly hidden from sight, a beautifully smooth copper button. It was a Gothic Revival drinking fountain, just the thing for this Disneyland. Jill would have been pleased.

I leaned in to press down on the button, but at that moment the Trumbull car finished backing out and turned onto High Street. It shifted gears and accelerated away. Behind it the garage gate swung back on its hinges to shut, and I was left in darkness.

3

20

I checked my watch as I opened the passenger door of Brook's Wagoneer and stepped into the first random snowflakes of the season. It was ten minutes after eleven on Thanksgiving morning and the wind was stinging cold. Brook had parked on Crown Street, several blocks outside of campus, and a few doors down from a doubtful-looking variety store called Cozzy's. Along this same street, about a week before, crowds of alumni and students had streamed toward the Yale Bowl for the annual Harvard-Yale football match, also known as The Game, better described as cocktails for sixty thousand, and the families who lived in the muted, dilapidated houses along the route had rented out their driveways and lawns at five, ten or fifteen dollars for the afternoon's parking, the price increasing as you got closer to the event. To get my mind off of Jill I went, drank myself sick on peppermint schnapps and saw little but rows and rows of grimly sophisticated Peters, Brooks and Pascales ten or twenty years into the future. I knew that Jill had never attended a college football game, but the very absence of women like Jill in the crowd made it hard for me not to think about her. And the circle of silent picketers who squeezed their WHO KILLED JILL LANIGAN? signs into the space between two portals during the fourth quarter made it impossible not to. The fact that some people booed the protesters amazed me. Had Flavia not grabbed my arm and swept me along to the concession stands I might have joined them. I looked for Lauren.

Most of The Game passed in a blur, and I seemed to hear Jill's voice admonishing me as the tips of my fingers froze in the waning afternoon: "I warned you how empty this would make you feel, and now you're going to sit around at dinner and pat yourself on the back like the rest of the complacent boys and girls." Jill had been dead for three weeks, yet she was still talking nonstop inside my head.

At that moment I saw Brook shoulder open the door of Cozzy's, close it behind him and slip on his shades. I leaned back against the scarred trunk of an elm tree, faint with relief. Brook had gone into Cozzy's to score some pot before we drove up to his grandmother's house in northern Connecticut for the weekend. Two large men in black parkas had entered the mom and pop store a few minutes after Brook, but no one had come out or gone in since then. As Brook approached I wondered: what would he have expected me to do if things took a bad turn—burst into the store and scream that both our families knew several superb lawyers? He didn't look too worked over, whatever the delay had been. He zipped up his blindingly bright yellow, blue and turquoise ski jacket and pointed to the bulge in his right pocket with a sly smile. At the same time I noticed that he was chewing the piece of gum I'd given him like a squirrel devouring an acorn. At the tree he tore off his sunglasses and held up his big arms.

"Now we're ready."

I shook his hand in congratulation. "Did anything go wrong?"

He wrinkled his nose. "Nah. I asked for two bags, so they had to pack the second one downstairs. You should have seen the two motherfuckers who were hanging out in there, though. Every time I moved one of them went for his belt!"

"I still don't see why you couldn't have scored from one of your famous Darien connections."

"No way. They sell shit; this stuff is great. Peter knows what he's talking about. Let's go, man. I'm gonna be the life of the party."

Brook let a couple of exhilarated hollers fly as we got onto the highway north out of New Haven. I couldn't quite match his enthusiasm, but I was glad to be getting away from the lifeless, unreal atmosphere of the campus minus ninety percent of the students. Brook had stayed on, ostensibly to write an overdue paper for his gut physics class on the history of Carnegie Hall and to see Pascale off to California to visit her evil father. But, as he mentioned when he asked me to come along for the weekend, he was also avoiding Campbell's Falls, Connecticut, until the last possible moment. Campbell's Falls, home of and mostly property of his grandmother, Eva Voigt Massey, caused Brook dread because mandatory visits consisted of not much more than an elaborate game of kissing ass so as to keep the family ensconced in Grandma's gargantuan will. He was, he claimed, the only one who really cared about the woman.

I was hanging around campus too, ostensibly to make some Christmas travel money working at the library, in reality because I had two late papers that hadn't got beyond the research stage after Jill's death. When I tried to work on them I would hear her talking, or see her doing the most mundane things over and over, taking a five out of her wallet or wiping her lips, and an hour would pass and I'd be on the same paragraph. Peter and Flavia made several attempts to shake me up, and treated me to waffle cone after waffle cone of ice cream at Ashley's, but by the time they took off to New York together I sensed them getting tired of my long face. I couldn't really blame them, but what could I do with any of it? Waking up with Jill racing around in your head was like waking up with a thudding toothache while on vacation in a foreign country. Where were the dentists? How did you inquire about one? Wasn't it somehow better to suffer until the pain went away, ignoring it even as its persistence undermined you? I drifted along in vague lockstep this way and took the days with me.

We reached the tiny, idyllic town of Campbell's Falls at half past twelve and turned right at the single stoplight into the commercial plaza, which featured six idyllic shops and a beer and wine store, or what Brook called a "packie." Brook got cigarette papers and a case of beer while I popped into the country market next door, scruffed my feet over the idyllic wood chips on the knotty pine floor and bought some party snacks and a deck of cards for bridge. My mother insisted on the phone that I take a nice arrangement of flowers or a book of Maine photographs, but Brook said that a deck of cards would be much more appreciated. He promised to teach me bridge after we had done some skeet shooting.

I stared out the window as I stood in line for the cashier and watched Brook dump the beer onto the back seat and then stretch his legs beside his Wagoneer. He looked relaxed and at home. A man in a dented pickup truck backed in beside him, talking on a cellular phone. His bumper sticker read, HICKORY MONTESSORI. I smiled and looked down. My usual experience of driving north included the dirty, prefabricated backs of logging towns and an ever increasing frequency of bad heavy metal on the radio. Here at the mountainous corner of Connecticut, New York and Massachusetts, I sensed only the quiet, insistent repetition of immense wealth: safe, self-fertilizing money reproducing itself forever and ever in the preppy acres; a world historical, immovable and utterly foreign to me.

"See someone you know?" Brook asked when I got outside.

"You've got to be kidding."

He slammed the door of his truck and rubbed his hands together to warm them. "You're right, dude, this is Pineyville. The biggest thing that ever happened to me here was seeing a deer jump through the window of the elementary school."

With that, we struck out for Grandma's house.

The old homestead, Massey Hollow, lay several miles outside of the town. To reach it we turned onto a private road and drove up at a steep gradient for nearly five minutes. At the peak of this long hill a tiny glacial valley was spread out below. There was a three-story stone house with a wide bay window, a hothouse and an outdoor flagstone patio; a clay tennis court way up the hill on the hollow's other side; and a small cabin with a thick chimney a hundred yards off into the green-black firs, where Grandma Eva fired her sculpture. All was dusted in a light layer of white. The paddle tennis courts, the livestock, the horses and the stream, Brook said, were on the other end of the property, a run of about four miles.

"Naturally."

"You're getting the best view now," Brook added as he idled his engine. "It gets so green you can barely see the house in the summer."

"It's simply fetching."

He grinned. "Don't be an asshole. Dad loves you and my sister's a bitch to everybody. All the other relatives are conceited as hell; they won't pay any attention to you. We'll definitely have to come back in the spring when all the other morons aren't around."

"Sounds great." I started to think, as we drove down to the other cars at the big house, that if Jill *had* skipped every Yale football game, surely she had spent some Thanksgiving vacations alone in New Haven, and no doubt had emerged stronger for the experience. What I was about to do made going to the black-tie Commons party look like a sharp political swing to the left. If only the empty campus didn't remind me of her so much. If only taking advantage of places like the one spread before me, places I would be permitted to experience once or twice in college, and rarely—if ever—after that, didn't make me feel like I was signing a part of myself away.

We left our boots and bags in the mud room of the big house and received instructions from the maid, Wanda, to go directly to the parlor, as Grandma Massey had just sat down at the piano with the guests. Brook cringed and I reluctantly followed him through a swinging door out of the bright kitchen, which was fragrant with the smells of basted turkey and a braised smoked ham that sat cooling in a pan. We turned left at the end of a long hallway hung with antique guns and saw the first few seated people beyond the far end of a large mahogany dining table which was set for dinner with pewter plates and silver cups. The bay window in the living room took in most of the hill we had just descended to arrive at the house. Opposite this window was a crackling fire, toward which I gravitated. I could practically see my breath in the rest of the house.

"Koobie, you made it!" a voice called as we stepped into the room. Dr. Morehouse was wearing a Massey Heavy Machinery baseball cap on his substantial head and drinking scotch. Brook only nodded to him on the way to his grandmother. Dr. Morehouse feigned mirth at his son's enthusiasm and crushed my hand in his.

"Alex, I'm glad you could come."

"Thank you for having me," I said, my voice nearly cracking. "This is a beautiful place."

"I hear we won The Game."

"Yes, apparently."

"Get any pictures, Koobie?" a man near the bay window asked.

Brook bent over at the piano bench. "Yale's been using the same plays for twenty years, just dig out an old program. Hey, Grandma, guess who?"

Now the piano music ceased, and the rest of Brook's relatives turned from a burnt-leather couch which angled away from the front door toward the fire. I felt myself shrinking under their lacquered, collective gaze. Seated at the piano was a short, jubilant woman of about eighty with very thin white hair pulled up into a loose bun atop her head, and little white tendrils cascading down either side. She was wearing a faded red paisley dress and pearls. Although the flesh around her cheekbones had sagged and the rest of her ruddy face was a blizzard of wrinkles, I could see from a wedding picture on an end table that she had once been a great beauty. She stood slowly, with gentle authority, gripping a tall art deco floor lamp and then Brook's arm, and introduced me around the room from her piano stand. There was her daughter, Brook's mother, and her husband; her daughter Joyce, her husband Montrose and their three children; and finally Ranney and Carter, her son Eliot's boys, who were in their late teens and worked with the horses on the property. Eliot and his wife Anna were visiting Anna's mother in Nahant. Brook's sister Olivia and her escort, James, were in the pantry getting a drink. Brook was easily the most attractive person in the room. Everyone else's face showed the genetic disadvantages of unmixed bloodlines. Ranney, for example, looked like a Pilgrim come back from the grave, and scared the shit out of me. Brook was correct, though: no one deemed me worthy of any attention. As I considered a large oil portrait on the wall behind Mrs. Massey, she caught my eye and turned. There was a strong resemblance to Brook in this painting.

"Just in case Koobie hasn't told you," Mrs. Massey said, "my husband died in 1977, and that is his portrait. It was done by a descendant of Henry Alken."

"How wonderful," I noted.

"I think it's quite the worst piece of junk," she said breezily. "Now do bring in the others and set yourselves up a couple of drinks. If your mother is allowing, Koob. We're about to do the Teddy Dewey song."

"Please, Grandma," Brook said. He helped her sit down and started back through the room again. "I'm a big boy now."

But Mrs. Morehouse spoke up. She was only slightly taller than her mother, with a dark, almost Spanish complexion, while her face, unattractively exotic and nothing like Brook's, suggested a deer. She wore an elegant tan knitted suit and several strands of gold chain with attached heart-shaped charms; she was the only person in the room dressed for a formal dinner and she looked acutely dissatisfied that this was the case.

"Not so fast," she said, butting out her cigarette. I waited for her to clear the frog from her throat, but she continued in a deep smoker's growl. Something about her sophisticated tone brought Mrs. Lanigan to mind. I think it was the way they both said "fast," as if they'd imitated a common source.

"You're on a two-drink limit this afternoon, mister. We may need you to pick up a couple of things later."

"Jeez, are we out of tonic water here too?" Brook bent toward me. "Let's get baked, right fucking now."

I spoke into his ear. "Surely you jest."

Mrs. Massey played an anticipatory arpeggio. "And bring a bucket of ice, Koobie."

We retreated back through the dining room. I felt like setting a place in the kitchen after such a warm welcome.

"Your grandmother doesn't look crazy to me."

Brook wrenched his shirt collar out of his sweater and hand-combed his hair. "I'm sure Mom pumped her full of tranquilizers for the weekend."

"I noticed that she introduced everybody relative to women. Is she a feminist?"

"Yeah. Maybe you can both castrate something later." Brook frowned with effort and pushed through a small, freshly painted door. We stepped down into an enclosed outdoor porch with a refrigerator and a deep freeze near a second entrance to the kitchen. The walls here were thick, rounded and whitewashed, as if the room had been hewn right out of the side of the hill. A couple in their late twenties poked their heads from behind the refrigerator door.

Olivia Morehouse resented her brother; I could see this at once because the origins of this resentment were written all over her face. Brook was tall and broad-shouldered, with a strong Roman nose, deep-set eyes and a carved knob of a chin, and so was

Olivia. She was, simply put, a female Brook, and the results were disastrous. Her escort, slim and blankly handsome, was equally resentful, but of both of us.

"Hi, Koob," Olivia said, as if she'd seen him that morning.

"Hey," Brook said guardedly. The man stepped forward and deposited his beers with Olivia.

"Brook, I'd like you to meet James Wrigley. We met in Hong Kong in July."

James extended his hand without wiping it. "How do you do. It's Wrigley as in the gum. With the *e*. Good to know you."

When I saw that Brook was going to begrudge his sister an introduction, I stepped forward and shook hands. "Hi, I'm Alex MacDonald. As in the hamburger, but with an *a*. Brook and I are roommates."

Brook turned his back and coughed with violent pleasure. Olivia's mouth tightened and she dropped my hand. Even her fake smile was more pleasant than the look she gave me. "Hi. We'll see you inside."

"Did you bring all your roommates?" James asked Brook. He said that he was geared up for a big game of "touch" after dinner. I assumed that he meant football.

Brook shook his head. "Sorry, it's just us two."

James frowned. "How's your grandmother's passing game?"

"Come *on*, James," Olivia called, "you'll miss the Teddy Dewey song."

Olivia and James left. " 'As in the hamburger,' " Brook said. "That was awesome."

I smiled. Olivia did look as lacquered and stifling as everyone else, but the fact that I'd insulted her boyfriend and gotten away with it so easily, either to please Brook or to force her to notice me, made me depressed. I wanted to close my eyes and be back in my room, eating saltines and listening to Van Morrison.

"What's this Teddy Dewey thing?"

Brook stared after his sister and seemed lost for a moment. "What did you say, guy?"

"Nothing. Teddy Dewey."

"Oh. Big holiday tradition. He's some guy from the town who went to school with my grandfather. There's this inane drinking song named after him. Here, listen." He surged up to the door and pulled it open. I heard a lusty chorus from the living room, led by Mrs. Massey's full-bodied playing:

> Drink beer, drink beer, and drink more beer!
> Bump bump bump bump!
> We are the Teddy Deweys!
> Get drunk, fall down, sleep in your car!
> Bump bump bump bump!
> We are the Teddy Deweys!

There was laughter and applause, but when the voices picked up the song again they started over at the same point. This second run-through accomplished, the clan moved on to "Don't Sit Under the Apple Tree."

"Doesn't anybody know the next verse?"

Brook shook his head. "That's the point, there's only one. Teddy's been dead from liver cancer for ten years anyway. And you're supposed to sing it when you're crocked off your ass from a case of beer, not in the middle of the afternoon."

"Well," I said, "for Teddy's sake I'll have a beer, then. Beer, as in the bottle."

Brook's response boomed from behind the refrigerator door. "Let's get wasted, as in 'with drugs.'"

Since Brook was showing me my room, my bathroom and the new computer den where we could work on our papers during the weekend, we sat down to the mahogany dining table last. The only free seats were on either side of Mrs. Massey, who presided at the head of the meal. At close range she looked more delirious than jubilant. Her expressions were exaggerated and changed very quickly, as if she'd lost control over her face and arms. But she waved off the maid and brought the platter of turkey meat to Brook and me herself.

"Which do you prefer?"

"Grandma," Brook said, "you know I like white."

"White'll be fine." She turned to me after Brook had filled his plate. I smiled politely.

"I'll take white as well, please."

She gasped and took a step back. "Bigotry."

Brook began to laugh at this, but I felt an icy silence emanating from the rest of the table and didn't join in. Then I remembered the maid who stood behind us at the end of the hall. I told myself to watch for signs of what was considered generally humorous and stared at the framed fox-hunting prints beyond Brook's head. Mrs. Massey began a rambling, nondenominational grace, which opened in Latin and touched on the food, the birds of the air, and all women in the world who did not yet enjoy the right to vote. She let her half glasses fall to her bosom and slid the printed card with the grace under her plate. For the next fifteen minutes everyone dined elegantly, but no one said a word about anything except the food. The turkey and six side dishes had been painstakingly prepared and presented, but the family looked eager only to get the meal over with and return to the living room. Brook, also sensing the rush of the meal, filled his wineglass continuously while he had the chance. I was confused —was the whole party waiting for me to introduce a topic as a new guest? Was that a rule at Massey Hollow? Was I committing an egregious conversational blunder, was I just being ignored as Brook had promised, or was I making everyone so self-conscious that they wouldn't speak about family matters? I began to sweat freely under my shirt. Luckily, Mrs. Massey noticed my discomfort and spoke up.

"So, Mr. MacDonald . . . ." Her voice broke through the embarrassed clatter of forks and knives, which concealed the sounds of gulping and swallowing. "Do you hail from the Massachusetts MacDonalds or the Virginia MacDonalds?"

I thought of my Uncle David, though he had emigrated to Boston in 1968. "I'm from a small set of MacDonalds from southern Maine, actually."

"Really?" She leaned toward me, nudging one of the dozen or so pewter candlesticks on the table, which Brook's hand shot out to save. She found her wineglass and swallowed from it with some difficulty. "Do you know John and Martha MacDonald, from Kennebunkport?"

"No, I'm afraid not."

"They've been friends for years," she said. "Martha and I were Communists in New York in the late thirties. And we're both very cozy with the Delaware DuPonts. Little Koobie goes riding there in the summers."

"I haven't gone riding with the DuPonts since I was eleven," Brook said.

Mrs. Massey's head turned, frighteningly absent of expression, until her eyes landed on Brook. "Koobie! When did you come?"

"I've been here for an hour, Grandma," he said grumpily.

"You have?" She drew herself up into a sort of regal surprise. "And you haven't even told me how I look?"

A knowing glance passed between the two, and Brook smiled slightly, chewing his turkey. "You look just your age, Grandma."

Her eyes widened, and she lifted a bony, shaking forearm to her brow, as if in distress. "But what about my hair, Koobie?"

Brook squinted. "What hair?"

To my astonishment, both of them broke into laughter together. This time I didn't dare join them. Now Mrs. Massey laid a gnarled hand over Brook's arm.

"Is that your Saab in the drive, dear? You didn't take that nasty train, did you?"

"I hate Saabs," Brook said. "I drive a Wagoneer."

She nodded. "Well, you used to have one, didn't you?"

Dr. Morehouse cleared his throat. "Eva, you know we haven't had one in years."

"Why not?"

"Mother, please," Mrs. Morehouse insisted.

"That's precisely why I wondered!" Mrs. Massey exclaimed. "Don't you think I remember anything?"

"Whose is it?" Brook demanded.

"It's mine, Mrs. Massey," James Wrigley called from down the table.

"Oh." She drew back, and the room relaxed. "Is it a turbo?"

James paused unsurely and looked to Olivia for assistance, but Olivia, like Dr. and Mrs. Morehouse, was staring at her dinner. "No, it isn't."

"Well," Mrs. Massey said, "then it's a 900."

"No."

She laid her fork down and shook her head. "You poor thing."

Brook leaned forward into his napkin and coughed, though I could tell from the way his shoulders rose and fell that he was laughing. His face was flushed from all the Chardonnay he was tossing back. Still, he called for another bottle from Wanda. His mother seemed not to notice.

"I have a little Mercedes convertible," James insisted, "but Olivia thought that the Saab would have better traction in case it snowed over the weekend."

The explanation was to no end, and silence fell again. I had just managed my first mouthful of turkey and yam, using the European manner with my cutlery, when Mrs. Massey drained her silver cup of ice water and slammed it onto the tablecloth.

"I've had enough dinner. Yes, I've had enough. Wanda, please bring in my dessert!"

The nearly spherical maid left the room and returned bearing a covered, rectangular silver tray. She placed it before Mrs. Massey's plate, which the old lady bade her take into the kitchen. Brook shifted uneasily. The lid of the tray was covered in a light hoarfrost from a freezer.

"What is it, Grandma?"

Mrs. Massey broke into a gleeful grin. "I made it myself. It's a surprise, isn't it, Wanda?"

The maid nodded. "She threw me out of my own kitchen while she was puttin' it together."

"The suspense is killing us down here," Olivia said blandly. "Let's have a look."

Mrs. Massey acquiesced and lifted the top. "You might find it a little tangy, but I think it's wonderful. It's a recipe from my own granny. My granny was a suffragette, Mr. MacDonald from Maine."

"Was she really?" I looked down at the fluorescent log on the tray. "Wonderful, it almost looks like frozen orange juice concentrate." Within three seconds my face was reddening, for this is exactly what it was.

Brook's eyes flashed malevolently at me before he grabbed the tray cover and slammed it down. "Wanda, take it back. It needs another few minutes in the oven."

"What was it, Eva?" Dr. Morehouse called good-naturedly. "We didn't even get a look at it down here!"

Mrs. Massey stiffened. "Koobie, don't be vulgar. That's a frozen dessert; it doesn't go into the oven!"

"Take it back," Brook said. Wanda's left hand, still sheathed in a tartan oven mitt, descended again. Mrs. Massey started and slapped the hand away.

"No, leave it here! What's gotten into you, Koobie; are you mad?" She pulled the cover off and lifted the tray toward me. "Would you care for a piece, Mr. MacDonald from Maine?"

"A piece?" I glanced up at Brook, who was stewing quietly in his own juices. I wondered, if she threw kerosene over the rugs and set the house on fire, would anyone but Brook try to stop her? I already had a tight, gaseous stomachache from eating so quickly, so I supposed that adding in something frozen and acidic couldn't do much more harm.

"Yes," I said. "It looks great."

"Save a little for us!" Dr. Morehouse called heartily. His wife had lit a cigarette, pushed her chair back from the table and crossed her legs. She was tapping ash into her pewter side plate.

"Here you go, dear." Wanda stepped between Mrs. Massey and me and shaved an inch from the orange log. I caught the maid's eye but she neither frowned nor smiled. There was laughter, though. I heard Jill's sarcastic, delighted laugh echoing over my right shoulder as if she were secreted away in the kitchen and sitting at the little table where I imagined myself enjoying the meal. "Welcome to the leisure class!" I heard her say. "Time to get cozy with your Suffragette Surprise!"

I smiled into the first mouthful of icy tang, but when I bit down the nerves in my teeth throbbed painfully, as if I'd started chewing on a ball of aluminum foil. The maid excused herself and moved on to Ranney's place beside me. I decided not to warn him.

21

"Now come on, open up your stroke!"

I tensed as a ghostly tennis ball appeared out of the blank wall of white in front of me, several feet to the left of where I predicted it should fall. I erred again in favor of a short, clipped squash backhand, and yet another one of my returns snagged the net. The snow clinging to the white mesh there shivered to the ground. I stamped back to the edge of the base line and turned, mumbling. The dark clay footprints in the white space around me looked like a dance-step diagram gone berserk.

"I can barely see the ball, much less the net!" I hollered back. The friendly jollity stuff had just about worn through. Brook ran out of the blowing snow on his side of the court and scooped up three yellow balls in his gloved hands. He rubbed them clean and pocketed two, then began walking back.

"Brook—" The soft hiss of falling white seemed to enclose us in our own strange world atop Massey Hollow. "One more game and we're going in. I feel like I'm catching pneumonia out here."

He pointed with his racquet to the house, which looked more like a square yellow beacon through the high fence. "You wanna go back in and jam with the Dysfunctionals, be my guest."

"I *am* your guest," I whined. "Let's at least go hang out in the Wagoneer, my feet are soaking. Or call it a draw on account of the weather."

"When I'm ahead 6–4, 3–1?" He shook his head firmly. "No way."

"All right!" I held up both arms in a V. "Let it be written that Alex MacDonald forfeited the final match of this year's Massey Hollow Invitational to Brook Morehouse, Esquire!"

Brook slid up to the net and jumped over it. "He clears the net, his publicist goes wild!"

I walked forward and shook his hand, then turned my glove into a microphone. "But will you take home a substantial purse from the tournament, Mr. Morehouse? What does the Massey Hollow offer to its first-place winner?"

Brook studied my face for a moment and raised his eyebrows. "First prize is a one-day visit to Massey Hollow. Second prize is ten visits."

"I was thinking about the tea," I said. "The teapot."

"Of course, we have to visit Mary Jane!" Brook walked over and scooped up his portable boom box, which had eaten his Aretha Franklin Greatest Hits tape at the end of the fourth game. "I'll run back to the house and get some provisions out of Wanda. Here." He tossed me a package of matches. "There's no lock on the door of the sculpture shack. Light a couple of candles and I'll meet you there in ten."

I slid my borrowed racquet back into its case. It was wood and weighed about eleven pounds. "Don't you want a fire?"

"Can you build one?"

"Screw you, of course I can build a fire."

Brook turned and ducked through the little opening in the fence. "Good, I always do a shitty job. Don't get lost, you'll probably die of exposure."

I ran toward the darkening pattern of Grandma Massey's sculpture cabin by the last daylight that reached the hollow. The snow
had already drifted several inches up the door and was filling the
branches of the trees. I started a fire in a cast-iron stove using
some yellowed newspapers and kindling stacked in a corner. The
cabin, which couldn't have been larger than twenty by twenty
feet, held a dense, numbing cold within its split-log walls, but I
quickly domesticated this chill once I got the fire feeding. I found
a bare electric bulb hanging from a cord in the ceiling but lit
several candles instead and spread them over the worktables
which lined both walls and defined a thin path between the stove
and the door. Now I saw that each table, and the surrounding
wall shelves, were crowded with cast ceramic busts, unfired clay
busts and even a few armless torsos in 1:2 scale. Most of the work
was stiff and academic, but as I moved a candle along one wall I
immediately recognized a group of head studies devoted to
Brook, charting his growth from late infancy through early ado-
lescence. I guessed, given the thick grime in the firing stove and
the fact that Brook had been left off at about fourteen, that the
cabin hadn't seen much use in several years. Koobie was certainly Mrs. Massey's favorite grandchild, though; there were at
least a dozen of him to prove it. A dozen Brooks—I shivered and
sat closer to the fire. I had just had dinner with a dozen Brooks.
Maybe if we smoked some pot I'd get to know my Brook a little
better.

I heard boots scuffing at the door and reached down beside the
stove for the poker. Instead I brought out a life-size, ceramic
cucumber with a ball attached to one end. I held it up to the light
as Brook wedged himself between the worktables toward the
stove. Now I saw that it was life size, all right, but it wasn't a
cucumber.

"Let's get hosed." Brook laid a six-pack of beer and two bags
of chips on the floor. He brushed the snow from his black hair
and jacket.

"What you got?"

I made a move to slide the piece under the stove but thought better of it. "I guess it means I'm happy to see you."

His face turned sour as he examined the ceramic penis. "Jesus Christ, Grandma." He flung it behind him and there was a dense crash in a dark corner of the room. "This must be the new work she told me about on the phone. Maybe she writes dirty limericks too."

"It was under the stove." I pulled a short stool over for Brook to sit on. "At least she's modest about it."

Brook sat down roughly but began to laugh, shaking his head. "What a fucking family." He produced a bag of pot and picked over the buds, laying the best ones in his big palm. "You cold, man?"

"No, not really. I'd be dead if we hadn't played tennis."

He nodded. "Got to keep you in practice. You wanna roll this?"

"No, I'm horrible at it." I opened two beers and set them down beside our stools. "I wish we had a bong."

"We've got enough here so we can make a few mistakes." He worked the crumbled pot back and forth within a rolling paper and slid his tongue over the gummed edge. "Oh, I almost forgot. I called our machine from the kitchen and got some messages. Some chick named Katharine called you."

"No way."

"She's your ex, right?"

"Yeah." I was genuinely surprised. "I thought I was still on her Most Wanted list."

"She left a number. Fish it out of my left pocket."

I zipped open the breast pocket of Brook's ski jacket but he shook his head and fished it out of his shirt pocket instead. I read the numbers over like a safe combination. "Is that a -4762?"

He turned up to me with a strange smile on his face. "Yeah, sorry. I was afraid that Mom from Hell might come into the kitchen."

"Does she know where we are?"

Brook lit his joint and blew on the little flame at the end until it went out. "I told Wanda we were going into town to play pinball." He took a long toke and I sat down on my stool. Now our knees were practically touching. "I suppose we could have gone curling too. That's another gung-ho sport in Campbell's Falls. They have these little tournaments, what do they call them? Bonspiels! Grandma's got about twenty trophies."

I partook of the joint and handed it back. It had a spiky, rough taste, like badly raised homegrown, which, of course, is exactly what it was. "What are the prospects for your grandmother?"

Brook drew back self-defensively. "She's an old lady, what do you expect? She's got the best care money can buy."

"That's true, I suppose." I fished around for my beer and took a long drink; I couldn't think of anything else to say on this subject. I was trying to keep my mind off of Jill, but now that I was alone with Brook and away from New Haven I also wanted to jog his memory about Dave Freitag's party again. I had thought about this during the drive up, imagined myself drawing lines of evidence back to a single attacker, having this person thrown out of school and charged with manslaughter or assault. It was the stuff of fantasy, all right—ten weeks had gone by and the administration still wouldn't touch the issue because the party had been held off campus and the New Haven cops were called first. Maybe there were some autopsy records somewhere. I should call Dr. Moran when I got back to town.

We passed the joint back and forth a few more times, trying to savor the tangy smoke, which now combined with the wood smoke from the stove. I felt my joints begin to relax, and watched as the little cabin became very specifically the cabin, the only place that existed with such clarity. Brook, whom I'd never gotten stoned with, was withdrawing into himself. He folded his hands, took deep breaths that lifted up his wide shoulders and stared quietly into the fire. I pushed the hinged window in the stove door almost shut and took off my bulky jacket.

"It's getting warm."

Brook nodded and eased off his bomber. "Yeah."

"It's getting large."

"That too." He chuckled absently, without turning his head. I watched his dark eyes as they searched the fire. In some ways Brook seemed ten years my senior. Did money do that to you? I wondered. That begged the question, at what point did you start using money to make yourself look ten years younger than everybody else again? In the here and now, the extended Morehouse family seemed to have bought into a myriad of complexes and neuroses whose cost would probably make my head spin. There were so many undercurrents at that dinner that I couldn't even begin to understand. The more attention Brook gave to his grandmother, the snittier his mother got, which made his father drink faster, which embarrassed Olivia, which made Brook give more attention to his grandmother, and so on.

"Hey, Koob." I reached over and touched his shoulder just below his neck. He was as tight as an iron spring. "What are you thinking about? You feel pretty wound up."

"Yeah. I can't get loose around here during the holidays, I guess."

I stood up. "Slide forward a little." I stepped in between the back of Brook's chair and one of the worktables and started to massage his shoulders. Katharine had taught me a superb massage of pressing into the flesh like modeling clay with the tips of all ten fingers, over and over. It never failed.

"Ohh . . . yes." Brook wrenched off his sweater and leaned forward with his forearms on his legs. "I'll talk, I'll talk."

I leaned forward expectantly, but he didn't elaborate. "How do you feel?"

He shook his head in luxurious tragedy. "I'm blasted, dude. I'm not even here any more."

"I agree. Where are you?"

He didn't answer for a long time. "You know, my grandmother swears this house is built over an Ojibwa burial ground."

"Come on. She's only a thousand miles off."

"There is something. You can feel something going on once you've been here awhile. We'll have to ask her about it at dinner tomorrow."

"But you lived up here too, right?" I said. "Didn't you mention a deer jumping through a school window?"

The question hung in the air until a small log popped and sizzled in the stove. Brook let his head loll back, searching my face out in the deep shadows. "Why do you want to know?"

"No reason, I just do."

"Don't play mind games."

I frowned. "Don't be a paranoid schizophrenic."

He went back to watching the stove. "I lived here when I was fifteen, okay? My dad did a year of surgery in the Philippines and I didn't want to go with the family."

"What's wrong with the Philippines?"

"That wasn't the point," Brook said. "I had some 'discipline' problems, that was why I didn't go."

"Oh."

"But I'm fine now."

"How was life up here?"

"The worst. I'm amazed I got into Andover from this shitty educational system."

"What about your grandmother?"

"She was the only good thing. You should have seen her with a skeet rifle, man—unbefuckinglievable. She's gone downhill, though. It kills me to see it. She used to let me drive my mom's car all over the property. I accidentally trashed it, of course."

"Was it a turbo Saab?"

"And a 900."

"Now I get it."

Brook nudged a piece of kindling with his boot. "Why is this so fascinating to you?"

I rolled my eyes. Brook was an open book, as usual. "I'm not building evidence against you, I just want to know. As your friend."

"Sorry. Like I said, I can't get loose around here right now."

"That's understandable." I stared at Brook sympathetically. Still, I wondered why had he gone to so much trouble to get me up to his place for a weekend, spring for pot and beer, and offer a great old cabin to build a fire and get better acquainted if the company paralyzed him?

When my fingers tired and I sat down again, Brook stood and stretched.

"Where are you going?"

He let out a long breath and squeezed himself between the tables. "Piss. Roll another if you're so inspired." He moved away into the deep shadows.

"Brook?"

"Yeah?"

"I don't get it," I said. "Am I screwing you up? Did you want to smoke this on your own or something?"

"Of course not. I'm glad you're here." He picked up a sculpted female head and held it beside his own. "Hey, Alex. 'Your gaze hits the side of my face.' Remember?"

"I remember."

He grinned and wrenched open the door. "Thanks for the back rub."

The door slammed. I looked over at the nearest table and was met by the garish marble stare of Brook Morehouse circa 1980, the masterpiece of the Massey collection.

"You're welcome."

Sometime after midnight I got into my room, my head heavy with wood smoke and pot fumes. I was in the bathyscaphe portion of the stone, when you feel underwater in an above-water world and the only remedy for the relentlessness of gravity is sleep. This sunken feeling was helped along beautifully by Brook's opacity.

Getting baked without toppling barriers and developing intimacy was like dry humping as far as I was concerned. I hadn't had such a dull time toking since a spring night in the tenth grade, one of my first such excursions, when I got separated from my devil-may-care buddy Jerry in the woods behind Hollier Prep and ended up with the cool boys from the basketball squad. The evening's festivities from that point forward consisted of discussing who the class nymphomaniac was currently "woofing," and walking up the hill to the Dairy Queen to watch some jerk get his jaw dislocated in a fight lit by a half circle of headlights in the parking lot. It finally occurred to me that no one would notice if I left, so I got up and walked home. I could easily paint Brook into the same scene, though he would be sitting up on the hood of his Wagoneer in swim trunks and an Andover T-shirt, displaying Pascale, his tan and his shirt, in that order. To make the Massey Hollow evening complete, Brook followed me into my room, mumbling about having to play a "major slumber gig," and passed out on the tiny guest bed. Trying to wake a six-foot-three stoned jock who's passed out in your bed was right up there with trying to force a couch down an attic stairwell without twisting it. I wrenched off his boots and covered him with a blanket, then put out the light and walked along the creaking, uneven floorboards with my toiletries kit and a Hudson's Bay blanket. I remembered seeing an olive cot in the computer room, and planned to crash there unless one of the Morehouses discovered me and sent me to a bedroom of my own.

I got settled in this makeshift bed with a needlepointed pillow, shut out the light and at once found myself wide awake. My mind felt like the Crab Nebula, nothing but swirling, unresolved clouds. Jill was stuck in my craw like a hard ball of gum, refusing to dissolve or digest. I imagined her poking through the sculpture cabin with me and the two of us deciding to glue the ceramic dick to one of Brook's heads. I saw her painting this neomorph black, calling it *Post-nuclear Boy* and taking it back to New

Haven for the undergraduate art show. I saw her winning first place and soundly beating out Gore Heilbroner's tray of sculpted Vaseline. I saw her headlining picture in the *Daily News* and her cool, subversive smile. I saw her at my door with champagne afterward, ready to toast to our victory.

I swung my legs out of bed and slipped back to my old room. I felt around in my duffel bag in the dark while Brook snored, face down into his pillow. Then I opened a side pocket and dug around in there. After a minute I pulled out the Ziploc bag with Jill's senior essay disk inside and hurried back to the computer room, my heart thudding.

I sat down in the black drafting chair before the McIntosh and turned it on. Luckily both my disk and the drive were double-density, so the little archetype disk on the screen smiled back rather than giving me the animated dead X-eyes, and I was in business. There was only one text file on this disk, titled "Senior Es Dft," so I clicked into that and waited for the window to come up. It seemed to take an hour.

I found myself in the midst of a paper, near the end of a section discussing Lily Briscoe from *To the Lighthouse* and a poem by Emily Dickinson. The page was numbered 32. I read aloud in a quiet, halting voice:

" 'As she begins to paint, Lily Briscoe loses speech, expression and community. It is indicative of her representative failure that what arrests her attention most strongly in her first brush stroke is what she cannot see, to her practical consciousness the gap between her artistic ideal and the amateurish reality of her work, on a more vital level the pauses between her painter's strokes that articulate those strokes. What is "at the back of appearances" is the structure of appearances, the as-ness that even the most realistic portraiture cannot escape.' "

I looked off and stared at an antique hurricane lamp on a shelf. Speech, expression and community seemed a lot to lose for picking up a paintbrush. Still, this was exactly the sort of writing I expected from Jill. "As-ness." Julia Westerbrook would lap that up.

" 'Lily's space of artistic production is also a blank, a silent, empty space that she calls the most formidable thing imaginable. Since she has been responsible for its production, Lily tries desperately to imbue this difference with life as it "suddenly laid hands on her," and thus find a way to control and then dispense with it.' "

My mind strained to take in what Jill was writing about. How the hell could you control and dispense with the structure of appearances? I cursored forward and found the last paragraph of the section.

" 'As Dickinson's language has already shown, this is the inevitable wreck of representation, where the mind and eye must always be stilled by the inherent and constant presence of non-suggestive non-Being, non-Truth, stasis and death.' "

Below this last paragraph there were several blank lines, then a screen and a half full of lower-case *m*'s. In the middle of a line Jill had broken off and written in, "Jesus Christ, I've just dozed off with my nose on the M-key." There were several more spaces, then this sentence, the last bit of text in the file:

"If I short-circuit myself maybe I'll burn brighter."

I stared at this for some time, lost and regained track of my concentration, reread the short section where I'd started and then lifted the curtain and stared out the window at Massey Hollow, now glittering like a field of diamonds in the clear night sky. What did Jill mean by short-circuiting: something about living on the edge? I let my fingers slide over the fat plastic keys. There was no way to know.

"Alex."

I gasped and turned from the keyboard. Brook laughed and shushed me simultaneously. He was naked, holding his clothes in a rolled-up ball in his hands, and swaying slightly from side to side.

"What are you doing in here?"

I caught my breath. "You passed out in my bed, remember? I'm in that cot, but I can't sleep."

He dropped the ball of clothes and walked over. "I mean what are you *doing?*"

I grabbed the McIntosh mouse and moved to close Jill's file. "Just reading an old paper."

Brook leaned over my shoulder. "What is it?"

"Nothing, a paper. I'm going to crash." I waited for the original disk window to come up, then saw, too late, that Brook could read the name of the disk on the primary screen: "Jill L. Essay I."

"Alex."

I pulled down the menu to eject, grabbed the disk from the computer's plastic lips and stuffed it back into the Ziploc bag. "It was given to me, I didn't steal it."

Brook put one hand on the back of my chair and one on the edge of the computer table, then leaned so far forward into my space that I could see the new black stubble on the edge of his upper lip.

"What are you doing?"

I looked away but Brook wouldn't move. When I stared into his eyes I saw that he wasn't going to take no for an answer. My heart began to beat faster. For the shortest second he hesitated, as if about to come even closer, then I drew back.

"Brook, I want to know what really happened at Dave Freitag's party."

He closed his eyes and took a deep breath through his nose. "I *told* you already. There were two dykes and their Eurofag buddies crashing a party they weren't supposed to be at, and when they were asked to leave they laughed in Freitag's face."

"Exactly like that? I thought you were out in the hallway getting a drink when it started."

Brook's right hand came up so suddenly that I tensed and squinted my eyes half shut. But he only patted my cheek. "Alex, you've got to understand. A guy like Freitag doesn't get to be captain of the football team by letting people walk all over him in his own house."

"Let's say you were at a party with Pascale," I said, "and someone called you a moron. Someone you've never met. What would you do? Would you call them on it, or would you let them walk all over you?"

"No." He pushed away from the desk and stood. "Finito, okay? The way everybody's head was screwed on that night, it was just *going* to happen. And by the time I started pulling people off it looked like a fucking cartoon. Harper, Talbot, Freitag, everybody got dragged in. It's impossible to say who started it."

"All those guys against two women? At a school where everybody crashes parties?"

"Alex, let it lie. It'll drive you crazy. And you weren't even there, remember? Would you just trust me?"

"I do. But Jill was a friend, and I loved her. No, I *did.*"

Brook tried to suppress a long, weary yawn. "How? How could you love her? You didn't even know her."

"I've known her longer than you've known Pascale."

"But I *sleep* with Pascale," he insisted, searching my face. "I know everything about her. She keeps me up at night, filling in every detail. I know about her father's nervous breakdown, I know why she cries when she comes half the time, I know *everything.* You didn't even sleep with Jill once."

"Yes, I did."

Brook relented a bit, then shook his head with decision. "Well, forget it. Throw that thing away. Why don't you use the phone number I gave you and call Katharine? I've seen the picture of you two, she's your type."

"Fuck my types," I snapped. "I'll be obsessed with whoever I want."

"Fine." He walked through the room to the door, scratching at the downy black fuzz on his lower back. "Screw it up yourself, I don't care."

I swiveled all the way around and stretched out my legs.

"Brook, you don't understand. I don't want to look back at my freshman year and only remember this nonrelationship. I want to find out more about Jill. I want to make it mean something. Didn't you get the point I was making at the memorial service? The space between tolerance and acceptance is too wide."

I waited in the silence. After a moment Brook gave a cotton-mouthed cough.

"All right. If that's what you want to spend your time doing. I'll see you in the morning."

"Brook, wait a second."

He widened his eyes. "Yeah?"

"Have you ever wanted to short-circuit yourself?"

He laughed sleepily. "Only around here." He picked up his clothing and took a step out into the hall. The floorboards creaked and snapped and carried him out of sight. I stared at the empty door for several minutes before I turned back to the computer. I slid the disc back in quietly and opened a new file. Onto the empty screen I typed the words "Talbot, Harper, Freitag." After a long pause, thinking of the blood on Brook's arm and the look in his eyes that night, of him trashing his mother's car, I added "Morehouse."

The computer wouldn't let me close the file without naming it, so I did. The new file was called "Participants."

22

The first thing that greeted Brook and me as we drove back into campus on Sunday night was a large black banner hung over the Phelps Gate arch of Old Campus, precisely in the spot where the "Welcome Class of 19—" banner hangs for the first week of September. Lengths of rope leading from each end of the banner disappeared into a pair of third-floor classroom windows where they were secured. The banner said, in neat white painted letters, JILL LANIGAN, R.I.P. Underneath this, in smaller letters, it said, CAUSE OF DEATH: HOMOPHOBIA.

Brook pulled up under the banner to drop me off before returning his Wagoneer to the parking garage. He stared at the granite arch with tired eyes but didn't respond. We hadn't said much of anything on the way back to town. In fact, Brook had clammed up the morning after Thanksgiving when we were obliged to pass the time with the family, and left me an open target for the ruthless games of bridge which Mrs. Massey arranged every afternoon, and of which she never seemed to tire despite my spectacularly bad beginner's play. On the floor near the gearshift was a bag of snacks which she had made up for the drive. Although it started to leak out of the bottom as we left Campbell's Falls, neither of us had dared to touch it.

The next morning, returning along College Street from my French class, I saw that the banner had been removed. While I stood looking up at the empty arch I became aware of someone else staring in the same place, and looked over my shoulder. It was Brad Lee, the Eurasian in the evening dress. We hadn't spoken since the Sexual Progress party. That morning he was back into his usual chinos, alligator penny loafers and field coat.

"Good Thanksgiving?" he said.

"Hey, Brad," I said, "you going to English?"

"Wouldn't miss it. Have you done the reading?"

"Two chapters. Notice how I drop completely out of the discussion after the first ten minutes."

"Don't say anything brilliant, she'll expect you to keep pace." He walked forward until we were standing abreast. "Are you doing some investigative work or something?"

"What do you mean?"

"About Jill. The sign."

"Not really." I looked up at the bare arch. A class that had finished in one of the Phelps Hall rooms was pushing through the stairwell doors and spilling out onto the street around us.

"I just wanted to know who took it down. Is someone doing an investigation?"

"Not yet," Brad said. "But there were a lot of alums at The Game asking who Jill was. Some of them nabbed the prez at Coxe Cage afterward."

"Really?" I wondered why it was that I never saw things as they happened, even if I was there. "So who took it down?"

"Yale cops. I saw them on my way back from breakfast." He paused and let this sink in, but when I didn't react, or didn't react enough, he said, "I was actually up in time for breakfast, can you believe it?"

"I can't. How long was the banner up, do you know?"

"Long enough for Sarah Auerbach to get a picture of it."

"Who is she?"

"A friend. She strings for the *Times*. She told me it might get into the Metro section tomorrow. That'll get the old wheels rolling." Brad removed a pair of thin black leather driving gloves from his pockets and slipped them on. "I liked your thing at the service. I didn't realize that you and Jill were so close."

"I wouldn't let just anybody put makeup on me."

"Jesus," Brad said. "You look like an accountant when you say that." He started to move off, but after a hesitation I caught up to him.

"That's why I was so distracted at the Alliance party. It was Jill, she was blowing me off. It was nothing personal."

"Don't worry about it, everybody gets blown off." Brad quickened his pace. He walked as if diving weights were attached to his feet; the heels of his shoes scraped the pavement lazily.

"We're going to be so late." He checked his right wrist, and I saw a flash of tiny translucent pearls.

I pointed to his sleeve. "Brad, what a beautiful bracelet."

"They're cultured. Mikimoto, they were my grandmother's. Thanks a lot."

We cleared Phelps Gate and rushed along to class. Brad was always late for English, but exactly the same number of minutes late each time, and I didn't want to throw him off. I made a mental note to pick up a *Times* the next day.

When I got back to my suite after class I dialed Jill's number on the common-room phone. It took me a few minutes to find the phone, since Peter's mother had come in over the weekend and done some "choreography" with our furniture. Now it almost looked like we were unpacking again. The phone on the other end was picked up on the second ring.

"Yes?" a voice demanded.

"Hi, is this Lauren?"

"Who is this?"

"The banner's been taken down. This is Alex MacDonald."

"I have it, thanks," Lauren said.

"I have something else of Jill's that you might want. Is there a time—"

"Drop it in the mail, it'll get to me," she said, and hung up.

Drop it at the Women's Center, drop it in the mail—they were made for each other. I was still sitting on the white couch holding the phone when Brook and Pascale walked in. They had croissants and coffee from the new place Jill had raved about which roasted its own beans. They were on their way to Brook's room to play; I could see it in his eyes. Pascale rushed over and kissed me.

"Hi, darling! What a treat to be with real people again. Brook picked me up in Newark, isn't he the best?"

"Brook," I said, through her hair, "I have to borrow your car."

The scene when I pulled up in front of Jill and Lauren's triple decker was more like the Labor Day weekend moving festivities than the end of November. Six book boxes were stacked on the edge of a brown lawn, a rental van was parked haphazardly in the potholed driveway and a pair of well-intentioned but confused-looking parents were standing by, caught between packing and carrying. Like a lot of Yale parents, they were overdressed for either option. I locked Brook's car, gripped the keys tightly and walked up to them.

"Excuse me, do you know where I can find Lauren Bozorgi?"

"I'm her father," the man said in the loud, overgenuine tone parents use with their children's college friends. "She's upstairs."

I glanced at the boxes and at the van. "Are these Jill's things?"

Mrs. Bozorgi's face darkened, and she looked down at the sidewalk crossly. "Those things are already gone."

"Did you really need to see her?" Lauren's father asked. "She'll be in New York, you can write to her at our address."

I backed away. "I've just got to give her something. I won't be a minute."

I jogged around to the back of the house and started up the rickety wooden stairs. Lamps, open boxes of books, stereo equipment and hangers full of clothing were sitting on all three landings. Jill and Lauren's kitchen, I saw through the window, had already been stripped bare. A youngish guy with a closely shaven head saw me peeking in and opened the door. I took him to be Lauren's brother.

"Hi," I said, "I've got to see Lauren for a second."

"Who are you?"

"Alex MacDonald. I'm a friend of Jill's."

He stared at me and stepped back. "You must be the freshman."

"Yes." They sure were a friendly bunch.

"Lauren!" he called. "That freshman is here!"

I froze when Lauren entered the room. She was wearing torn jeans, an olive V-neck sweater over a T-shirt, a small khaki army jacket and black gladiator sandals. I guessed from her drained look that she had picked up the same flu I'd had. I guessed too that Lauren's parents didn't know the origins of her outfit, that the sweater and jacket had been Jill's. She saw me staring at these items and spoke.

"You'll have to excuse me if I seem rude, but I've got this cold." She rubbed her open hand up over her nose and sniffed. "I wouldn't advise you to stick around if you don't want to catch it."

"I've had it already." I pulled the disk out of my jacket pocket. Unless I looked Lauren in the eye I had the freakish sensation that I was speaking to Jill. "It's dangerous to send these through the mail. I think they can get erased. Dr. Moran asked me to deliver it to Julia Westerbrook, but she doesn't need it."

"Thanks." Lauren took the disk out of its Ziploc bag, flipped it over and tossed it onto the stove. "Is that everything?"

"Yeah." I looked around the bare room. "Are you really moving back to New York?"

"Is that what my parents said?"

"Uh-huh."

"No, I'm just getting a smaller place, is all." She folded her arms and rubbed one hand back and forth over an olive sleeve. "It's too big in here for one person."

"Yeah. Much."

Her expression softened a bit. "But I am taking next term off. My parents are just being good watchdogs."

"I get it. . . . You gave a beautiful eulogy, Lauren. I wish we could have met before."

"Was that what it was, a eulogy?" She leaned back against the stove, gripping the black handle of the oven door. "I guess it was."

"I had *The Magnet Book* too, a hand-me-down from my brother. It was the coolest."

"Well, I never really got to use mine, like I said."

"Didn't Betsy Mendez loan you hers?"

Lauren shook her head. "Amy Johnson stole Betsy away. They went to Amy's house in the Adirondacks for a whole month in the summer. My first heartbreak. I didn't mention any of that." She turned around and picked up the disk from the stove. I watched her fingers slide over it.

"But Jill was easy to love?"

"Is this all you wanted?"

"I'd like to help," I said. "Is there anything I can do?"

Lauren looked over her shoulder at me. She dropped the disk again and walked out of the room. As I stood there, two men entered with a small armchair on a path toward the back porch. One was Lauren's brother and the other one was the tall man in the black T-shirt from the memorial service. They lowered the chair to the porch and went back through the kitchen into the bedroom again. Lauren passed them on her way out to me. I thought that she might have gone for good.

"There is this." She handed me a medium-sized brown bag. There was a name, "Julie Shipley," scrawled on the front in red marker, and an address in East Haven.

"Jill never got around to dropping that off to her friend. I've been trying her apartment but she must be at work or something. My parents won't have time."

"I'll make sure someone gets it." I added, after a moment, "Someone told me that there's finally going to be an investigation."

"Sure, now that the football season is over."

"I know," I said, though this fact had never occurred to me. "And I hear there might be a piece in the *Times* tomorrow too."

"Wonderful." Lauren's impassive face trembled. "I'll make sure to pin it to my bulletin board."

She turned and made for the hallway. There was an exchange of voices within the apartment, a door slammed, then heavy footsteps started toward the kitchen. I took a last look around and left quickly. When I got to the bottom of the stairs I took a peek inside the bag. It was a white blouse from Ann Taylor.

I ran a red light on the way back to campus and was nearly sideswiped by a diaper service van. I was actually thankful that the van's screech snapped me back to my senses, because I ran the light deliberately. It was something I'd always longed to do in my parents' truck in McMurtry, to run the stop sign at the end of

our street and let the consequences try to catch up—neighbors, a
local cop, a kid on the corner who would memorize my plates and
tell his parents, whatever. I always stopped when I got to the
corner, though; even if I was driving back from Katharine's at
three in the morning I stopped. I never felt that I had justification
to break a sensible rule for the hell of it. A ticket would blot my
record and its taint might stick for years. The colleges I was
applying to would find out and drop me for another applicant
from a low-density state like Nebraska. I'd lose points on my
license, catch hell from my mother, and Katharine, upon hearing
of the infraction, would thumb up one of my eyelids and pretend
to take a look around to see if anyone was home. On the way back
from dropping Mrs. Shipley's blouse, though, at the corner of
Chapel and Audubon at three in the afternoon, I accelerated into
a red. I expected that my chest would rise and my head would
swim as if I'd inhaled a hoseful of nitrous oxide, but there was
only a sinking, disoriented feeling followed by the visual jolt of
the van's rapidly approaching front grille and its industrial-
strength horn. Perhaps you didn't burn brighter when you short-
circuited yourself. I didn't, at least.

I drove around the campus for half an hour: down High Street,
around Tower Parkway, down Broadway and Elm, down College
and half a block up Chapel to High Street again. As I drove
through this pattern my mind went back to the first-day agenda
that the comedy magazine was distributing when I met Jill:
"Freshmen: Crying. Upperclassmen: Euphoria, which dissipates
as you see all the people you hate." I drove the same pattern over
and over, looking for another red light to run and waiting for the
disoriented feeling to go away. The leaded windows and
pseudomoats and high granite walls sped by, the students swag-
gered from one corner to the next in their wool and cashmere
overcoats and ski bombers, and the professors rushed between
these students to their offices and meetings. The gym inhaled and
regurgitated its charges, the half dozen homeless panhandlers
held their own in front of the convenience stores on Broadway

and all the bricks in the windows of the secret societies held tight. The doorman at J. Press was blowing his nose; there was a black stretch limo with Maryland plates at the door. Everything was running smoothly, and the investigation would start as soon as football season was over. At Yale Station Jiffy Smith ran up the stairs onto Elm Street and paused before the brightly painted line of audition sandwich boards below the first-floor windows of Wright Hall. She tore a copy of *FMR* out of its protective plastic skin. Between her teeth an onion-skin envelope was dipping forward to show its corner of foreign stamps. Everyone, it seemed to me, might just as well be wearing the advertising boards which Jiffy stood in front of. Jiffy could draw her family crest on the front of hers, and nail the new *FMR* under it. She could have someone carry her sandwich board behind her, better yet. We could tie it to Brook's ski rack and hook up a PA system.

On my sixth time around, low on gas, I saw Peter crossing over from Chapel to High. I laid on the horn and jumped the left front wheel onto the curb in front of him. Peter seemed to know that I was coming; he just glanced up at the profile of the Wagoneer and ran around to the passenger door. He was in his tennis sweater and winter white corduroys and was carrying his duffel. He didn't seem to notice that I was driving until he shut the door.

"Alex! Delivering papers?"

"Running red lights. Where to?"

"Out to the gym." Peter checked his watch and rubbed his hands together briskly. "I may make the goddamn game after all."

"I'll give it a hundred and ten percent." I roared through a yellow and shot past Sterling Library. Peter punched down his door lock.

"How was your Thanksgiving?"

"Fine," I said. "Is your mother going to charge us for the choreography?"

"No," Peter said benignly, "she was just breaking our symmetry. She took one look at the common room and said, 'Peter, I've got to break this room.' "

"Why was she here?"

"She missed Parents' Weekend, that bugged her. And she was in the area anyway. Some client in Greenwich gave her husband five hours of Mom's time for his birthday. Now tell me that isn't some form of business prostitution—five hundred dollars to rearrange this guy's golf trophies and books."

"How does she get along with Flavia?"

"Alex." Peter smiled and hid his face. "I can't even tell you what Flavia and I did this morning. Mudd Library, in the conference room? We did it in there. I was sure we were busted."

"Very impressive." I glanced down at the duffel bag on the floor. "I didn't realize you had time for squash."

"It's just Price," Peter said, "then back to work. Who are you taking to Flavia's party?"

I braked at the corner. "What's that?"

"What's that?" Peter grabbed my arm and shook me lightly. I wanted to punch his face. "Haven't you been with us lately? Her parents are throwing it for her in New York, guy, first weekend of reading period. They rented a club, a bus to take us there, the whole nine yards."

I thought of Flavia at her own club. Would she wear a boa at the door? "Is this the birthday thing?"

"Her eighteenth. Imagine this: she's never had a birthday party in her life. She never wanted one. Mr. Nathan is even going in for the Whiffenpoofs. It's going to be the kickingest assingest."

I swung out onto Tower Parkway and crossed four lanes toward the gym. My knuckles were whitening on the steering wheel. "So it's on the Friday before exams start?"

"Five *days* before. If you can't cram a semester of work into your brain in five days you shouldn't be a Yalie. What a pleasure it's going to be to get out of this place for a while. Who are you going to take? You can go stag, of course."

"Don't worry, I'll dig someone up. Is this okay?" We were half a block down from the doors to Payne Whitney.

"Sure." Peter hopped out and heaved his duffel down onto the street. "Why did Brook let you have the truck?"

"Some errands. Remember to slam it hard."

"Alex, is everything all right?" Peter heard his name called and waved to someone standing beside the yellow crew bus. "You look tired."

"I'm fine," I said. "That was a convincing wave."

"What!" He laughed, his new single-outburst laugh. "You are on the rag today. Tell me what's up."

"I'm fine. There's no story here." I didn't even feel like looking at him. "Slam it hard."

23

The picture of the memorial banner did not appear in the Tuesday *Times* Metro section, but it did appear on Page 11 of the A section the day after. There was no accompanying story, just an inch-long caption which described the banner's location and intent, then tied its existence into a new phenomenon of gay bashing, which was "spreading nationally." The caption's last sentence read, "To this date, the Yale Administration has scheduled no formal investigation of the incident." Since the picture appeared in the A section, it was of course transmitted over a great deal of North America in addition to the tristate area. By 10 A.M. on Wednesday, it was impossible to reach any phone extension at Woodbridge Hall (even the janitorial staff phone, Brad told me), and the *Daily News* had planted a photographer and reporter outside the president's office. By noon, two hundred notices of an initial hearing on the Jill Lanigan case, to be held that very afternoon, were taped up on the walls of lecture halls and down on every major flagstone pathway of the college. Most of the outdoor notices turned to red and blue mush in the rain, but by third period the hearing was common knowledge.

I bumped into Brook at Commons at the tail end of lunch and we had a quick bite together. We talked about Flavia's party and a popular novelist for whom a tea was being thrown at Stiles College that day. I planned to go to the tea and asked Brook if he was skipping practice for it. He said no, but then asked me to buy the novelist's new book and wondered if I wouldn't mind getting an autograph. He handed me twenty dollars and told me to have the book inscribed to his grandmother so that he could "unload" it on her for Christmas. I agreed, and Brook told me to keep whatever change there was. I protested that he was too kind.

After we had parted out on Beinecke Plaza, I stood in the drizzle and watched Brook's tall, retreating figure. The reading was to run from four to five, and the hearing, which we had rather conspicuously not touched on, was to open at four-fifteen. I would of course go and get Brook's book signed, but I hadn't mentioned to him that I already planned to attend both events.

The tea went more or less as expected. The novelist, a lawyer from a Yale class of the mid-fifties, read from his sixteenth book and then answered questions. Each of his preceding books had been about someone who went to Yale and then went on to make a big success in New York or Boston or Cleveland. Some had intrigue plots, a few featured a murder or two. My mother used to take this man's books out from the McMurtry library and read them from her lap while she crocheted in the evenings, and occasionally I had seen a guest at our cottages bring one out of a wicker bag and place it on the gray-white sand next to their tanning oil. The latest novel concerned a Yalie who went out into the world and was a failure. The novelist said that the project had been a turning point for him. Only one other person bought the new book, so the novelist seemed eager to talk to me during the reception, but I saw that it was already five o'clock and grabbed a cookie and my coat and excused myself. The Master's wife shook my hand at the door and said that I must come again.

I ran all the way across the freezing center of town to Branford College, where the hearing was being held within the Gothic javelin of Harkness Tower. Every gate I tried was locked, as it now was almost pitch-black by five o'clock in New Haven, but eventually someone heard me calling and opened one of the heavy iron entrances. I was heaving out breaths, and the wind had pulled several drops of water down my cheeks.

"Thanks." I saw that I was standing before the black-haired man who had laughed during Lauren's eulogy. "Is everything over?"

The man looked at me as if it were extremely strange that we kept running into each other. "One of the provosts is still grinding away. I think after that it'll be over. Not that it really got started."

"Thanks again." I ran over a short flagstone path, splashing in a few puddles from the rain of that morning, and opened a wooden door that led up the seemingly endless spiral staircase of the tower. The walls smelled distantly of wet rock and plaster. I heard and then met a crowd of people coming down, their heels clicking against the tight twist of steps. Behind them came a thin black woman with a flash camera, and behind her was Peter in a pig suede cap.

"Alex!" he exclaimed. "You're late, my friend. We're down to meaningless closing comments."

For a moment I was too surprised to speak. "Pete . . . are you covering this for the paper?"

"Yeah. Jennie, this is my roommate Alex."

"Hi." The photographer smiled shortly at me, then glanced up anxiously at Peter. "Shouldn't we . . . ?"

"You going to add any new testimony?" he said. "I've got to—"

"No," I almost shouted, "I doubt it."

"All right." He squeezed past me. "But call at the *News* if anything else happens, would you? We may be stringing this for the *Times*."

"I will," I said. I nodded goodbye and rushed up toward the second-floor landing.

"Look," a deep, reasonable voice echoed down to me, "there's a lot of misunderstanding out there. And that's why we're here."

I cleared the last few steps and poked my head into a long, exquisite room decorated like a medieval Bavarian tavern. The walls were painted with white jumping stags and symmetrical flowering vines and two enormous electric candelabra hung from the timber-beam ceiling. About thirty dining chairs with high, carved backs were arranged in neat rows, but less than half of them were still occupied. A short woman was standing beside one of these chairs, her coat on, pointing to a handsome, balding man in a suit seated at a walnut table near the back of the room. A pitcher of ice water sat on the table next to a few glasses and a pass-around lapel mike. Lauren was seated up there, as were two white-haired men with red cheeks who seemed to be from the administration.

"Come *on*," the woman was saying in a loud voice. "You're here because you were embarrassed into it by the media. Your asses are on the line because now the whole country knows about your negligence." Three or four people applauded, but the room seemed to swallow the sound.

"Miss Sygevy," the man insisted, "there is no definitive evidence that Ms. Lanigan's death is in any way related to the injuries—"

"We're not going to let you forget, either." She turned and stalked away. It was Marissa, the woman from the happening at Jonathan Edwards. Everyone in the dining chairs applauded. The white-haired men looked at their notes as if they were going to tear them up. Lauren yawned. She was still wearing Jill's V-neck sweater.

"Everyone." The handsome man pulled at a pink tie. "The last thing we want to do is knowingly and intentionally cut any of you off from voicing your opinion, but it is getting late and we've got a lot to follow up on here. Let me just thank you for coming on behalf of the university and close the meeting. We'll keep you in touch if anything develops."

He switched off his lapel mike. My heart sank as Lauren's friends flocked around her and the two older men rose and slipped their pens away. I gripped Brook's new book hard and walked around the rows of chairs to the table.

The younger man seemed to know that I was coming. He looked up from his notes once, then held his glance and gave me a quick smile that seemed to beg sympathy. I supposed that I looked more like him than anyone else in the room, not counting the older men. Like an accountant, according to Brad.

"Sorry," I said. "I just got here."

"That's all right. It's a busy time of year." The man extended a finely tailored tweed arm. The soft brown of this tweed matched his eyes. "I'm Charles Jerome, assistant provost. How are you today?"

"Alex MacDonald. I'm a freshman." I had learned that saying "freshman" to anyone in the administration threw open formerly bolted doors in your wake. I tasted copper on my tongue, though, and I reddened as Lauren looked at me from within her crowd.

"Do you think I could have a word with you somewhere?" I looked at the provost and then glanced over at Lauren's friends. Mr. Jerome nodded and stood. I followed him to the other side of the room, trying to walk naturally. It seemed that we were there in three steps. He pointed to a pair of chairs sitting to the left of the door and cracked open a thin stained glass window. Although I had just come in from outside, the rush of air felt good on my hot face.

"You shouldn't feel nervous," he said encouragingly. "I think I know why you're here."

I took a long, slow breath and let it out. "I wasn't at the party,

Mr. Jerome, but I put together a list of people I think you might want to talk to."

He smiled. "Good, let's talk about it."

I emptied my wallet when I got back to my suite and uncrumpled Katharine's number from one of the side pockets. I punched the eleven digits into the phone before I lost the nerve. The crushing feeling in my chest was so strong that I felt like I might throw up. The line only rang twice, and caught me by surprise.

"Hello?"

"Hi, is this Katharine O'Brien?"

"Yes, it is . . . wait a minute." Her voice dropped. "Is this Alex?"

"Yeah." I chided myself for calling without thinking anything through. I was still wearing my soaking gum boots, and my shins were aching. "Are you busy?"

"Am I busy? Why are you calling me?"

"I know," I said nervously. "I'm sorry it took so long to return your call."

"Are you back in the hospital or something?"

I was afraid that if I answered no she would hang up. "I'm just calling to see how you are."

"Do you care how I am?"

"Of course I do! I've known you for eleven years, why wouldn't I?"

"I don't know," Katharine said. "I feel very distant from you right now, Alex."

"I know." My head was already beginning to feel as if it were wrapped in hot towels. "I'm sorry about everything that happened. I really am. I didn't know what I was saying."

"I guess not."

Now my mind went blank. I couldn't remember the point of the call until I saw a copy of Flavia's invitation on the coffee table. "So, are you seeing anybody these days?"

"Are you?" she shot back.

"No. I had a good friend, but she died about a month ago."

"I'm sorry to hear that. Are you just dating *Yale* now?"

"Katharine, that's a low blow."

"Isn't it true?" she continued in the same tone. "Yale was like your idol, your myth. I just became this flattened, objectified thing."

"I'm feeling pretty flattened myself these days. Has Orono been good?"

"It's great. I've been spending a weekend or two a month at home." Katharine seemed to be holding the receiver several inches away from her face. "I noticed you weren't in McMurtry for Thanksgiving."

"No. I was too broke to go anywhere. Mom and Dad understood."

"It's too bad I didn't know that," she said. "I was down at Wesleyan visiting Marybeth about that time."

"Would you have offered me a ride if you knew?"

"You're right. I suppose you were at 'The Game' anyway."

"Oh yes," I said. "That was impressive."

"I'll bet."

I grimaced as my mind blanked out again. I felt as if the walls of the common room were closing in around me. Brook and Peter were due back at any minute, and I couldn't talk to her with them around.

"Katharine," I said firmly, "I called because I'd like to see you. I'd like to see you before Christmas. I'm actually calling to see if you can come down here for a party that a friend of mine is throwing in New York. It would be on the thirteenth. There's free bus service there and back, so you could just park your car here in New Haven. But only if you want to go."

She seemed to put the phone aside and walk away from it. She said something that I couldn't make out, then: "I don't believe you, Alex. You're asking me on a date. You're asking me to come to New York for a party with you?"

"But I really want to see you," I said. "I just don't want to see you in the McMurtry context right now."

"Did it ever cross your mind that I might not want to see *you?*"

"Come on. We've been friends forever. You're one of my best friends, Katharine."

Katharine seemed to put the phone aside again. I could imagine her looking around the room, shaking her head. I was about to speak again when she came back on the line.

"Can't you even get a date down at *Yale?*"

"Of course I can. I just want to see you. And don't worry, I've eaten the words I said to you five hundred times since I've been here. I want to make it up to you a little. As friends. You still mean a great deal to me."

"You figure I can just drop everything and get in my car and drive seven hours to see you."

"But it's New York. It'll be fun. And it's only five hours to New Haven."

"New York . . . the Upper East Side, knowing you. I suppose you've been meeting the right sort of people?"

I cringed at this jab. "How is everybody at home? Did you see my mother?"

"The day after Thanksgiving. Your mother started aerobics, you know. She's lost about fifteen pounds."

"Thanks for the warning." I sat up on Brook's couch and stretched out. "Did they give you a pecan pie to take home?"

"As usual. They had a lot of leftovers. Marty had to stay on in Los Angeles for a story."

"Yes, he leads a very tough life."

"By the way, I got the letter you wrote from the infirmary. It was a little fragmented."

I smiled. "I didn't think you'd even read it."

"I nearly didn't."

I heeled off my gum boots, rolled over and looked at the ceiling. "So."

"So, New York on the thirteenth. I haven't been in New York for three years. And I have got these exams and things. Don't you?"

"But it'll be an amazing time," I said. "My friend Flavia's talked her parents into renting out a whole club for her. You'll love her. And I'll have a shitty time without you."

"I'll bet. How long will it go?"

"One or two, I guess. No longer. You could sleep over or sleep on the bus and drive back to Bangor the next morning if you wanted."

"It's Orono." Katharine laughed a little, her fed-up laugh. "I don't see how I can refuse you if I'll make the difference between shitty and amazing."

"You always did in McMurtry."

"Alex," she said after a moment, "why do I let you talk me into everything? You are such a pain in the ass. All right, when did you say it was again?"

After I hung up I put the phone aside and stared at the frozen sweeps of plaster on the ceiling. An enormous sense of relief in my chest almost overcame the feeling that I had just betrayed my roommate by giving the list of names to Charles Jerome. I'd nearly forgotten what it was like to have a conversation with another rational human being—the ground under me had hardly shifted once. Surely there had to be a few Katharines in New Haven. The question was, where the hell were they hiding?

24

Flavia Mothership One and Flavia Mothership Two, as we dubbed the pair of coach buses, were raising clouds of blue exhaust in the near darkness when Peter, Flavia, Katharine and I finished our impromptu cocktails in Flavia's common room and ran down through Phelps Gate onto College Street. Katharine lost a flat in the rush, and I ran back to help her. It was twenty-two degrees without adding in the wind chill. Phelps Gate, of course, was built like a wind tunnel.

"Hang in there!" I called as Peter turned around. "We're coming!"

Peter shouted merrily as the first bus pulled forward and away. "Looks like we're in Number Two!"

"Looks like it!" I snatched up the flat and ran to Katharine's foot, which she had curled tightly around its muzzle of hose. Another crowd of invitees rushed past us, shrieking against the wind. Two women had wrapped long cashmere scarves around their heads like wimples.

"Hurry up, I'm going to pull a muscle!" Katharine was wearing a sleeveless cornflower-blue dress with a big bow in front under my thin black trenchcoat. She shivered miserably. For a second her pale face was lit up by a wedge of light from an opening stairwell door under the arch, and I remembered that at the Hollier Prep graduation ball, in the same dress, she had been a splotchy sunburned red from sitting out trying to get an early tan in McMurtry. We couldn't dance any waltzes that night because her shoulders were so painful. I knew that my trenchcoat was unlined and practically useless, but I felt an embarrassing impulse to press it on Katharine. Her dress had looked so simple and elegant in June compared to the purple poufs and wide skirts of the other prom getups, but among all the Little Black Dresses of the Yale women who were running to the buses it was just short of hokey.

"I don't see why we have to rush so much." She gripped my head for balance as I knelt with the shoe. "We could just take my car. I've been in it for hours already today."

"Are you ready to pay seven bucks an hour for parking?"

"That depends." She wobbled and pulled my trenchcoat close around her body. "Are you ready to sit with those people all the way to New York?"

I looked up at her and smiled. Predeparture cocktails, for which Katharine and I were half an hour late, had consisted of one bottle of cheap vodka with flat tonic and no lemon and listening to Brook wonder aloud whether he'd be tapped for the secret society Skull and Bones before he got around to breaking into its two-story crypt, which had barbed wire and surveillance cameras on its roof. Further entertainment was provided by Peter, who passed around the new copy of "Cliffman Doings," a twenty-page pamphlet with green and red marbleized covers that his great-aunt in Montreal printed each December as an international family yearbook. Peter had written that he was dating a nice Jewish girl at Yale, and sure enough his great-aunt had changed "nice" to "wonderful" and left out the Jewish part. Flavia dashed in and out of her bedroom, torrential with apology, taking last-minute calls. Katharine sat in her blue prom dress, fiddling with the bow and nursing a head cold she'd brought with her from Maine, and I drank like a fish.

"I feel like I'm at a country club," she whispered as I poured off the last of the vodka.

"Get used to it."

"Oh, my God." Flavia ran in again, panting, and knelt beside her warm highball. "*More* stress. My laundry pile today was so enormous that I just went to Macy's and bought three pairs of panties. Don't you find yourself doing that constantly?"

Katharine, taken by surprise at this question, had simply stared at Flavia, and Flavia had stared back, moving her head forward slightly as if my ex-girlfriend might be whispering her answer. Fortunately Pascale ran in at that moment to report that Sasha was on the line from New York again and needed a "quiche flavor firmed up" with the caterers. Brook left with Pascale soon after, claiming, "I know of some people who know I'm waiting to be contacted." Peter sniffed loudly and I nodded at him. Katharine fell asleep from exhaustion against my arm for the rest of the festivities, and now looked wildly disoriented at Phelps Gate, as if I'd dropped her into a bathtub of ice water.

"It would look ridiculous if we didn't get on the bus," I said. "We're going to be with them all night anyway." I sat back on my heels and gripped Katharine's ankle. "Don't you feel well enough to go?"

"I'm fine. Don't you want to go?"

"That's why I invited you."

"Then let's go!" Katharine knocked the top of my head with her tiny purse and ran on, rubbing her hands violently up and down her arms. It occurred to me as I passed her and climbed the four steps into the blue plush of the bus—a blue plush, I noted, that perfectly matched the blue of Katharine's dress—that I had never paid Brook back what I owed him for the tux I was wearing. At that point in the term I couldn't afford buttons for my trenchcoat. The draining sensation this produced made me want to turn around and climb off again, as a hundred things that day had made me want to scuttle the party, but Katharine was too close behind me. I couldn't let her down after all the buildup.

"You just made it," the driver said. "Anybody else gonna walk." He let us pass and pulled the door handle to. It closed off the cold with a vacuumlike suck and he threw the cornflower-blue bus into gear.

Katharine had pulled into town early that afternoon, found our suite faster than I could find it after I'd lived there for a week, and surprised me in the McClellan Hall computer room, where I was applying a verbal Band-Aid to a tourniquet-sized wound in the logic of my final English paper. The stress level in the basement room of McIntosh stations on the thirteenth of December made the midterm and pre-Thanksgiving rushes look like coloring-book parties. I had been living on this pressure for a week, and over a seven-day stretch I had written one paper each day. The whole university had shrunk into a general, unspoken tension, but in fringe sites like the McClellan basement there was no capping it. The floor was a sea of Diet Coke cans and candy bar wrappers. Half the chairs had white foam wounds in their dark

Naugahyde flesh, or no backs at all, two lo-fi printers screeched and ate computer paper nonstop, and at the cubicles crouched figures sat with two or three open books in their laps and thin slicks of oil on their faces, trying to stay sharp enough for another ten-pager on Spenser or Paul deMan, demanding silence from their neighbors while they whispered fanatically to themselves. This excluded the few veteran *Daily News* staffers who always haunted the room and had degenerated, as Flavia put it, "all the way to zits and cellulite."

It was not, in short, a place conducive to brilliant critical insight. But since the administration had started calling up witnesses from Dave Freitag's party for interviews, neither was my suite. Brook's return from his "discussion" lingered in my mind. I had been on the phone again with Katharine, giving her driving directions, when he stormed in. His cheeks were red and he was smiling, but I could see that he was shaken. He nodded at me once and walked down to his bedroom, where he slammed the door so fiercely that the wood split over a knot in the side that faced the hallway. Until the afternoon of Flavia's birthday bash I had steered clear of Brook, but when I passed him digging around in our refrigerator that day and asked him to direct Katharine down to McClellan Hall, he seemed perfectly himself. Of course this was the last thing in the world that could have put me at ease.

"Sure, Alex." He leaned around and tossed me a Diet Coke from his six-pack.

Katharine greeted me by sliding her cool hands over my eyes. I got a strong noseful of jasmine perfume and menthol throat lozenges.

"You get one guess."

I found my keyboard and typed "Katharine?" onto the screen. Actually, my fingers slipped a key, and it came out as "Lsyj-stomr?"

"Close enough," she said hoarsely.

"Oh no," I whined, "you have a cold!" Then I looked back at

my screen and slid her hands down to my lips. "Hi! How were my directions?"

She laughed for an answer, pulled her hands away and was shushed by one of the *News* people.

"How do you like Old Campus?"

Katharine knelt down on the torn carpeting beside my chair and blew her nose in a balled-up Kleenex. She was wearing a blue parka over a pink sweatshirt and jeans. Her voice rang through the room even though she was whispering. "It's great. But this guy who gave me directions was so scary!"

"I can't wait till you meet everybody else."

After I printed out a copy of my paper I took Katharine to a very late lunch at Louis. We ate fat hamburgers on toast with warm Pepsi under the Tiffany lamps. Over coffee at one of New Haven's ice cream boutiques she updated me on all the McMurtry gossip. The new bowling alley was filled seven days a week, the mayor had broken his leg in Florida, and of course there was my mother's aerobics mania. When I brought the discussion around to our personal lives, Katharine became cautious and said little. She didn't look pleased to hear that I hadn't been having a great term, but she didn't look teary with concern either.

Back on the campus we walked around the sculpture garden and went into the art gallery. I directed Katharine upstairs to my favorite Van Gogh, *The Night Café*, and we sat on the parquet floor in front of it until the gallery closed.

"This is practically the best museum I've ever been in," she whispered. "And this all belongs to Yale?"

"I think they lease the plants."

"*I'd* be pretty happy about it if I were you. Orono barely has a gallery."

"You don't have to whisper in a university museum," I said. "Nobody ever comes here anyway."

Katharine pulled her denim shoulder bag to her side and started poking through it for another Kleenex. "All right. I said, all we've got are slides and posters!"

"Shh." I smiled. "That's too bad. You can't really get a grasp of the way Van Gogh's palette matured without the real McCoy."

"Alex"—Katharine spoke into her Kleenex—"please stop."

"Stop what?"

"Stop talking like that. You've been doing it all afternoon and you sound silly."

I blushed defensively. "How do you want me to sound, like some hick from McMurtry?"

She gave me a very unpleasant look. "What do you mean, hick? We both grew up there."

"Whatever."

"And I didn't really come all the way down here to talk about art."

"Fine. I see you changed your White Girl, then." The White Girl was what I called Katharine's Jell-O-mold haircut. Now it was styled like Louise Brooks, all bangs and straight as a stiff brush. "You're not going chic on me, are you?"

"No," she said more calmly, "I was just getting sick of brushing it out of my eyes."

"It looks great."

There was a long silence, as if we were on the telephone to each other again.

"So you were saying about Jill?"

"Jill Lanigan."

"Right." She turned her pale blue-gray eyes on me. "You really think you were in love with her?"

"Love, fascination, curiosity? I don't know any more."

"I wish I could have met her." Katharine went back to staring at the Van Gogh, biting at the nail on her left index finger. "I still can't believe you said you're less sure about everything than you were the day you got here. What's happening?"

I slid my knees to my chest and wrapped them with my arms. "I don't know. I've been to all these parties and seen all these people, and it's like that Lyon contingent from Hollier Prep all over again. Be a dweeb all week and on the weekend stand around a keg like an asshole. I don't need any more of that."

"You knew what Lyon was like," Katharine said, "and he came here a year before you. Don't say you weren't warned."

I stared at her intently. The disoriented feeling was building in my chest again. "Do you remember doing that Eliot poem with Mrs. Kuniski sophomore year, with the line 'How should I presume?' Prufrock?"

"Sure. I had to memorize half of it."

"Well, that's what it's like here half the time. How should I presume? It's like I'm a spectator watching all these lives that are so much bigger and better than mine, and I can't get my own started."

Katharine rubbed my back gently. "What about your roommates? They obviously care about you."

"As long as I behave."

"They seemed pretty nice to me. Although Brook . . ."

"No," I said. "Brook I like. He comes right out and says what he's feeling, at least."

"Unlike Lyon, that jerk." Katharine rubbed the knuckles of one hand along my cheek, as if Yale were an awful lot for an imbecile to bear. "Do you ever see him?"

"He lives out at the yacht club. I don't see him much."

Katharine closed her eyes and stretched out. "Alex, let's go. This painting is making me dizzy."

Pascale and Brook were already at the back of Flavia Mothership Two, stationing themselves along the cushioned banquette below the one-way glass of the rear window when I got on with Katharine. Peter and Flavia had just joined them. Flavia and Pascale were in nearly identical black taffeta dresses, though Flavia had added elbow-length silk gloves, and their outfits were to susurrate continuously for the two-hour trip. Brook and Peter were dressed to the nines as well, looking as more themselves in their shawl-collar tuxes as I felt less myself in my still unpaid-for vintage-store peaked-collar number. Everyone applauded Katharine as we brought up the rear. The banquette was really built for four, but the Whiffenpoof singers had engine trouble with their van and had rushed the second bus at the last minute, filling (like the true gentlemen they were) every free seat in the first three rows, so it was basically make cozy in back or sit on the floor. At least I couldn't hear them tuning up so clearly over the motor. I'd had a lifetime's fill of Yale songs at The Game.

"Kate, did you get your shoe?" Pascale called.

"I did, thanks."

"Thank God," she said, as if a tiresome gag was now over with. "You both look so cute! It's going to be such an awesome time. Where are you sitting?"

"Here," I said. "Where do you think?"

"Alex," Flavia said, "we booked ten extra seats over the invitations. Didn't you check the bus?"

"The Whiffs are in those seats. They had a little van trouble, didn't they tell you?"

"Are you sure you checked everywhere?" Katharine said.

"All right, if you don't believe me." I turned and made my way back up the aisle, looking over the back of every seat as I approached the front and looking deeply into each seat as I made my way back. Flavia rolled her eyes as I leaned toward her again.

"Excuse me, madam. Is this one taken?"

"All right, sweetie, I believe you."

"Alex, I can just drive," Katharine said. She was leaning against the back of the last row of seats with her arms folded. "I don't mind."

"*That* would be fantastic," Pascale said breathlessly. "Kate, you're wonderful. There's barely enough room for four here as it is."

"In case you haven't noticed," I said, "we're half a block from the medical school already. Do you think the bus driver's going to just turn around?"

"Alex is right," Peter said. "Everybody stop being so Jappy and put your coats up in the back window. When I was in Venezuela I had to share my bus seat with two chickens."

"In that case," I said, "I promise not to shit in your lap."

Brook gave a nervous, coked sigh through his nose and Pascale picked at her rolls of taffeta as if she couldn't possibly clear another inch, but I managed to install Katharine and squeeze onto the end of the banquette with my right leg hanging off the cushion. I knew that my back was going to be throbbing painfully in half an hour, but as I looked up and down the bus and along our window seat I began to feel distant from the scene, or maybe not distant so much as distinct, unmoored from all the loyalties and connections. The exhausting but invigorating plunge into academia over the last week had reminded me of what I originally came to New Haven for, and the arrival of Katharine, who stood out from the crowd in the same sore-thumb way I had done during "Camp Yale," was now giving me a sense of fresh definition. Even if her dress did announce itself like a Down East accent, her presence allowed me to have someone to stand out *with*. She had fleshy arms and full breasts, not the attenuated, boyish builds of Pascale and Debby Bass and the rest of the chic set. She had a crooked front tooth and thick eyebrows and average Irish looks. She was wearing a high school prom dress to a New York party, and she had called me on breaking into a speech about Van Gogh's palette, which I knew next to shit-all about. She was fallible and lacquer-free. And how long had it been since I could really let my guard down around anybody? I could hardly remember.

"Katharine," Flavia began, ignoring Peter since he'd called her Jappy, "I haven't had a chance to talk to you yet." She smiled with deep cranberry lips. "Or should I say, Alex hasn't let us get at you for two seconds. How are you liking Mount Holyoke?"

"Mount Holyoke!" Brook exploded. "Is that where you go? Wow, my mother went to Mount Holyoke!"

"I go to U. Maine Orono," Katharine said. "Who told you I went to Mount Holyoke?"

I reddened. "I just mentioned that you got into Mount Holyoke but didn't go."

"You never said she didn't go to me," Flavia said.

"You must not have been listening."

"I thought the campus there was beautiful," Katharine put in, "but I wanted to be closer to home my first year. How did your mother like it, Brook?"

"Oh, she grew all over it." Brook sniffed voraciously and exhaled into a long cough. "My dad met her road-tripping to Smith."

"Brook, you've got to tell this story," Pascale said. She encircled Brook's chest with her arms and pretended to fall asleep against him.

"What's the story, Koobie?" Peter said.

"It's great, it's great." Brook slid his arms around Pascale and gripped her tightly. "My dad was just back from the Korean War. He was in Yale Med, and he and his buddy Jake were tripping up to Smith to meet Jake's girl Betty. And Dad had this gorilla head with him. A friend who was working out in Hollywood gave it to him when he got back stateside."

"This better not be gross," Flavia warned. Now she had Peter's hand resting in her lap.

"Absolutely not." Brook was so wired that he was having problems with words over two syllables. "The story starts when they were about just outside of Providence—"

"About just outside of?" Peter cut in.

"Chill out, dude!" Brook shouted. There was a cheer from up the bus and he raised his fist. "They were passing all the cars on the road, and then they pulled up alongside this Simca. There's a woman in a kerchief driving and a twelve-year-old kid in the other seat. For a gag, Jake gets Dad to put on the gorilla mask, and when they've passed the Simca Dad jumps over into the back and sticks his head up in the back window with this mask on. And the kid starts having an epileptic fit!"

Katharine looked from Brook back to me. "That's horrible."

Brook ignored her and pinched the tip of his nose. He looked like a Norman Rockwell policeman on speed. "Then they pull over, and my dad is like dyin', and Jake's trying to get this kid's tongue out of his esophagus, and the chick who was driving the Simca takes off her kerchief and starts cursing Dad up and down the highway—"

"And the rest is history!" Pascale exclaimed. She spoke at about half Brook's speed. "Dr. and Mrs. Morehouse have just met."

"Was the boy all right?" Katharine said.

"You bet," Brook said. "It was Mom's brother, Eliot. His sons Ranney and Carter work for my grandmother with the horses. Alex, you met them up at the Hollow, remember?"

Katharine looked at me with a knowing smile. "Sure, Alex knows how to meet all the right people."

I linked one of her hands in mine. "Ranney and Carter. They had the blond hair, right?"

Once within the New York City limits, Peter stepped in as Flavia Mothership Two's copilot. To the delight of the restless crowd, he ran to the front and directed the driver, Jerry, down Seventh Avenue, then, just shy of the Casbah Club, the site of the party, he made some sort of request. I saw the driver's head turn, and Peter drop a little vial of white into his hand. We made a very sharp turn over to Fifth. Flavia and Pascale also rushed forward to look out at the canyonlike streets of Manhattan. It was snowing heavily, and several of the California freshmen on the bus had rarely seen snow that didn't come out of a machine on a slope, and several of the Midwestern freshmen who had seen lots of snow had never seen Manhattan, so there was some excitement.

"What's the deal?" I whispered to Brook. Katharine had fallen asleep on my shoulder.

"Peter and I chipped in on something. We've just got to pick it up."

"He didn't get her the reptile clutch from the Coop?"

"No, I think her parents got her that. We got a special discount at Fortunoff. The son is on the *News* board."

"I see. May I . . . ?"

"No biggie," Brook said. "Just a little something for her neck. What about you?"

"Just a book."

"What kind?"

I held his stare. "Etiquette. She mentioned that she wanted one." I didn't add that I'd bought it for two dollars at Bookhaven since I was nearly broke.

"Good idea." Brook nodded noncommittally and headed for the front of the bus. I nudged Katharine awake.

"Hey, we're almost there."

She rubbed her eyes and yawned. "Almost where?"

25

When we pulled up to the mosaic tile sidewalk in front of the Casbah Club, I saw that the receiving line twisted through the vestibule and stretched all the way out the door to the edge of the Turkish canopied entry. Coattails and hair whipped in the wet, freezing wind. The women shivered and the men jumped up and down in their black shoes. Flavia ran ahead with Peter to get things under way, but Katharine and I sat in the front seat of the bus with Jerry until the line proceeded. Brook and Pascale had disappeared through one of the side doors, as if ducking photographers.

"How was the driving?" Katharine said. She was refreshed and energetic after her sleep and swayed against me to the tinny big band music on the driver's transistor radio. I'd never met anyone who could sleep so successfully on a bus.

"Okay now, but it's gonna be comin' down." Jerry looked straight ahead, seemingly transfixed by the fat, regular sweep of the windshield wipers. "That radio's predicting six inches by morning." Katharine's eyes widened as Jerry accidentally pulled out his vial along with his handkerchief. The tiny half-filled bottle rolled over the blue carpet and stopped at her feet. She leaned forward and picked it up.

"Here you go."

Jerry extended his hand gratefully. "Don't wanna lose that."

"The line's moving, let's go." I got up quickly and stood out in the narrow aisle.

"Have a good time, you two." Jerry pulled the door open. "Save a little fun for the other people."

"Thanks!" We slid out together. Katharine gripped my arm over the already slushy pavement.

"Alex, let's take the other bus back, okay?"

"Fine with me."

"And promise you won't do any coke."

"Come on," I said. "Who do I look like, Lyon Gregg?"

She tugged at my arm. "Promise, Alex."

"Okay, okay! Jesus Christ."

Peter had briefed me on the Casbah Club while Flavia dozed and Katharine slept and Pascale crashed from her own little vial. The Casbah had once been a fashionable *boite* where the likes of Joan Crawford and other stars with sharp white teeth had gathered in the forties and fifties, then it had suffered a decline and become a retro bar and a tourist trap recommended by hotels like the New York Penta. Recently, however, the Casbah had begun a rapid upward climb and had almost risen past the point where it now wobbled, as one of about fifteen possible venues for the coming-out parties of wealthy Manhattan and Long Island debs. Since the late summer, it had become a once-weekly site for invasions by the uptown set. Soon, Peter predicted, it would become truly chic again and no one would be let in. Whatever the uptown set was, we weren't about to meet them that night because Flavia's father had rented all the rooms on both floors. I wondered which had cost more: my parents' house and land or the rental of the Casbah for ten hours.

In the foyer we passed a pair of short, dark doormen dressed in the Foreign Legion style and I dropped my trenchcoat with a squashed-looking woman who did not appear to be in the mood to cater to the whims of a hundred and ten Yalies for the rest of the evening. She flicked a ticket onto the burnt orange and blue counter and wrenched my coat around a thin wire hanger. Katharine straightened and adjusted her blue bow and slipped through the smoked glass door I held.

"She was nice."

I took her hand. "Many people are nice."

When we entered the main room of the brilliantly lit club, my eyes were drawn to a poster of Flavia at age three. She was sitting on a dull gold Louis XVI chair and speaking into an antique phone. Her hair was in long blond ringlets, and she appeared to be referring an upstairs maid to a downstairs maid. Even at that age she had mastered the no-hands receiver technique she now used in our common room. Beside this photo was an equally large sweetheart shot of Flavia with Peter, both of them staring up into the camera from a green lawn, each wearing a Yale sweatshirt. After this display the animate members of the receiving line began. About twenty couples were to proceed through it before us.

"When could they have taken that kissy one?" I said with wonder. "It looks like the first week of September." I looked past the large, gazebo-like bar *à la Casablanca* opposite the reception area and into the lounge and dance floor beyond it. There were mirrored balls and bowls of cigarettes on thin, stemlike tables. There were two dozen semicircular booths with black and white zebra upholstery, and beyond the booths, at the edge of the blue and orange Arabian carpeting, there was a hardwood cul-de-sac of a dance floor with three gently curved walls of mirror around its perimeter. A balloon arch in pink and white along the longest mirrored wall spelled out HAPPY 18TH TO FLAVIA.

As we moved along, two tenders appeared behind the gazebo bar. They looked like Mafioso put out to pasture—one wore Porsche sunglasses and the other was bald and yawned and checked his watch. There was bad disco playing at low volume, nearly drowned out by the chatter as the crowd rushed for a first drink. Everything struck me as half F. Scott Fitzgerald and half Cyndi Lauper. I had expected something more like a sleekly renovated bank or a church, but then again Flavia's father was a Yale alum, so conservative retro-chintzy nightclub was what we got.

"Alex!" Katharine called. "We have to sign the picture."

I turned and examined the young Flavia poster carefully. The border was strewn with signatures and best wishes in light pink marker, excepting a word balloon drawn above Flavia's three-year-old head which read, " 'Pascale, can I tell you?' Happy 18th! Love you! P.T."

"You sign it," I said. "Something touching."

"What am I going to say: 'I hope you get all you want in life'?" Katharine took the marker, then she brightened suddenly. "Remember that rhyme you put in my yearbook in seventh grade? 'When you get old and out of shape—' "

" 'Remember that girdles are $3.98!' Come on, put that down."

"That might look rude, we'd better not." She scribbled out our names and the word "Yeee!" and slid the pen back into its Velcro holder on the easel leg.

"Right on time, guys," Flavia called down the line. "I'm only ready to drop from starvation."

"God, I hope they got the quiches straightened out." I took Katharine's hand and led her forward. We were indeed dead last in the receiving line. If I found a booth it would be a minor miracle. We stood and waited patiently for the people in front of us to be greeted.

Mr. Nathan was a short but tightly built man, loud and jocular, and wore top-heavy black reading glasses with his tuxedo. He beckoned me forward and shook my hand aggressively. During Parents' Weekend he had taken all of us out to Naples for pizza and reminisced about his years at Eli, when you could still buy a good English or history paper from the back room of the campus dry cleaners. Maureen Nathan, originally from Michigan, was a tall, patrician woman with Flavia's blond hair and a strong, boxy Germanic face. She wore a short, gold-embroidered wool spacesuit dress with black gloves and matching bag. She remembered me from Parents' Weekend too and kissed the air beside each of my ears. My head swam with Joy. Flavia's younger brother Sasha, who looked like he lifted a lot of weights to compensate for his being only an inch taller than Mr. Nathan, was half hiding behind his mother and sticking out his hand. Katharine nudged against me as the line stalled and I realized that I'd forgotten to introduce her. I turned us back and put my hand on Mrs. Nathan's arm.

"Mrs. Nathan, this is my friend Katharine O'Brien."

"Welcome! I'm delighted you could make it." She showed her perfect teeth again and spoke close to my ear. She was one of those women who had to get very close to you to speak. "Alex, Flavia had to run off to check on a few things, so why don't you say hi to Sasha and start enjoying yourselves right away?"

"Thanks, Mrs. Nathan, we will." I looked down past Sasha: Flavia and Peter were indeed gone, why hadn't I noticed it? Katharine gave me another nudge and I moved along. Sasha had a broader face than Flavia, but the same eyes and round mouth.

"How's it going?" I said. Sasha shook my hand and gave Katharine, who was now speaking with his mother again, a lewd once-over.

"How's Yale?" Sasha spoke as if I must have gotten in via a clerical error.

"It's great," I said evenly. "Are you still at Dalton?"

He brushed his substantial head of blond hair back with a thick hand. "Yeah, but I'm going to Princeton. I just got in Early Entrance."

"I'll bet you did."

"You can throw your present on the pile there." Sasha indicated a low hill of ribboned and wrapped boxes behind the closest booth, which had a dozen yellow roses on its table in a vase.

"Thanks." I walked off to lay the package down, marveling at the scale of the fete around me. It was the way of the rich, I supposed: rent out substantial places and invite people over to see if they could lay it on that they were at least as substantial. That was how "A" and "B" and "C" lists grew, depending on how well you kept up your side of the unspoken social bargain. The thought of entering this kind of adulthood sent a wave of nihilistic nausea through me, and I looked around for Katharine, who was, I saw, still talking to Mrs. Nathan.

Now the whole reception area dimmed and the dance music roared up to full volume. It was like the cabin lights in an airplane going down as you lifted off after dark. I turned to the booths as they began to empty out toward the dance floor and more people started sauntering down to the bar. The booth scene looked just like the black-tie Commons dinner, with only the dweebs weeded out. Two women in basic black and pearls broke off from the bar-bound crowd and walked up to me. One, a horsy redhead from Vermont named Pam, I knew slightly from my "Great American Novels" class. Pam seemed to see in me a version of her middle-class New England self which she was trying hard to grow beyond, or was at pains to suppress, so if she was about to talk to me it was probably to ask where the bathrooms were. I saw that without Katharine as an escort I would have spent the whole night playing third wheel to little groups like Pam and her buddies. "B" groups and "C" groups, I supposed. But what did that make me, a "C–"?

"Alex, hi," she said. "Do you know what we do with our gifts?"

"Right here." I pointed to the pile and laid Flavia's wrapped etiquette book down on top of a sturdy box done up in brilliant silver paper. "How's it going?"

"Real good." Pam laid her gift down and stood off slightly, looking back at the reception line. "There it is, you see? The sleeveless one? I tried that on at Saks."

Her slender friend nodded unsurely. "Wait, you mean the blue one?"

"*No.*" Pam put her hand over her mouth. "The blue one speaks for itself."

I stood rooted to the spot, praying that Katharine would walk over and embarrass the hell out of Pam and her friend, but she and Mrs. Nathan appeared to have hit it off.

"Alex," Pam said, "weren't you sitting with Brook Morehouse on the way down?"

"That's right. He's my roommate."

Her affection for me swelled noticeably. She placed her hand on the hip of her little black dress. "I didn't know that! He's a great guy."

"Isn't he though?"

She stepped closer. "Is it true he's carrying blow tonight?"

Blow. Pam must have gotten that one from a "Starsky and Hutch" rerun. "I've never known him not to be. It's kind of like a talisman with him."

Pam's friend nodded thoughtfully. "Have you seen him around?"

"No. I know that he's waiting to be contacted, though."

"Alex." Pam looked tremendously relieved that I could use the right euphemisms and pecked my cheek. "That's great of you. We'll be cruising around in case you see him, okay?"

"I'm sure I'll see you later." I left my fellow classmates and had a drink at the gazebo bar. I smarted inwardly as I watched Katharine look around the large reception area for me in her dress, and for a second I nearly didn't signal her. Then I shot Pam a murderous glance.

"Psst!"

Katharine ran over and gave me a little push on the shoulder. "How could you leave me alone with her?"

"Ow! With Mrs. Nathan? She doesn't bite."

"I'll say. She wants us to come down to Barbados for spring break and stay at their time-share!"

"Really?"

"Yeah." Katharine picked up a cocktail napkin and prepared to honk into it. "What's a time-share?"

"It's a condo thing. Don't worry, she was just talking trash."

"She sounded serious to me."

"Honey." I handed Katharine her cranberry juice. "Don't you remember *The Great Gatsby?* They never mean things like that."

"Well, excuse me." She took a sip and frowned. "Let's sit down."

"Don't you feel well?"

"No, I just want to sit."

Katharine wove through the drinks line with me and out into the club proper. She gazed at the garishly bright décor as we found our own little booth, set off from the dance area behind the closest glass wall. This booth actually looked like it had been moved there by someone who had forgotten to set it back in place with the rest.

"I feel like a doll in here." Katharine threw her purse in as I slid around on the zebra fur. She stepped back and stiffened her arms and expression into that of a plastic-jointed woman. "Don't you, Alex? Isn't it. Like. A giant. Dollhouse?" She tipped forward and I caught her with my hands.

"Come on in here." I gave Katharine the better part of the view, slid my arm over the booth behind her shoulders and lit a cigarette from the bowl. The cigarettes were Marlboro Lights, brand of the young and trendy. I remembered parties at Hollier Prep where I would be talking to a circle of people around a table and look down to see six or seven packages of them. I smoked so rarely myself that I had to concentrate on not hacking out the first drag.

"Are you doing that now?" Katharine glanced at me discouragingly.

I shook my head and took another drag. "Barbados. Where the hell do they think I'm going to come up with the cash for a ticket to Barbados?"

"They'll probably pay. She said 'fly everybody down.' Where is everybody, anyway? I haven't seen Brook or Pascale since they got off the bus."

"Who cares? I'd rather hang out with you."

"I'm just wondering."

"They're having one of their little cabals, I'm sure. To hell with them."

"You don't think they want you to go find them?"

"I think Brook is more in the line of being 'contacted' tonight."

"Find them, contact them . . ." She wiped her nose in another napkin. "What's the difference?"

"It's beneath you."

"Do your friends play a lot of practical jokes on you or something?"

I mumbled an answer and put out the cigarette, embarrassed that Katharine might be embarrassed for me. All afternoon we hadn't run into a single acquaintance on the campus save Brad Lee, who ignored me, so this left me with a universe of four college buddies to show, four buddies who, I had no doubt, were somewhere in the bowels of the club getting cranked without me. Okay, Alex, I thought—which unspoken rule did you break this time?

"Come on," I said suddenly. "I want to dance."

I had forgotten how much Katharine loved to dance, throwing together all the goofy styles she knew (including the Bump, which I adamantly refused to do), so we spent a good hour out in the mass of well-dressed, heavily scented bodies under the flashing banks of lights before I had any notion of time passing. All the music sounded like Top Forty of the previous two years until I recognized a new tune, called something like "Not Gonna Fall in Love." It seemed to be the most popular tune of the evening, if not the whole semester, as I recalled hearing it at most of the Yale parties I'd attended, mixed somewhere into the "Mirror in the Bathroom"/"Good Lovin' " tapes that every party-thrower on campus owned. At the same time, I'd never been able to remember it clearly the day after. When the chorus of this song came around for the second time I realized when I'd first heard it.

"Yes!" I called to Katharine. She was bobbing her bare shoulders up and down to the music, spinning all over the place.

"What's wrong now?"

"I danced to this with Jill one night."

"Wait, don't tell me. She was a fantastic dancer too, right?"

"I was just saying. They had it cut in with a professor's tape on a Hegel paper. In September. It was so great."

"I thought you said you smoked your short-term memory away already."

"Very funny."

Someone started clapping to the bridge of the song and Katharine instinctively raised her hands to join in. She tried to get me to follow her lead but I kept on dancing—the bridge was the best part of the song as far as I was concerned, and shouldn't be tainted by an inane round of audience participation. When I continued to resist, Katharine reached down and took my hands in hers. I fought against her pull until I saw her face darken; then I brought my palms together. She moved us a little closer to one of the mirrored walls as a space opened up on our right. She began a pattycake game in time to the beat.

"Come on, Mr. Cool!" she shouted. "I've seen more life in a hat tree!"

I grinned and started to clap my hands together and then meet hers. The "Not Gonna Fall in Love" song was slowly mixed into a funk number more suitable for pattycake, so Katharine insisted on continuing the game, clapping and sniffing and throwing her cornflower-blue hips from one side to the other. She looked somewhat absurd, but why not? She didn't have to finish out her postsecondary education with the people around us. I laughed at my snobbery and turned to the reflection we made in the glass wall. The rhythmic pattern of clapping had increased with the new song, and now Mr. and Mrs. Nathan stepped out for a twirl. I actually liked the way Katharine and I looked in the mirror, and tried to keep my hands synchronized using our reflection. When I got this pattern down I looked beyond my reflected hands for a moment and watched the swaying crowd. A huge guy with blond hair passed, several people back, but paused when he saw me.

I stopped and stared with upheld palms, which Katharine continued to assault. When I turned away from our reflection and looked out into the crowd I saw no one but a group of Flavia's friends from Welch. I looked back in the mirror, and after a few seconds the head was there again. This time it was moving to the beat, but every minute or so it stared menacingly at me. It took me a while to recognize the guy. His hair was a little long, but there was something about that pneumatic-drill chin cleft . . .

"Hey." I got Katharine's attention and indicated a direction with my head. "I see Bob Talbot over there. Who the hell invited him?"

She raised her eyebrows and stepped in closer to me. "Who?"

"He's—" I broke off, aware of his reflected stare again. I felt that it was very important to keep dancing and speaking, put on a studied blasé look the way Lauren or somebody would, but even though I picked up the beat again I couldn't pick up the thread of what I was going to say. I looked into the mirror and waited for Talbot's reflection to meet mine. He seemed to be fading far back into the crowd, so the next time he appeared I caught his eye and raised a stiff middle finger. He fell out of my line of sight, but when our eyes met for the last time he had raised a finger too, his index finger, which he pointed at me. Then he left the floor with a tall blond woman and disappeared.

Katharine and I stayed out under the lights and mirrored balls for several more songs. I let her move me up and back on the dance floor, as she always liked to do, but I couldn't have named the title of anything that we danced to after that. I kept seeing that wide, pointing finger of accusation. Only when she was completely exhausted and begged for a break did I focus in and remember that we were there together.

"I need to replace some liquids!" She picked up the front of her damp dress.

"Good idea."

I got a shot of Cuervo Gold with lime and salt at the bar, and a cranberry juice for Katharine. She stared at me doubtfully as I winced and ordered another.

"Why are you rushing?"

I patted a napkin over her damp face. "Am I?"

"Hello, Earth to Alex." She put a hand on mine and removed it from her cheek. "Come on, let's put some food in your empty stomach."

We walked across the breadth of the club to the caterer's display. Katharine made three Brie and water biscuit sandwiches and handed them to me with a smidgen of pâté and a few seedless grapes. The food table, which was nearly invisible in the deep shadows where the caterers had relegated it, had hardly been touched. She asked me if we could slip the round of Stilton into her purse unnoticed and get it back to the bus.

"They're serving a full breakfast at four-thirty, too," I said as I chewed. I was looking around for the reappearance of Bob Talbot. "You might want to save room for a melon."

"What?" Katharine stared at me in surprise. "It's going that long?"

"Sure. All these clubs stay open till dawn. Have you got to be back for an exam? Tomorrow's Saturday."

"No." She looked away for a long moment, considering. Finally she slid a sweet thing onto my paper plate and balled up her napkin.

"I've got to make a call, all right?"

"Sure." I handed her her purse. "The Nathans probably know where the phones are."

"Good." She patted my arm. "I'll be right back. See about that Stilton."

"Will do."

I watched her walk confidently toward the Nathans, who appeared to be bemoaning their short-winded performance on the dance floor. As for Katharine, she did not look of the crowd around her or try to appear above it. She was supremely unselfconscious, and I saw how several men followed her with their eyes. One guy even missed what his escort was saying, and suffered for his ignorance. At the birthday booth Mrs. Nathan took Katharine's hand in both of hers, beaming as if she'd taken her up on the Barbados adventure (wouldn't Katharine love to watch me eat my hat over that one), and begged her to sit for a minute. It was pleasant to watch Mrs. Nathan with Katharine. I was happy for my old girlfriend. She could sleep on the bus and drive away from New Haven in the morning and meet whomever it was she had waiting for her up in Orono by the afternoon. I already suspected what type of phone call she was going to make; I was no idiot. For a long time after she left the Nathans' table I watched her pale, pale shoulders weave through lines of tuxedos and dresses. She was living an hour from home, loving college and partying on a head cold, and I was gathering a "silly" vocabulary and a new wardrobe in anticipation of the day when I could walk through the doors of Lawrance Hall with Brook and Peter at my side, all of us wearing our team jackets. I wanted it to be my graduation prom again so badly that I had to have my arm nudged to give up the cheese knife I was gripping.

"Excuse me, hello?"

"Sorry. Hey!"

It was Pascale. She was staring at me from the other side of the food table in her low-cut black taffeta sheath. She had a meal-sized paper plate half covered with goodies, some of which I probably hadn't noticed under all the canopies of lettuce leaf and sculpted fruit on the table.

"Pascale," I said, "what's the deal?"

Pascale was so wired that her lips quivered. She wore a teasing, knowing smile that was also accusatory. She looked shocked with, delighted by and disappointed in me.

"Hi." She used a red toothpick to skewer a few grapes.

I smiled back at her, though my mind was on Bob Talbot again. "Where've you all been hiding?"

Pascale shrugged. "Around. Big mouth."

I looked at her dumbly. I wondered, why would Talbot point at me unless he knew that I had turned in a list of suspects to the inquiry committee? Then I realized what Pascale had said and started out of my fog.

"Come again?"

"I'd stay away from Brook, big mouth," she said carefully, then gave a low laugh that was also a hum. I had no idea whether or not I should take her seriously. She was using that Californian singsong voice that made my fillings ache.

"Thanks for the advice, smarty pants." My voice came out as if I already did know what was going on and was drowning in guilt over it. Another fall from grace, another rise from shame, more grist for the mill, one orbit further from the center. *Champagne? We asked for wine, stupid! Wine? We asked for champagne, stupid!*

Pascale laid the cheese knife down with another hum-laugh.

"Catering somebody's stone?" I said.

"No. Bye."

She proceeded down the table, grabbed a bottle of corked German beer from a large glass bowl of ice water and headed toward the Nathans. The beer label slid off and floated over the sloshing surface. I watched it as it sank. It depicted three cherubs, each running with a mutant raspberry balanced on its head.

The cherubs had puckers of baby fat, bright white hair and a mantle of strung green leaves at their waists to cover up their little cherubic genitalia. The strung stems of the raspberries made up their garters. Unlike most beer labels I had seen, this one seemed to have a plot. Something about ecstatic escape. I reached down into the bowl and started turning over bottles, but apparently Pascale had snagged the last one, because my freezing hand only came up with splits of sickly sweet spumanti.

Flavia, I saw, was a few feet from the end of the food table, her back to me. She was deep in conversation with one of her Welch girlfriends and didn't notice my approach. My cheeks felt very hot, and I remembered the tequila shots. Now I was mixing that with spumanti.

"That's great." She gave a laryngitic squeal. "She used to come in with these bags around her eyes and say, 'I've got *such* Letterman rings.' I never believed her for a minute."

The woman glanced at me twice before Flavia looked over.

"Alex!" Flavia put a hand on her chest, as if she'd accidentally tripped her mother. "That was so *rude* of me to ignore you. I'll have to consult my new guide."

"Will you?" I said. "I guess you couldn't have known that it's bad manners to open one birthday gift before all the others."

"But, Alex, it's my party."

"It sure is."

"Look at Jenny," Flavia said, "she's so lost. Letitia Baldrige here gave me an etiquette book."

The woman smiled. "I get it."

"Which I did not in fact open."

"I guess somebody just told you about it. Just a rumor that went around."

Flavia stared at me quizzically. "Alex, you are totally drunk at my birthday party."

"Which way are the phone booths?"

"Follow the bathroom signs, sweetie. Left at the end of this corridor and then all the way down the hall. Go down the stairs and you'll see them. And if you see my rumored boyfriend tell him he's dead meat. He abandoned me thirty minutes ago, thank you very much."

"He has terrible manners."

"Alex, you're incredibly angry at me for some reason, but you're not going to tell me now, are you?"

"I'm not angry at you," I said. "I'll talk to you later."

"My thank-you card will be in the first post tomorrow morning, I promise!"

Flavia's instructions took me past the back of the longest glass wall, where I could just make out the tip of the balloon arch bobbing on its line of cord, and down a dimly lit hallway no wider than the passage in a train car. Here I heard faint strains of Arabic music coming from behind a door, and passed several dome-shaped mirrors hung at regular intervals along the orange and blue paisley wallpaper. I passed Pam with a new group of friends and got a knowing smile, then I passed the stairs and had to double back. Above the lintel of the doorway was the dimmest EXIT sign I've ever seen. From here the dance music was only a distant, repetitive thud.

"Alex!" Peter ran up the stairs smiling. "We were looking for you."

"I was in the club," I said. "Where were you all?"

"Brook's looking for you in particular," he said. "I hope you brought a bulletproof vest."

"What'd I do now?"

Peter put a hand on my shoulder and slid his eyes all the way left and right, like an undercover agent. "He's not telling me, whatever it is. Where's the Flav-monster?"

"With the food. You'd better borrow my bulletproof vest."

"Shit. I'll see you later."

"Okay."

I walked down the stairs slowly, my ears ringing in the quiet. The landing at the basement level was carpeted in black and orange. Two English phone booths stood side by side, both fire-engine red, their windowpanes shining, and flanking them sat a pair of Barcelona chairs in black leather. The washroom doors were labeled Mesdames and Messieurs. Katharine wasn't in either phone booth, so I guessed that she was in the Mesdames blowing her nose or rolling out some toilet paper to stuff in her purse. I took a seat to wait. I fell into one, actually, and was at once unsure whether I could get up again.

Brook came out of the Messieurs taking great breaths through his nose. His bow tie was undone and he had splashed water through his thick black hair. He didn't see me at first, but when he did he walked over and stood a few feet from the edge of my chair. Pleased he wasn't.

"Is this where you've been all night?" I said.

He nodded. "I guess I'd better be, now that everyone's looking for me. Thanks for sending Pam my way, asshole."

"Didn't you want to be contacted?"

He wiped a hand through his hair. "It's none of your business whether or not I want to be contacted."

My heart began to pound in my chest, but I was determined not to fall apart and placate Brook because he was pissed off. "You'll have to be more specific."

"Don't shit me," he snapped. "They called my parents, you know, that board. They wanted to know if I had any violent behavior in my past. Dad was delighted. So there went my Mory's application right out the wazoo. One phone call to his buddy the board director and they canceled it. The car goes next. And if I don't come up with straight As he'll probably cut me off completely."

I watched Brook in the dim light, feeling my own anger rise. "So you just felt obliged to unload this on Bob Talbot? You should have seen the looks he was giving me."

"And for that you give him the finger? Butthead! You're god-damn lucky I saw him before he got to you. Flavia would have loved a fight at her first birthday party."

"Was he planning a few kicks to the head?"

"I'm going to ignore that."

"Did you tell him I turned you in to Big Brother or some-thing?"

"Talbot was in the office at Woodbridge when I got called over," Brook said. "I suppose you gave his name too, while you were at it."

"Lauren and all her friends gave it before me, I'm sure. What's it to you?" I wrenched myself out of the deep chair. "And if you broke up the fight, testifying was the least you could do."

"Did it ever occur to you that I might testify voluntarily?" Brook's voice dropped to a whisper. "When are you going to listen to me? That fight was over who was invited and who wasn't, and *everybody* was at fault. And it was *dark*. You're way off base."

"And you seem to forget that Jill's in a fucking vase at her parents' house! I don't care if I'm way off base."

"Ohhh, man." Brook rubbed his face and looked the way his father did when he brought the highball glass down on his attic stairs. "You are really starting to get on my nerves."

"Then get some new nerves," I said. "I want to set this thing to rest as much as you do, don't you understand that? If it had been handled the right way in the beginning we wouldn't even be arguing about it." I saw Katharine come out of the bathroom and walked around Brook. I was surprised that he let me pass.

"How'd your phone call go?"

"Fine." She looked a little guilty to find me waiting for her. "What's wrong?"

"I don't feel like staying. I must be catching your cold."

Katharine glanced from me to Brook and back again. "Are you sure?"

I checked behind me. Brook had taken my place in the Barcelona chair and was staring straight ahead, hands folded, trying to keep himself under control.

"I'm sure."

"Where are we going?"

"Anywhere. Come on." I started for the stairs, and was nearly there when I heard Brook's voice.

"I thought you trusted me."

"Brook." I turned around and faced him. "I told Jerome you were there, that's all. I would never say a word about anything else. I'm sure you were the only person at Freitag's who gave a clear account of it."

"Is that right?"

"Yes. I trust you, that's why I wanted you to testify. Who knows what they'll find when they put all the accounts together?"

He shook his head. "You're dangerously optimistic, guy."

"I know," I said, "you told me. I'll see you tomorrow."

I joined Katharine at the stairs. "Have you got enough to get us back to New Haven?"

She stared down at her purse, as if reading its mind. "I think so."

"Good. Let's go."

The coat check lady was asleep and had to be roused. She blinked unhappily and flung my property back over the counter. Katharine slipped into the trenchcoat nervously, as if I'd set a bomb in the club while she was on the phone. With the production of two dollars a Foreign Legion doorman stepped out to get us a cab. One event blurred into another with a reckless speed that always set in after five or more drinks. I hardly remember what I said to Flavia and Peter. Something about Katharine being on death's doorstep. Flavia hugged Katharine and said that I was showing good etiquette to take my date home even though I was at such a fabulous party.

"Why were you so mean to Brook?" Katharine said, gathering my trenchcoat around her.

"Was I?" I was pacing in the vestibule. "I thought I apologized. Didn't I?"

"If you say so." She shivered. "Maybe I am getting pneumonia."

I slid my arm over her shoulder and pulled her to me. "I shouldn't have made you go. We could have just hung out and drunk tea in my room or something."

"Don't be silly." She slid her arms around my waist. "What are you going to do, though?"

"Keep pushing with this until I alienate everybody, I guess."

"I mean generally."

I thought for a minute. "Get a new frame of reference, first off."

"What do you mean?"

I stepped back as a strong gust of wind slid under the swinging doors and filled the vestibule. "I'm not sure. I'll let you know when I get there."

She dug around to get another Kleenex. "I think you're right, in case you're interested. You don't really fit into this crowd."

"I'll take that as a compliment."

"I mean you don't look like you're having any fun. If I know one thing about you, I know when you're having a bad time." She dropped her head and honked into the pink ball in her hand.

I heard footsteps running toward the vestibule as the doorman stuck his head in and touched the brim of his hat.

"Taxi, sir!" he called. "Did you want this taxi?"

"We'll be right there!" I stepped up to the hard plastic dome shape cut in one of the swinging doors and looked out, buttoning up my tux jacket and putting on gloves. My eyes were dazzled. Midnight New York was lit and shadowed in a tenuous layer of white. I was about to tell Katharine that the scene reminded me of my favorite Childe Hassam painting of Manhattan, but instead I called her up to have a look with me. She said that it was nice. I kissed the raw red tip of her nose and agreed.

When I looked back in Brook was standing in the vestibule, offering his hand. I hesitated and then took it.

"Come on," he said. "Come on in and have a drink. Forget the train. Everybody wants you to stay."

"Last call on this taxi!"

"Thanks, Brook, but I don't feel up to it. Apologize for me, would you?"

"Okay, I tried." He released my hand. "I broke it up, Alex, I really did."

"I know, I believe you."

"Bye, Brook." Katharine kissed his cheek and ran her finger over the spot to remove her lipstick. "Thank Flavia's parents for us. It was a great time."

Brook nodded at her, expressionless, and we stepped out into the cold night. Katharine held my hand tightly until we got across the street to the cab. It was very hard to walk away. I pulled the back door shut and we headed downtown.

26

Six weeks later, the Yellow Cabby left me off half a block from Phelps Gate and deposited my luggage on the ice-slicked street with a hernial grunt.

"Any more Yalies on that train?" He flipped through the dollars I handed him and nodded his approval.

"I don't think so. Probably the next."

"All right, buddy." He slammed the trunk. "Go easy on that ice. Happy New Year."

"Right. You too."

I hoisted on my shoulder bag and picked up my duffel. I also had a shopping bag of Christmas gifts from my parents that was ready to drop its bottom. The sun had just cleared the Presbyterian church on the public green and was melting the coating of ice from its spire. As the cabby drove away I stood out in College Street and listened to his receding muffler. It was too early in the

morning for many cars to be on the road, and most of the secondary streets were still strewn with branches and power lines that
would be cleared in the coming hours and days. Everyone had
missed a picnic of a storm, the cabby had said. Down toward the
Taft Apartments a forty-foot elm had given under the weight of
the ice and split right down the center, like a piece of broccoli.

I glanced up at the brick facade of Lawrance Hall as I
crunched along. It looked like someone had scrubbed and shined
over the Christmas break until each stone in the building glowed
with its original ruddiness. More likely it was the contrast after
three hours of murky Amtrak interior and three weeks of driving
past the peeling sides of tract houses in McMurtry. Rivulets of
water dropped from the peaked roof of Lawrance to splash over
the plots of ivy before the sidewalk, where the snow was gathered
in mounds. Farther along I looked up at our fourth-floor turret;
one of its rectangular windows was still open.

When I turned right into Phelps Gate, I smiled. Up ahead,
where the arch framed the Old Campus quadrangle, the elm trees
stood like clutching hands above a cover of white that was catching the first slanting lines of sun. I slid my bags off and walked
up to the edge of the arch's deep shadow. From Vanderbilt Hall
across to the leaded windows of Dwight Chapel and all the way
along the cast-iron fence to the Elm Street steps, no feet had gone
wide of a single path which had been plowed through the flagstones. Otherwise the snow was unbroken. Away from the traffic,
the soft patter of dripping ice sounded like rain over a summer
field.

I looked up into the sky, rippled blue and white in the center
like the fan of a mackerel's skeleton. At that moment it was
possible to imagine a winter version of Brook Morehouse striding
out of Yale Station and across the snow, the zipper of his fluorescent parka dancing with lift tickets (Deer Valley, Mont Ste. Anne,
Gstaad), downhill skis in a bag over his shoulder, rubbing sun-
guard off his nose as he marched forward to life's next slalom
run. From the fresh look of the snow cover, though, I guessed that

Brook and the rest of the students would be several hours or days yet in coming. For a while I had the campus to myself, and felt that I might be able to work through the feeling that Old Campus was more a home to me now than the place three hundred miles north where I had grown up. I had denied the feeling before I went back to McMurtry, with Christmas coming and an excited exodus of people swirling around me, but now that I was back in New Haven, and alone, the feeling was just as strong. It was as if I'd never known another place, or a place that was so fully real.

I took a few steps back from the edge of the arch and picked up a pay phone, then dug around in the pocket of my jeans for the sheet of bond paper I'd been scribbling on as my train pulled into town. Katharine's machine in Orono kicked in after six rings.

"Hi. I thought of the Stevens line I was telling you about, the one about horizons? 'It was her voice that made the sky acutest at its vanishing.' That's what I've got down here, anyway. I thought of it on the train. Give me a call when you get in."

I replaced the receiver, walked out to the quadrangle and tossed the piece of paper into a wood-framed trash barrel. On the other side of the sheet there was a letter from Charles Jerome, Assistant Provost. It was warm and friendly and full of phrases like "I cannot thank you enough for your attention in this inquiry" and "We are committed to issuing a full report no later than January 31st." Brook got a Charles Jerome letter during break too, in fact, and told me about it when he called from a raucous fondue party in Darien. I read my letter back to him and we discovered that they were identical. I was incredulous at first, and then angry, but Brook only belched on his rum punch.

"Christ, Alex, what did you expect? I'm tossing mine after I hang up, in case my parents find it lying around."

"I guess you don't have high hopes."

"If they can narrow it down to one person, it won't be because of anything I said."

Brook went on to say that we should meet for squash in the new year, as soon as we got back. He also wished that I was there at his fondue. I couldn't think of anything to say, and eventually one of us wished the other a Merry Christmas and hung up.

As I stood there thinking about my conversation with Brook, I realized that he was right: Charles Jerome's letter was just the sort of document you were supposed to read and throw away once you saw how clear it was that any future developments were out of your control. That was precisely why I had to get it back.

When I had pulled the letter out of the barrel and slid it into my pocket again I took a deep breath of cold air and walked up to the edge of the green. A few minutes passed, perhaps more, and gradually I felt the tips of my ears freezing. I realized that I was staring at the spot where I'd picked up my Women's Center survey, and I would now never see Jill trudging through the impossible inconvenience of snow or nursing a winter cold down in Machine City. I'd never know how she would have felt or what she would have done as spring came back to New Haven, what sort of subversive smile she might have been wearing as she passed through Phelps Gate for the last time in May, to graduate. And though I tried to deny it, I wasn't naive enough to believe that all my real memories of Jill wouldn't inevitably begin to fade too, the way an image etched on a copper plate starts to blur after three or four hundred pulls. My mind would print a handful of scenes over and over and after a while, and maybe even a short romance, I would think of her again and realize that she had slipped a mental notch from familiar to face, and then, after another interval, from face to name, and then from name to word, and then—what? I was already losing track of so many things from the fall: dashes into the shower during the heat of the first month, all-nighters pulled in the law school library with Brook, even the grip of a long, cool hand tightening around mine as I was led through the crush of a party.

But Jill's presence was still there. Perhaps, for me only, there would always be something uncanny about that spot a few feet out from the fence at Lawrance Hall, just beyond a September

sign that urged a new freshman class on to involvement in its
college. If I concentrated, perhaps this vague plot of patchy grass
would evoke a presence far longer than memory dictated, a presence with the prick of truth about it. It was toward this spot on
the snow-silent green that I finally raised my hand.

About the Author

Hugh Kennedy grew up in Boston and Nova Scotia and attended Yale University, from which he graduated in 1987. While at Yale he wrote for the *Yale Daily News* and received the Gordon Barber Prize for undergraduate poetry. In 1992 he was awarded an M.A. in English with Creative Writing concentration from Cleveland State University. He currently lives in Boston, where he is at work on his next novel.